Hurricane

Book 2

SERIES
STREET RATS OF ARAMOOR

written by

MICHAEL WISEHART

Copyright

HURRICANE is a work of fiction. Names, characters, places, and incidents are products of the author's imagination or are used fictitiously. Any resemblance to actual locales or persons, living or dead, business establishments, or events, is entirely coincidental.

STREET RATS OF ARAMOOR: BOOK 2
HURRICANE

To View Map in More Detail

« www.michaelwisehart.com/city-of-aramoor »

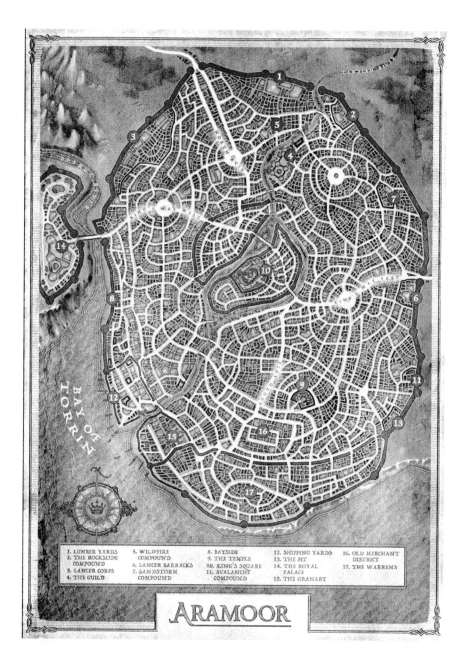

1. LUMBER YARDS
2. THE ROCKSLIDE COMPOUND
3. LANCER CORPS
4. THE GUILD
5. WILDFIRE COMPOUND
6. LANCER BARRACKS
7. SANDSTORM COMPOUND
8. BAYSIDE
9. THE TEMPLE
10. KING'S SQUARE
11. AVALANCHE COMPOUND
12. SHIPPING YARDS
13. THE PIT
14. THE ROYAL PALACE
15. THE GRANARY
16. OLD MERCHANT DISTRICT
17. THE WARRENS

ARAMOOR

Foreword

HURRICANE IS THE second book in the Street Rats of Aramoor series, an off-shoot of the Aldoran Chronicles saga. If you haven't yet read the first book, *BANISHED*, I recommend doing so.

Books

THE ALDORAN CHRONICLES

Book 1 | The White Tower

STREET RATS OF ARAMOOR

Book 1 | Banished

Book 2 | Hurricane

Chapter 1

MY JOURNEY was nearing its end.

After leaving the *Wind Binder* and her captain and crew behind on the Shemoa River, I traveled east around the Sandrethin Mountains with Magistrate Sirias and his family. The trip had taken nearly two months, but we were in no rush, and with having the magistrate's resources returned after freeing the slaves at the Cylmaran mining camp, plus the share I'd received from Captain Treygan for my part in the rescue, we decided to take our time and enjoy the trip. After our harrowing experiences over the last few months, it was a welcomed gift, a time to heal both physically and mentally.

Once we had rounded the southern tip of the Sandrethins, we parted ways. Magistrate Sirias, Merilyn, Rosella, and their infant son continued south toward the coastal cities of Vinten and Fayburn, while I took the west road to Aramoor.

Not wanting to waste my coin purchasing a horse, I spent the next couple of weeks enjoying the open road on foot. A day outside of Aramoor, I was lucky enough to be picked up by a farmer and his family, where I found myself bouncing along in the back of a wagon filled with half a dozen large melons and a barrel of cucumbers that smelled of last week's pickings despite the FRESH CUT label on the front.

They told me no thirteen-year-old should be out on these roads by themselves. There could be highwaymen just waiting to snatch me up. I almost laughed.

Their son, who was seated across from me on a small crate of lettuce, was several years younger and definitely not shy about speaking his mind.

"What's wrong with your eyes?" he asked, his head cocked slightly to the side. "They look funny."

"Hush, Enon. That's rude." His mother was trying her best not to stare herself.

Enon reminded me of my younger brother, Jorn. He was about the same age and just as feisty.

The little boy folded his arms. "Well, they do."

I smiled. Having passed through as many cities, towns, and villages as I had on my way to Aramoor, I'd grown accustomed to the stares. It would seem colorless eyes were something of a rarity. Growing up in the Lost City of Keldor, I'd never known anything different. I was just as amazed at the variety of color I'd seen.

"All of my people have the same eyes," I said.

The farmer's wife twisted in her seat. "Your people?"

"The Upaka."

The woman's expression darkened, and her husband threw me a sharp look over his shoulder. "Upaka?" There was a hint of concern in his voice. "That's a name I haven't heard in quite some time. What are you doing this far south?"

"It's a long story," I said, not feeling in the mood to share the tale of my banishment with strangers, even strangers kind enough to give me a ride.

They got the hint and didn't pry further. I doubted their silence had anything to do with common courtesy. After all, my people were well known as mercenaries for hire.

A gust of wind caught my hair and sent it whipping behind me. It had grown long enough to tickle my shoulders, nearly half as long as my sister Rianna's, which would have earned me some time with Mother's shears were I at home.

We crested a small rise, and I could see Aramoor looming in the distance. It was larger than anything I had imagined. The capital city of Elondria was the home of the High King. It was also the largest city in the known world. Nothing in the five kingdoms came close to its magnitude. The thought of calling it *home* both excited and terrified me.

"So, this is your first time to Aramoor, is it?" the farmer asked.

He'd turned his attention back to his team as the horses plodded down the main road leading toward the city.

"Yes, sir."

He smiled. "Bet you've never laid eyes on the likes of it before."

"I haven't."

"That wall is one of Aldor's great wonders, if you ask me."

I stared off into the distance at the protective barrier surrounding the city. Its white stone could be seen for miles in all directions.

"I can see why."

"They say it was built by wizards after the defeat of the Kuhl hordes. It was probably one of the last great feats of magic before the Purge." The farmer shook his head. "It's hard to believe something as evil as magic could create such beauty."

I bit my tongue. Having magic was no more likely to make someone evil than having too much gold. I could speak from personal experience.

The road grew more congested, the closer we got to the city's eastern gate. It was as though the townsfolk from the surrounding communities had decided to make a sacred pilgrimage to the capital, all at the same time.

We passed a number of other wagons toting wares to sell to those living within the protection of the great wall.

Our pace slowed as we reached the first of two gatehouses leading in. This close, I could see that the blocks used to build the fortification were as wide as the farmer's wagon. I wondered at the amount of magic it must have required. The wizards from that age must have been truly powerful.

A sentry waved the cart in front of us on, through and we pulled forward to the first checkpoint. "State your name and purpose," the guard said. He bore the insignia of the Elondrian Lancers—a high sun overshadowing a golden crown.

I'd seen pictures of that emblem in my studies back home. I'd been required to learn of the various militaries within the five kingdoms. Their crests and colors had been just as important to memorize as their styles of combat.

"The name's Neelan," the farmer said to the guard. "We're from Cadwyn. This is my wife and my two boys. We have fresh produce to sell at the lower market on South Avis."

The guard stepped over to my side of the wagon and looked in. Thankfully, my back was to him, so I didn't have to worry about hiding my eyes. One quick glance and he was walking back around to the front. He waved us forward. "Move on through."

We passed a second guard station once we were through the gate, but no one bothered stopping us. The lancers at that station were concerned with traffic leaving the city.

"Where would you like us to drop you off?" Neelan asked as we started down the main thoroughfare leading into the heart of Aramoor.

In the distance, I could see great domes and spires rising above the dwellings we were passing between. They reminded me of the snowcapped peaks of the Northern Heights back home.

With this being my first time inside the city, I needed to get my bearings before attempting to explore any deeper.

"I'll get off here, thanks."

"Here?" The farmer's wife turned in her seat. "Do you have family nearby?" She looked at the closest buildings as if expecting to see some nice couple standing there waiting on me.

"Uh, yes," I lied. "Uncle Fen . . . der . . . stad." Of course, I didn't have an uncle, and if I did, his name certainly wouldn't have been Fenderstad. I wished I'd given it a little more thought.

The farmer directed the horses over to the edge of the road and stopped the wagon. "Are you sure? It's easy to get lost in here if you don't know where you're going."

"I'll be fine. He doesn't live far from here." I grabbed my travel bag and slung it over my shoulder before hopping down from the back. "My parents gave me directions. Thank you for the ride. It was most kind." I waved, not giving them a chance to argue. I was too embarrassed to tell them I was homeless with nowhere to go.

"Well, good luck to you, lad," Neelan said with a concerned look and a polite wave. "If you change your mind, we'll be on South Avis. It's off of King's Way East." He pointed at the wide cobbled road in front of us leading into the heart of the city. "Just follow this to the main square and then turn left. You'll find us somewhere near Marrow Lane in Cheapside. You can't miss it. We usually sell out before dusk, so if you can't find us by then, just wait for us at the east gate."

"Thank you. I will." I waved once more and casually walked down the first street on the right. I hoped it looked like I knew where I was going. Behind me, I could hear the farmer snap the reins and the wagon wheels thump over the cobblestones.

I stopped at the corner of the next building and listened as the wagon blended into the cacophony coming from those on their way to market. Taking a deep breath, I scanned the street, mesmerized by the flow of the crowd. I was surrounded by more people than I'd ever seen in my life, and yet I had never felt so alone.

I knelt and adjusted my boots. The coin pouches were starting to chafe. With the money my father had given me, along with what I had salvaged from the two dead highwaymen, and the proceeds I'd received from Captain Treygan, I hoped it would be enough to keep me sheltered and fed until I was able to find some type of work or purchase an apprenticeship with a local merchant.

At the thought of my father, I lifted the thin chain from where it was safely hidden under my tunic and stared at the ring hanging from its end. The black onyx band had a single white rune at its center, the crest of my clan. Tears welled near the corners of my eyes, brought on by the thought of once again being alone. Being this far from home, now, more than ever, it was the small things like this ring that helped remind me of who I was.

I tucked the chain back into my shirt and pulled the hood up to hide my eyes as I made my way north up the street. I let the natural flow of the people move me along. The farther I walked, the more the crowds began to dwindle. I kept an eye out for a place to stay, somewhere not too far from the eastern gate, in case I needed to take Master Neelan up on his offer.

I was looking for somewhere reputable, but not too reputable or the cost would be too high. I would have been fine with four walls and a mattress, as long as it came with clean sheets and an owner who wouldn't try mugging me in the middle of the night.

The farther I traveled from King's Way East, the more dilapidated the buildings became, not to mention the people mingling around them. I generally judged a location by the hairs on the back of my neck. So far, they hadn't risen, which meant it was a reasonably safe place to find a room. But I couldn't quite shake the feeling that someone was watching me.

Across the street, a sign swung back and forth with a rusty moan. The faded gold letters under the painting of a large buck proclaimed it THE WHITE STAG. It seemed a typical name for an Elondrian inn. Many carried the names of wild animals: The White Stag, The Wild Boar, The Dancing Bear. Although I found it hard to imagine a bear dancing.

The building looked reliable enough. A couple of windows on the upper floors were lit, letting me know it was in use, so I headed across the street. I reached for the front door, but a sharp cry kept me from entering.

"Help! Someone please help!"

A young boy, several years younger than myself, was being dragged by two older boys into a narrow alley a few buildings away. The bigger of the two slapped the kid across the face.

"Shut your mouth or I'll slit your throat."

I looked to see if anyone was going to help, but the few people I saw didn't seem to care enough to stop what they were doing. For most, that meant sitting around, smoking pipes and nursing drinks while pretending nothing was amiss.

I knew I shouldn't get involved. I looked away. The last time I got involved, it had me attacking a Cylmaran compound. I tried to act like the rest of those sitting around and ignore the problem, but the boy's desperate pleas stopped me, and I turned back.

What kind of citizen would I be if I just let this kid be taken without trying to help? My father's voice answered from somewhere in the back of my mind: *A smart one.*

I sighed, dropping my hand to caress the hilt of my dagger. With a quick adjustment to my pack, I took off for the alley. *It's just a way to test my training,* I told the voice in my head. *Don't want my skills to get rusty.*

I didn't believe that for a minute.

CHAPTER 2

BY THE TIME I reached the small opening between the buildings, the boys were gone. Whoever they were, they were moving fast, probably spurred on by their victim's loud outcry.

I pulled my dagger and started through the narrow alleyway, keeping my eyes open for anything suspicious. I picked up speed, the closer I got to the other end.

The buildings in this part of the city looked older than those near the gate. They rose like a gnarled forest, blocking out the sun and paving the streets in eerie shadows.

The alley ended in a split. I looked both ways and spotted the kidnappers to my right. They were racing for the next street, so I took off after them. The boy slung over the larger one's shoulder wasn't moving. I hoped he was just unconscious.

They turned left at the next street. I stopped at the corner and found they'd only made it a couple of buildings up. This was my chance. The vacant road was wide enough for me to move freely, so I tightened my grip on my dagger and took off.

I kept to the balls of my feet, softening the noise of my approach. They seemed unaware of me, and I willed them to remain so.

Apparently, I was in good standing with the Creator. Not only did they not turn around, they actually stopped, and the larger boy removed the small kid from his shoulder.

The boy didn't seem to be unconscious after all. Neither did he seem to be all that scared. I slowed. Something wasn't right.

The boy turned and smiled.

I skidded to a halt. The hairs on the back of my neck weren't just standing on end; they were hopping around like jackrabbits. I had taken the bait and the cage was about to close.

"Gets 'em every time," the small boy said with a disturbing chuckle.

"What did I tell you?" the boy who'd done the carrying said. His own smile revealed he was missing most of his front teeth. "I can always spot the heroes."

I took another couple of steps back, but at the sound of footfalls behind me, I realized the cage door had been shut.

"What's your rush?" the gap-toothed boy asked.

I turned. There were kids moving in behind me, cutting off my escape. They carried rough-looking bludgeons.

More filed in from nearby alleyways.

Their weapons were a mismatched assortment of clubs, poles, wrapped pieces of glass, and a few knives. One boy had a long dagger sticking out the back of his trousers, while the kid with the missing teeth wore a rusty shortsword.

I shifted my travel pack around to the front. Everything I owned in the world was in it.

Toothless, as I decided to call the boy with the gapped teeth, smiled. The sight of him would have made me laugh if I hadn't already been too preoccupied with devising a way to get myself out of this situation. I scanned the faces surrounding me, searching for a weak spot. Their eyes told me I wasn't going to be able to talk my way out. For that reason, I was thankful for my Upakan training, not to mention my other gifts.

"How about you give us a look-see inside that bag?" Toothless said, stepping forward and reaching for my satchel. He clearly felt he had nothing to fear with his fifteen-to-one odds.

I clutched my bag close to my chest and pulled back my hood, hoping my eyes would be enough to make them think twice.

"Are you going to hand me that pack, or am I going to have to pry it from your dead fingers?"

This was just my luck. I hadn't made it a single morning inside of Aramoor, and already I was being accosted by a gang of rabid hooligans.

"You take another step and you'll be sucking soup the rest of your days."

Toothless stared at me and then turned to the others, confusion written on his face. They seemed to share his bewilderment. A few of the kids shrugged, and the large boy turned back around. "What?"

I rolled my eyes and pointed at my mouth. "Your teeth. I'm going to knock out the rest of your teeth." Not only was I being robbed, I was being robbed by a gang of imbeciles.

His puzzled look quickly turned to anger.

I tightened my fingers around the leather grip of my dagger. My eyes darted from one kid to the next, waiting to see who'd make the first move. I slowly slid my right leg back and shifted my weight to stabilize my stance.

I was about to lift my blade when something inside of me changed. I'd never felt anything like it before. It was as though part of me had died. The heat I normally felt from my magic had gone cold, and not by my doing. I panicked.

My magic was gone.

"Who do we have here?" someone called out from behind the blockade of kids.

They parted far enough for me to see the girl standing behind them. She had black hair like mine and a red vest.

Up until this point, I had assumed Toothless was their leader, but even he retreated far enough for the girl to see me. She didn't seem to want to get any closer.

"New arrival," Toothless said. "Seems to think that bag belongs to him."

"Does he?"

Things were getting worse by the minute. Taking on five or six kids was one thing, but those numbers had tripled, and I couldn't reach my magic. I was going to have to do this the hard way.

You don't realize how much you depend on something until it's gone. My abilities were a part of me. I'd ever had to fight without them only once before, and that had been a personal choice. With this many kids, I could have really used my visions.

"Stand back," Toothless said, drawing his shortsword and waving for the others to give him some room. "He's mine."

Most of the belongings in my sack were clothes, so I held it out as a padded shield against strikes while gripping my dagger with the other hand. The sack wouldn't do much good against a sword, but it might stand up against the clubs if it came down to it.

I raised my blade.

Toothless rushed forward, clearly anxious to finish me in quick order. He swung directly for the top of my head. Even without magic, I could see it coming. He clearly had little experience using the weapon. I sidestepped and rammed the butt of my dagger straight into his mouth. There was a loud cry of pain followed by blood. Lots of blood.

Toothless dropped his sword and covered his face with both hands, trying to hold in what was left of his front teeth. He stumbled backward, tears coursing down his cheeks. "Kill him!"

The others took up the call and charged.

I didn't have time to worry about my pack, so I dropped it and grabbed the discarded sword. I'd barely had time to turn when the first wave hit. They were about as skillful with their weapons as Toothless, but with their numbers, proficiency didn't really matter. All it would take was one lucky strike.

I blocked with the sword and cut with my dagger. Kids all around me began to drop. I took a club to my right arm and nearly dropped the knife since I hadn't seen it coming. I was off balance without my magic.

I pushed through the thinnest point in the lines to keep from having to fight everyone at once. I managed to keep two or three of the kids between me and the rest as I fought my way closer to one of the buildings. I needed to keep my attackers from flanking me.

Toothless was still screaming at them to kill me. Even their leader shouted her disappointment. "What's wrong with you? He's just one boy, you pack of pathetic weaklings! Are you going to let him embarrass Wildfire like that?"

Their leader's shouts seemed to spur the kids into an even-greater frenzy. I dodged left, twisted, and spun right, fighting to stay clear of their clubs. Going for the legs worked best. Once a kid was down, they were less likely to get back up, not to mention the added benefit of the other kids tripping over them to get to me.

My movements felt sluggish, forced. I had to devote most of my energy to compelling my limbs to respond, something I'd never had to do before. For the first time, I felt what it was like to be normal.

Along with my visions, another gift I had lost was the ability to remember coordinated movements and replicate them. While others had to spend hours training every day in order to master a particular skill, I only had to do it once. My mother said I was a repeater, a very useful tool when you found yourself being robbed by a herd of bloodthirsty thugs.

On my right, I ducked a boy's swing and kicked him in the knee. He screamed and went down. With my sword, I parried another strike, giving me time to stab a lanky kid in the thigh with my dagger. He went down just as quickly.

I couldn't keep this up. There were just too many of them.

One of the girls got too close, and I head-butted her in the face. She squealed and swung wide, clubbing the kid beside her, who took two more down with him. A wild swing with a knobby table leg struck me in the thigh, causing the muscle to cramp. I was barely able to put weight on it.

I blocked two more attempts at my head. They almost had me up against the wall. If they got me there, it was over. Fighting to keep from being overwhelmed, I kicked off the stone wall behind me and shoved my way into the middle of the pack. It was a lot harder for them to swing their clubs in close. They were just as likely to hit each other as me. I stabbed three legs. Three cries followed. Three more kids went down, leaving a small opening for me to escape.

I was halfway through when something heavy struck me from behind and I went down. I tried to get up, but whatever it was, it was still on top of me. I was pinned. I tried wiggling free, but the remaining kids grabbed my arms and legs and held me down.

I twisted my head around just enough to see Toothless sprawled on top of me, blood dripping from his chin on the side of my face.

"I'm going to kill you . . . slowly," Toothless said before rolling off me. The kids still standing pried the weapons from my hands and pulled me to my knees.

"Move aside!" Their leader pushed her way through the on-lookers, nearly tripping over the injured still sprawled on the cobbles. Her face was as red as her vest, flushed with anger.

"Hold him still. It's my turn."

CHAPTER 3

T HERE'S NOTHING quite so humiliating in life as being beaten in front of a pretty girl, unless the one doing the beating happens to be that very girl.

I was on my knees, held in place by two thugs who looked like they'd rather eat me than fight me. She swung her fist and it connected with the side of my face, whipping my head to the right. Something popped. My jaw throbbed, but I held my tongue and hid the pain. I was Upakan, after all. We didn't break.

At least I hoped I wouldn't.

I was seeing double. The two older boys released my arms and

I collapsed, blood seeping from the corners of my mouth, pooling in the gaps of the worn cobbles beneath me. I rolled over to my back. The buildings on either side of the narrow street towered overhead like the audience from an ancient colosseum—bearing witness to my shame.

The pain was nearly as bad as the time I'd fallen from Pike's Bluff during one of my first solo climbs. That experience, however painful, hadn't been nearly as traumatic as getting pummeled by this girl and her band of psychotic misfits. There were dozens of them now, all standing around cheering her on as she bravely beat an unarmed, defenseless stranger.

She appeared quite fond of applying her fists to my face. The small part of me still clinging to consciousness wondered if it had something to do with the thrashing I'd given her fighters before they overpowered me. It had to be humiliating, a dozen of her best taken down by one boy. I tried to smile, but the muscles in my face refused to cooperate.

I stared up at her through blurry eyes. She couldn't have been much older than I, fifteen or sixteen at most. Her hair fell halfway over her face, only partially hiding the satisfied smirk.

I didn't lose. I didn't know how to lose. I hadn't been beaten this badly since . . . well, I'd never been beaten this badly. Why these lunatics were so intent on pummeling me into a sack of mush was beyond me. I should have followed my instincts and never gotten involved.

"What's your name?" the girl with the red vest asked. Her voice was deep. Deeper than mine.

I was having a difficult time focusing on her words. Her face was little more than a blur now that both my eyes were swelling shut. "Ayr . . . Ayrion."

"Where are you from, Ayr . . . Ayrion? I've never seen anyone with eyes like that. You sick or something?"

My head was spinning. "I, uh . . ."

"Well, no matter." I could hear the smile in her voice. She lifted my pack and waved it in front of me. "It was a pleasure doing business with you, Ayr . . . Ayrion." She turned and started down the street. "Oh, by the way, welcome to Aramoor."

I heard the faint sound of laughter as everything spun out of control and faded into darkness.

A splash of something wet hit my face and tore me away from the peace of my unconsciousness. It must have been raining. At least, I hoped it was rain. The thought of a stray dog marking its territory on my head was enough for me to wrench open one of the swollen masses that were my eyes.

No sign of a dingy cur, urinating or otherwise. I released a raspy sigh of relief. At least I had one thing going for me. Or I thought I did. A crack of lightning was the only warning I had before the sky opened and released its flood on top of me. I shook my head. Maybe the rain would wash off some of the humiliation.

The sun had set, leaving the lonely street covered in darkness. The soft glow from the lamp on the corner was hardly enough to cut through the shadows. I wondered how long I'd been out and why nobody had bothered to help. Had no one seen me lying there? What sort of a place let a wounded kid bleed in the streets?

I tried lifting my head.

Bad idea. My body felt like it had been trampled over by a herd of zyntar intent on pounding me with each of their six enormous hooves before passing. The searing pain shouted in my ear that I should just lie there and let the inevitable happen, but in the end, I managed to push myself into a sitting position. It was then that I realized that not only was my travel sack with all my worldly possessions gone, but I had been stripped down and left with nothing more than a thin pair of undertrousers. Of course, it wasn't one of my nicer pairs but an older one my mother had mended on more than one occasion.

I looked around for any sign of my things, already knowing I wouldn't find them. From what I could tell, I was no longer on the street where the fight had taken place. The buildings were too close. They must have stashed me in an alley somewhere.

My father always said if you're going to do something, then do it right. Apparently, the girl with the red vest lived by the same motto. Although, if she had meant to do it right, she probably shouldn't have left me alive.

Nauseated, I hacked up a thick wad of blood. I watched as it mingled with the pools of water around my legs. The dizziness had lessened, but my eyes were swollen enough to leave me nearly blind.

I slowly took stock of the damage. It didn't take a physicker to know some of my ribs had been cracked, if not broken. Every breath felt like a knife sliding farther into my chest.

I was rolling my neck when I realized the chain holding my father's ring was missing.

"No!" I spun around. Pain shot through my chest. I scoured the surrounding area.

No ring.

"Where is it?" I forced myself to stand and wobble across the worn stone. Desperation took over, and I fell to my hands and knees, crawling from one side of the dirty street to the other. I examined every crack, crevice, and puddle. But there was no sign of it.

I stumbled into one of the larger holes and lay there, too weak to move.

My world shattered. What started as a soft whimper quickly turned into a full-on wail as I suffered through the shame of having been beaten, the loneliness of having nowhere to go and no one to turn to, and the fear of having lost everything I needed to survive. Above it all, I cried because I had lost the one precious thing my father had entrusted to me. His warrior ring.

Never had I felt so alone.

"If you're looking to go swimming," a voice said behind me, "I'd suggest the potholes over in Cheapside. They tend to be a bit deeper."

I wiped my tears and turned around. A short figure stood near the mouth of the alley. He sounded young, but with the lamp to his back, all I could see was his silhouette.

I must have looked insane—sprawled out in the middle of the walkway with bare chest and feet, my hair matted to the front of my face—but I was too exhausted and in too much pain to care.

"If you've come looking for an easy mark, you're too late." I tried to get to my feet but collapsed back into the pool of water. "I don't have anything left but my undertrousers, and if you want those, you'll have to kill me first." I managed to stand, trying to appear capable of defending myself, but my traitorous legs quivered like a drunken sot with a full bladder.

The boy moved closer. He was shorter than I and walked with a noticeable limp. What I thought had been some form of mutation was actually a large satchel he was toting over his right shoulder. I hoped, for one desperate moment, it might be mine, but he took a step to the right, and the streetlight showed me it wasn't.

I lifted my fists.

"Easy," the boy said. "Your wet skivvies are the last thing I want."

The boy turned enough for the streetlamp to show his face, and I lowered my guard. He was younger than I was. His light brown hair was short and parted to one side, or at least it had been before the downpour. He seemed well kempt compared to the last group of kids I'd met, which meant his face appeared to have been washed within the last week.

"What do you want?"

"Clearly, I want your sodden undergarments."

I wasn't sure if he was trying to be funny or serious. He might have looked younger than I, but the way he spoke sounded like someone much older.

"Actually, I want to help."

"Why?"

"Why? Someone offers to help, and the first thing you ask is *why*? Not very trusting, are you?"

"Today's my first day in Aramoor," I said, pointing down at my lack of clothing. "Do I look like I need to be trusting?"

"Good point. You look like you received a royal welcome from one of the tribes and lived to tell about it."

"Is that who attacked me?" I tried to sound calm, but my desperation took over. "Where can I find them?" I stumbled forward, but the boy caught me before I fell.

"If you have to ask, then I'd say your best bet is to come with me." He worked his shoulder up under my arm. "I doubt you'd last the night without my help. With your luck, you'd probably run across the one ruffian out there who'd want your soiled skivvies." He chuckled to himself.

"I need to get my stuff back. I had a ring—"

The boy grunted. "Your stuff is long gone. You won't be seeing it again. The sooner you come to grips with that, the better off you'll be." He started us back toward the street. I couldn't tell who was limping more, he or I.

"You don't understand. She took my ring. I have to get it back."

"She?" The boy stopped. "She who?"

"The girl who took it."

"What did she look like?"

"She was about this tall." I motioned with my hand to show that she was a little taller than myself. "She had black hair down to here." I pointed to the middle of my back. "Wore a red vest." Describing her wasn't difficult. Her image was seared into my memory.

The boy released a heavy sigh and shook his head. "Yeah. That would be Red." He studied my swollen face. "What did you do to get on her bad side?"

"Do? I didn't do anything!" I tried to steady myself, but my legs were still shaking. Another outburst and I was going to send us both down to kiss the cobbles. "Two larger boys grabbed some kid and ran off with him. He was screaming for help."

The boy shook his head. "You fell for the ol' kidnap routine." He chuckled. "That hardly ever works. Most people are too scared to help." He gave me a curious look. "Where did you say you were from, again?"

"I didn't."

"So, what happened next?"

I took a deep breath and coughed. "When I caught up with them, I realized it was a trap. That's when they demanded my stuff. When I refused . . ."

"You're lucky she left you alive. Red doesn't like to lose, and if you ever embarrass her . . ." The boy *tsk*ed. "Let's just say it's not a wise thing to do."

"Where can I find her . . . this Red?"

"You won't. Unless she wants to be found."

We stopped at the corner. The main street was quiet. Most of the windows were dark, shutters drawn and occupants asleep. The boy turned us right, and we started walking again.

"Where are you taking me?"

"Home."

I was hardly in a position to turn down help. Instead, I focused on placing one foot in front of the other.

"I'm Reevie," the boy said as he strained to keep his balance under my weight. His crippled leg wasn't helping. There was something genuine about him, something that made me want to trust him.

"I'm Ayrion."

"Well, Ayrion, in case no one has said it yet . . . *welcome to Aramoor.*"

CHAPTER 4

SLEEP WAS SLOW in coming, and when it did, it left me wishing I were awake. My dreams were plagued with nightmares.

I was being hunted by someone in a red vest. Sometimes it was Red, while other times it was my sister, Rianna. My own mother wore the vest at one point and chased me out of the house with her ladle, shouting something about not letting a murderer live under her roof.

Through it all, Reevie never left my side. Each time I woke, he was there with another cool compress to place on my head, reassuring me that everything was going to be fine. The foul liquid he forced down my throat was nearly as bad as the injuries. That was my life for the next few days: wake, pain, compress, nasty liquid, and then back to sleep.

As unexpected as the cruelty of Red's gang had been, the kindness of this little crippled kid was even more so. Why was he helping me? Other than my family, this street kid was about the closest I'd ever come to having a real friend.

I tried lifting my head to see if Reevie was still there, but it took a few moments before my neck got around to obeying. My entire body felt strangely numb, my movements sluggish. The trembling was gone, it had passed sometime in the night, but the pain from my beating remained. It wasn't the shooting pain from earlier but more of a throbbing ache.

I immediately reached for my magic, desperate to make sure it was still there. I'd never had it disappear like that before and was afraid I'd somehow lost it. I released a short sigh of relief. Through the numbness, I could sense the small ember of heat inside where I'd kept it hidden. I didn't dare release it in my weakened condition.

After one of my first punishments by the Peltok had left me bedridden for three days, Mother had warned me not to use it. She said that my magic was fed by my own strength, and if I were to use too much of it while in a weakened state, it could kill me.

A floorboard creaked, and I forced my eyes open. "Where . . . where am I?"

"Ah, I was starting to wonder if you were ever going to wake up." Reevie's voice was soothing. "Still alive, I see." His expression was composed, pleasant even, despite the dark circles under his eyes. "You're in my home."

I turned my head slowly, but even that movement caused the room to spin. "I don't feel very alive. What did you give me? I feel . . . funny."

"Oh, that. That's just a tonic I made for times like these."

He limped over to a small shelf on the far side of the room and rifled through a collection of colored bottles.

"Bleeding pustules!"

My head shot up at the strange outburst. "What? Where?" I lifted my blanket to peek underneath. Realizing I didn't have anything on, I yanked it back into place.

Reevie glanced over his shoulder and giggled. "Sorry. I curse in sicknesses. Helps me keep the knowledge fresh." He tapped his finger on the side of his head.

I cocked my eyebrow. "Knowledge?"

"Yeah. I'm a healer. At least, I'm studying to be."

The little boy was growing odder by the moment.

"Aha!" He held up a small bottle with some sort of dark liquid and smiled.

"What's that?" I knew a thing or two about herbs. Upaka learn from a very young age how to survive off the land, what could be used to save life and what could take it. A very useful skill to have, especially when taking a contract could mean traveling from one side of Aldor to the other.

MICHAEL
WISEHART

Reevie shifted from one foot to the other as he held out his bottle of tonic. "I use a number of different herbs, but at the base are yarrow, willow bark, mandrake, and valerian." He seemed excited by my interest. Probably as lonely as I was.

"All of them have strong anesthetic properties, especially the valerian," he continued. "But they're diluted. A full dose would put you in a sleep so deep, you'd never wake up."

"That sounds pretty good to me." I rolled to my side, but my ribs let me know that was a mistake, and I quickly rolled back. "How do you know so much about herbs?"

"My father was a physicker here in Aramoor."

"Was?"

"The Black Watch took him. Lord Ackelman told everyone that my father was using magic in his healing when the lord's daughter died." Reevie tightened his grip on the jar as if getting ready to hurl it. I raised my pillow in case he did.

Reevie stared at the tops of his tattered boots. They were at least two sizes too big. "When they showed up, Father hid me in the cupboard." He took a deep breath. "I never saw him again."

"I'm sorry," I said, not knowing what else to say under the circumstances.

Reevie wiped his eyes. "My turn to ask questions." He pointed to my chest. "What's all this?" I didn't need to look to know he was referring to my scars. "And don't try to tell me it was from your fight with Red's beaters."

Each of those markings told a story. Some were training accidents, times where I'd failed to block an instructor's blade. The jagged scar on my shoulder was from being impaled on a rock while climbing without gear. There were burns from when I'd been dared to hold an ember in my hand. The worst of them, though, were the long, thin scars on my back from Master Dorin's whip.

Reevie was still waiting for my answer. I rubbed one of the healed-over cuts on my forearm from a failed parry several years ago. "It's from my . . . education."

Reevie's brows shot up. "Education? Remind me to never attend any classes with you. Why don't you have any on your face?"

The absence of scars on my face was something I was quite proud of. While most of my classmates had at least one or two scars, I had been able to avoid such damage, thanks to my magic.

I tried to sit up.

"Whooping cough!" Reevie cursed as he limped over to my makeshift bed of old blankets and mismatched cushions. He gently pushed me back down. "What do you think you're doing?"

"What does it look like I'm doing? I can't just lie here all day." A sudden wave of nausea hit, and I collapsed back onto the pillows.

"See? I told you." Reevie grabbed a cloth and wiped my forehead. "You're fighting an infection. You're going to need to stay in bed at least a couple more days if you want your body to heal properly."

"A couple of days?" I tried sitting up again, this time releasing an embarrassing yelp when I was hit by a shooting pain in my abdomen. I collapsed back onto my pillow and took several shallow breaths, waiting for it to ease. "I don't have time to waste. I have to find Red. I've got to get my father's ring back. It's my only tie to my family."

"Yeah, yeah. You've already mentioned that," Reevie said, waving off my statement with an unsympathetic flick of his wrist. He limped back across the room to his shelf of tonics. "You have to do this. You have to do that. What you *have* to do is rest and heal. Your stuff is gone. Shame, too," he said, half-mumbling to himself. "You could have fetched a good price for that green cloak alone."

"I'm not going to just lie here. I need to—" I quit fidgeting when what he said hit me. "Wait. How did you know I had a green cloak?"

Reevie froze, his back to me. "You told me."

"I didn't tell you I had a cloak, let alone what color it was."

Reevie turned. "I, uh . . . I'm sure you told me about it."

I glared at him.

"Okay, okay." He raised his hands in submission. "So, I might have been passing by your street a little earlier than I let on."

"Earlier? What do you mean, *earlier?*"

"Well, let's just say I happened to catch your little scuffle with Red's beaters." He took a step forward. "I've never seen anyone fight like that! You took down half her fighters before they knew what hit them. It was amazing!"

My mouth hung open. "Why didn't you do something?"

He looked at me like I was insane. "What was I going to do? If I'd opened my mouth, I would have been right there beside you."

"You could have gotten help! What about the patrol?"

Reevie started laughing. "Are you crazy? The patrollers are worse than the tribes." Before I could say anything more, he was back to his scavenging. So, I took the opportunity to get a better look at where I was. The walls were mostly brick with age-worn plaster. The ceiling joists looked to be supporting another floor above us, and by their size, a large one at that. There were candles scattered around the room on boxes, broken shelves, and old barrels. Reevie had found either an abandoned house or a shop with a storage cellar, or he had somehow managed to rent one. It was possible he was simply squatting there, but I didn't think that likely.

"Here, eat this." Reevie hobbled back to my bed and handed me a couple of slices of cheese and a hunk of bread. I stuffed both into my mouth and barely chewed before swallowing. Either it was the best-tasting cheese and bread I'd ever eaten, or I was a whole lot hungrier than I thought.

Reevie smiled at the look on my face. "It's not exactly fresh, but the bread's still soft."

"It's good." I licked my lips and belched my thanks.

"You can stay here as long as you like. I've got plenty of room. And there's more where that came from," he said, pointing to the remaining piece of cheese I had gripped in my left hand. "And once you get to feeling better, I can show you around Aramoor."

I coughed. "No offense, but I think I've seen enough of your city to last me a lifetime."

"Bloody flux!" Reevie said with a dismissive wave. "You haven't seen anything but the butt end. Just you wait; when you're back on your feet, I'm going to take you places that'll bring tears to your eyes."

"Thanks," I said, "but I think I've had enough of that already."

Reevie laughed, and so did I.

Chapter 5

ㅜHE DAYS SEEMED to drag on and on, and the nights
weren't much better. My jailer had me bound to my bed with
little to do but stare at the walls and rafters. By the time he let me
do anything beyond sitting up, I'd counted every brick within sight
at least four or five dozen times.

Every day, it was the same question: "When can I get up?"
Every day, I'd get the same answer: "Not long now." I was wearing
him down, though. I could see it in his eyes.

Sure enough, on the fifth day, he gave me permission to test
my strength. I made it all of two and a half steps before gravity

took over and I toppled to the floorboards, taking a set of boxes down with me.

Reevie just stood there, shaking his head with an I-told-you-so look smeared across his face. But I didn't let it get me down. With his help, I was back on my feet and moving about. That was, I was able to hobble from a stack of boxes to an old barrel and then back to my bed. The pain was still there but slightly duller thanks to the herbal tonics Reevie continued pouring down my throat.

Reevie was astonishingly resourceful for a crippled orphan. He had somehow managed to procure an entire cantermelon. One side was showing signs of age, but it was still sweet. I had no idea where the food came from, but I wasn't about to turn it down. I was more concerned with stuffing my mouth full of the fruit's soft yellow nectar.

"You're getting around better," Reevie said, limping his way across the room to my bedside.

It took me a while to answer. I was savoring the last bite of melon.

"I am," I finally said as I slurped in the juices seeping from the corners of my mouth. "When can I go outside?"

Reevie prodded a couple of my deeper cuts and then felt my ribs. I fought to hide how much they still hurt. "I'd give it another day or two. You need to get to where you can move around on your own before going up there."

I knew what he meant. I needed to heal enough to be able to survive on the streets. But there was more to surviving than just being healthy.

I glanced at his leg. "How have you . . ." I wasn't sure how to word it delicately.

"Managed to survive with this?" he asked, patting the top of his right knee. "Not easily." He sat on a small upturned crate labeled HERRING. "It's hard enough even without a leg like mine. The best you can do is beg, unless you find a group to take you in. Out there on the streets, you can't survive on your own. You need a place to belong."

"You seem to be doing well enough on your own."

"I might choose to live here, but that doesn't mean I'm on my own."

I glanced around the dimly lit room as if expecting some unseen occupant to come jumping out of the shadows.

"Not here, ninny. Out there. If you want to survive, you've got to band together. Find people you trust to watch your back. Where'd you think the food you've been eating came from?"

"I was afraid to ask." I doubted Reevie, in his condition, would have had an apprenticeship, so naturally, I'd figured he had applied sleight of hand to what he brought home.

"It's from my tribe," he said as he motioned for me to hand him my leg.

I lifted it slowly and placed it on his lap. "What's a tribe?" Reevie had used that word before when talking about Red and her gang.

"Don't you have tribes where you come from?" he asked as he began to pinch and wiggle my toes. "Where do all the street kids live? Come to think of it, where are you from?"

I was surprised he didn't already know. "I'm Upakan. I figured my eyes would have given it away. We live in the underground ruins of the Lost City."

"Hmm, I've never met an Upakan before." Reevie left off with my toes as he examined the bruising around my ankle.

"That's probably a good thing."

Reevie took a hard look at my eyes. "I just thought you had some form of deficiency. I guess your ability to fight makes more sense now."

"To answer your question, no, we don't have tribes or street kids. We have clans. Each is made up of a select group of families."

"That's sort of the same thing," Reevie said, a little too excitedly, as he managed to twist my leg and cause me to yelp. "Oh, sorry." He laid the leg down and motioned for the other one. "We just call them *tribes* around here. The Warrens have clans, but you don't want to go in there."

"The Warrens?"

Reevie sighed. "Forget about the Warrens. I keep forgetting you're not from here. Everyone on the streets belongs to a tribe. It's street law. If you don't belong to a tribe, you can't work, which means you can't get food. Basically . . . you die."

My jaw tightened. I didn't like the sound of that. To be honest, there wasn't much about this place I did like the sound of. I kept a close eye on Reevie's hands as he started in with his examination of my other leg.

"In order to become a member of a tribe, you have to be of some value. Typically, with a leg like mine, I would end up getting branded a reject, but because of my knowledge of medicines, I've been allowed a place."

Without realizing it, I had clenched my fists. Part of what he had said struck close to home. It reminded me of Upakan society. Those physically able to fight would be given the right to join the ranks of warriors, earning the respect of those within the clans, while those less fit were sent to the top to cultivate the crops and manage the livestock. Not saying there was anything wrong with that, but most tended to look down on those not wearing the black ring.

I had spent my entire life training so that one day I could claim the title of warrior. Had I been guilty of the same? Had I looked down on those not able to do the same? I hoped not. I'd never thought about it before. Just because a person had a disability didn't mean they had no worth. Reevie was living proof. If it weren't for him, I would probably have already been dead.

"There are five tribes. Each is named after a natural force." He pinched my toes, one at a time, as he listed them off. "There's Hurricane—the tribe I belong to—Avalanche, Rockslide, Sandstorm, and Wildfire. And then there's the Guild. It controls the tribes."

"The Guild?"

Reevie chuckled, taking a break from squeezing my calf. "Pretty silly, if you ask me. As much as those on the streets shun the idea of having some all-powerful ruling class telling us what to do, like regular society, we go and organize one of our own. The Guild acts like the senate in that they give themselves the authority to make the laws, enforce those laws, and punish anyone who doesn't follow them. Namely us"—he pointed to himself—"the poor workers who don't get a say. But in all fairness, if not for the Guild, we would be seeing a whole lot more street wars taking place."

I tried to wrap my mind around the politics of it all. I had a lot to learn if I was going to make it in Aramoor. It looked like I had a pretty good teacher in Reevie.

Reevie nodded, as if happy with the result, and finally lowered my leg back to the floor.

Of everything Reevie had tried explaining, one question still ate at me. "Which tribe does Red belong to?"

"Wildfire." He stuck his finger in my face, eyes narrowed. "But don't you get any ideas. You listening to me? Whatever you're thinking . . . stop."

I raised my hands. "Wouldn't dream of it." Reevie lowered his gaze, but I knew he'd be keeping a close eye on me from now on.

No matter what I decided to do about Red, the rest of my options seemed rather limited—join a tribe or starve to death.

I had the feeling I wasn't going to fit in too well.

CHAPTER 6

AFTER A WEEK and a half of sitting on my hands, I was eager to leave our candlelit hovel and take Reevie up on his offer to see the sights. My legs were weak but healed enough that I no longer needed assistance. The best thing for them now was to be put to use.

We started up the rickety staircase leading from our quiet hideaway to whatever lay up top. "Watch it. Don't step on that one," Reevie said, pointing at the step where I was about to place my foot. "It's for unwelcome guests."

My foot hovered as I studied the wooden plank. It looked safe enough, but the twisted amusement on Reevie's face said otherwise, so I followed his example and stepped over it to the next.

"The bottom is scored. If anyone were to step on it, they'd go right through and I'd hear them." The little boy chuckled. "Once their leg is caught in the hole, they're mine." He raised his hands in the air as if holding a bludgeon and whacked an imaginary trespasser over the head.

I wondered how I'd managed to miss that step when I'd first arrived. The night Reevie had rescued me was somewhat of a mystery. From the time Reevie had carried me home until the time I'd first awoken on his bed, I had no memory.

Reevie was still chuckling at his trap when we stepped out of his dark underground hideaway and into the building above. Damp air and iron-gray light greeted us. The new day had not yet fully dawned. I stretched with a yawn. Something about the morning sun always did that to me.

The space above our sleeping chambers was much bigger than I had expected. It had been a warehouse or factory but clearly hadn't seen service in years. The soft light peeking in through the windows filtered through a heavy layer of dust. Apart from the natural creaking of the building's timbers and the skittering of hungry rats looking for their next meal, the place was quiet.

"Where are we?"

"One of the old granaries from back when this used to be the main shipping district."

"Who owns it?"

Reevie shrugged. "Ever since they opened the northern port

and moved all the warehouses over there, most of these older build-ings have been left vacant."

"I'm surprised there aren't other people living here. There's plenty of space." I stomped my foot on the floor. "And it seems sturdy enough."

"It's not the building that keeps people away. It's the location. We're just south of Cheapside, which puts us on the outer edge of the old city. Most people refer to it as the Warrens."

This piqued my interest. "You've mentioned that name before. What is it?"

Reevie headed for the doors at the front. "I'll show you."

We stepped outside the granary and into a small loading yard at the front. The colors in the sky were breathtaking. Gold, laced with pink and burgundy, melted into a rich blue and lavender as the clouds stretched farther west.

"The next street up is Mora," Reevie said, pointing off to the right. "Once you cross, you'll be in the Warrens. It's said to be the oldest part of Aramoor. They cut the stone from the bay when the first High King decided to build his city here."

"Doesn't look all that scary," I said as my eyes hopped from one building to the next. "There's no one there."

Reevie snorted. "They don't live up here. They're down there." He stamped his foot on the hard-packed clay.

I scratched my head and glanced at the print his boot had made in the dirt. "Down where?"

"Underground tunnels. The Warrens is a network that runs under the old city. Some say it extends all the way across Aramoor.

No one knows for sure. Not even the lancers will go down there. Nobody wants to mess with the clans."

"Why not live in the old city above?" I asked, recognizing the irony of the statement coming from an Upakan.

"'Cause those buildings are over a thousand years old and half of them have already collapsed in one part or another. Not a safe place to lay your head, never knowing if the roof over it will land on you in the middle of the night."

"The Warrens sounds like the perfect place to hide."

"Yeah, if you want to wind up without your hands and feet. No one goes down there without invitation, and even having one doesn't mean you'll come back up." Reevie shivered. "Best to stay on this side of Mora, if you know what's good for you."

"Well, from what little I've seen of Aramoor so far, it is impressive."

Reevie burst into a fit of laughter that ended in a rather embarrassing round of snorting.

"What's so funny?"

"That's like looking at a girl's big toe and describing how pretty she is." Reevie shook his head and limped his way up the short drive toward the main road. "Come on. If you want to see Aramoor, I'll show you Aramoor."

I'd never seen so many people in all my life.

The streets were full of them: tall people, short people, fat people, skinny people, some with big eyes, some with round chins. There were narrow cheeks, protruding noses, wide foreheads, and bulbous ears; a few had hair down to their waist, while others had no hair at all. Not at all like Upakan society, where everyone wore very similar garb, the people in Aramoor seemed to pride themselves on their individuality.

Living in the underground tunnels of the Lost City tended to breed out one's fear of enclosed spaces, but here in Aramoor, the mere act of walking down the street was enough to send my heart racing. I clenched my fists to keep them from noticeably shaking.

Unlike the streets outside the granary, where half the cobbles were missing and the holes were large enough to bathe in, the streets and walkways within the newer districts were well maintained. Most of the stones looked to have been replaced within the last few years, judging by their lack of wear.

The city itself seemed to transform as we moved from one section to another. Not only did the styles and shapes of the buildings change, but the people as well. Clothing went from simple trousers and tunics of rough cloth and bland colors to costumes with so many shapes and layers that it was hard to spot the individual underneath. How they managed to suffer through the summer heat wearing sweltering amounts of opulent clothing was a mystery. I quickly realized our job was to keep out of their way as they strolled by, noses stuck in the air.

Another aspect that separated the sections of Aramoor from each other was the variance in speech. In Cheapside, the dialogue was loud, abrasive, with a touch of get-out-of-my-way thrown in for good measure. It was a dialect for people who didn't want to communicate: half-spoken words, arm and head gestures, grunts and whistles. Instead of politely asking someone to step aside, a whistle and a jerk of the thumb was all you got.

West of Cheapside, we crossed through the outer edge of what Reevie said was the new shipping district. Most of the residents were men who spent their lives on the open waters and women and children who waited patiently for them to come home. Of course, there were also plenty of the other kind of women, those with heavily painted faces and scantily covered bodies, also waiting for the ships to return. I tried not to look in their direction when we passed, but it was difficult with all the winks and calls they sent our way. It didn't take long to realize which houses were off-limits.

Most of the sailors went about their daily chores topless, their skin dark from exposure. Their trousers were baggy and tied off just above the calf. The old pair of trousers Reevie had lent me was short enough on my legs that I appeared to fit right in.

Seeing the sailors brought back memories of my time spent on the *Wind Binder*. Their speech had a strong flavor of the sea. To me, it sounded redundant at times. For example, their use of the word *be*. "Would ye *be* likin' a tour of our ship, young sirs? She *be* the finest vessel this side of the Blue Isles. And that *be* no lyin'." It was a fun way to talk, and I found myself smiling as I followed along.

Just north of the shipyards was Bayside with all its grand estates overlooking the blue waters of the Bay of Torrin. We hadn't wandered too far inside before one of the patrollers chased us back out. I doubted I would have liked it much, anyway. Trying to keep my nose in the air the way they did left a kink in my neck.

The closer we got to the merchant district, the grander the buildings grew and more packed the streets became: shoppers coming and going, street vendors calling out their wares—those unlucky enough to not possess the gold necessary to open their own shops. Dirty street kids with nimble fingers darted in and around the patrons while patrollers in their notable royal blue capes stood ready to give chase. It was a living, breathing chaos that moved in an order of its own. There was a natural sort of rhythm to it, like the water cascading over Triple Falls, moving from one pool to the next on its way through the tunnels back home.

The noise alone was enough to drown my thoughts. I fought the urge to cover my ears: horses' whinnies, riders' whips, merchants' calls, heavy-heeled shoes on stone, wagon wheels, children's excited shouts as they hurried their parents toward the next shop. Thousands of people, each unaware of anything outside their own small sphere.

"This way!" Reevie shouted above the crowd. "Don't stop in the middle of the road."

I followed his example and kept to his heels as we crossed. "Why's that?"

"It's the carriages. The drivers are ordered to—"

As if on cue, a large white-and-gold barouche flew around the corner, its top down in the summer heat. A fat man layered in blue and gold silks with a bored expression on his face sat in the back on blue velvet cushions, his wife next to him. The driver spurred the two horses with a crack of the whip. People all along the center of the avenue rushed to get out of the way, some practically diving to keep from getting hit.

A woman in the crowd screamed. "My son!"

There in the middle of the street was a small child making his way across the now-empty cobbles. He was completely unaware of where he was as he focused on trying to catch a large frog as it hopped from one stone to the next.

My breath caught. I looked at the driver; his eyes went wide, but he showed no sign of slowing the carriage. I looked back at the crowd; no one moved. Most were too far away.

Men shouted for the driver to stop, while women clutched their children and covered their eyes.

The young mother wailed, trapped too far back in the crowd to reach her son.

I was one of those at the front. I could feel the tremor of the horses' hooves as they beat the ground.

Without hesitation, I released the barrier holding back my magic. I didn't have time to worry about whether my body was healed enough to use it or not. If I didn't do something, the little boy was going to die.

As soon as the magic released, I was struck with my first vision. The horses pounding me into the road, their hooves stomping my chest, legs, and arms, followed by the weight of the carriage wheels.

MICHAEL
WISEHART

The pain in those moments was unbearable, then I was back suddenly on the side of the road watching the little boy.

I took a deep breath and jumped into the street and ran, leaving Reevie to shout at me from the side. My timing had to be exact, or I was going to end up trampled along with the boy.

The horses were right behind me.

I didn't need to turn to know how close. I could hear their snorts, practically smell the sweat from their hides. My mouth was dry, but I tried swallowing anyway.

Three. Two. One.

I dove.

My arms wrapped around the boy as his hands wrapped around the slimy croaker.

We tumbled to the side and rolled clear of the deadly hooves.

The horses reared.

Their sudden halt threw the overly dressed man and his wife across the carriage, where they landed in the seats on the other side.

The crowd gasped.

I felt like I'd just set myself back another couple of days of healing. My ribs and right arm burned from where I'd landed on them. I struggled to my feet and helped the little boy back to his before proudly turning to present him to his mother.

By the people's reactions, you'd think they'd never seen a selfless act before.

Then I realized they weren't looking at me. They were all watching the fat fop and his ugly wife get helped back to their cushions.

"Oh, thank you, thank you, thank you," the child's mother sobbed. She grabbed the two of us and pulled us close. I think she kissed me just as much as she kissed her son. "Laris, what were you thinking, running out there like that? What have I told you about leaving my side?"

"Mama, look." Laris raised his hands for his mother to see his slimy new pet. After everything I'd done to save its life, the wretched thing had the audacity to belch at me. I shook my head.

"Put it down. I told you to quit playing with those disgusting things." The woman reached into her bag and pressed a gold coin into my hands. "I can't thank you enough." She glanced at my sad state and patted me on the head. "Buy yourself some new clothes."

"Thank you, ma'am." I offered what I thought was an appropriate bow. I was about to ask her to recommend a good shop when a commotion broke out behind us.

"There!" The obese man in the white suit stood from his carriage and pointed at us. "That boy right there! He's the one! Get him!" I turned around to warn Laris, but neither the boy nor his mother were anywhere to be seen. Then it dawned on me who the overdressed pincushion was referring to.

Reevie rushed over, out of breath. "Black Pox, Ayrion! We've got to get out of here. Now!"

CHAPTER 7

FOUR BLUE-CAPED patrollers responded to the fat man's cries. They drew their cudgels and charged, shouting as they came. Reevie grabbed my arm, and we dove into the crowd. For the first time since we'd left the granary that morning, I was thankful for all the people.

"What's going on?" I asked as I fought my way through the sea of bodies to match Reevie's steps.

"We're being chased, is what's going on!"

"I know that much. But why?"

"Maybe because you just tossed Lord Gerrick and his wife

around like a couple of button dolls in the middle of the square. I'm sure he wants to decorate his study with your head."

"Who's Lord Gerrick?" I asked, already feeling winded. My body was on the mend, but it was far from being ready for an all-out street chase.

"He's only the *biggest* supporter for cleaning up the unwanted from Aramoor's streets." He glanced to his side. "Namely us."

I didn't say more. I couldn't. I had to put all my focus into breathing. What was it about this city that had me running for my life every time I stepped outside? We fought our way through the surge of bodies, skirting legs and dodging arms, praying we could duck into an alley.

We had one thing in our favor. We were the perfect size for disappearing. Reevie's head barely rose above the taller men's waistlines, while mine reached their chests. I was shocked at how well my crippled friend was able to move through the crowd. Even with his gimpy leg, he never missed a step.

I, on the other hand, was nothing short of a clumsy dolt. I'm pretty sure I hit more people than I missed. I was a little preoccupied with trying to keep my bare feet from being squashed by heavy boots and stray heels.

I knocked one lady carrying a small mountain of parcels off her feet.

I tossed a quick apology over my shoulder, but she was too busy hurling accusations and shrieking for the patrollers to hear me. She latched on to one of the patroller's legs, demanding he not only catch the dirty street rat who had tried to kill her but also that he help her up and recover her packages while he did.

I smiled at our luck and kept running.

I had no idea where we were going, and Reevie never once hesitated. Breaking out of the flowing current of bodies, we ducked between two towering stone buildings. I suddenly knew what it felt like to be an ant in a forest of elder pine.

Tripping over some discarded debris, I stumbled forward and went down. An alley cat leaped out of a bucket, hissing its outrage at having its meal disturbed. I apologized and pulled my sore foot out of the crate I'd just stuck it through. Thankfully, it hadn't found a rusty nail.

"This way. Hurry!" Reevie was already halfway down the narrow lane by the time I crawled around the piles of trash. I took off as fast as my legs would carry me. With nothing else blocking my way, I was able to catch up pretty quickly.

"Get back here!" The shout echoed off the corridor behind us. I turned to see three of the four men in blue capes working their way through the piled garbage.

"Stop, or you'll regret it!"

"I think we'll regret it even more if we do." I grabbed Reevie's arm and pushed him forward. Reevie grunted, half-running, half-hobbling between another pair of buildings as we rushed for the next street.

We spilled out of the alley and onto a small thoroughfare where the traffic wasn't quite bursting at the seams. We skirted the edge of the crowd, often only an arm's width from the shops themselves, the scents of each assaulting us as we passed: tanned leather, rich chocolate, fermentation, wood shavings, strong herbs.

Up ahead, the road forked. I had turned to ask Reevie which way when I realized my guide was nowhere to be found.

I froze.

I'd learned at an early age that the worst thing to do when lost was to wander about trying to get un-lost. Living in an underground labyrinth of tunnels as I had, getting lost had become something of a hobby. The best thing to do was to stop and wait for someone to find me, preferably while making as much noise as possible. Unfortunately, that particular approach would only get me captured.

I glanced left and then right, finally spinning in a circle as I scanned every face, frantically searching for Reevie. He wasn't there.

Behind me, the patrollers burst from the alleyway. The fourth man had apparently managed to catch up with the others. He was the first to spot me. He pointed and charged. I was about six or seven pavilions away, with a host of shoppers between, but that didn't slow them in the least. People—those too preoccupied with shopping or too stupid to move on their own—were thrown aside.

What had I done to deserve this? I had saved a child from a horrible death. Sure, some fancy lord had been tossed around in his carriage, but he'd landed on a pillow. I shook my head. Aramoor might have been spectacular to look at, but it was as dangerous as an Upakan blade and growing more cutthroat by the moment.

I turned to run, but someone grabbed my shoulder.

I spun, fists up.

"It's me!" Reevie hissed and pulled me toward one of the shops. "This way!" He ran through the open door, taking me with him.

That was a mistake. At least outside, we had the ability to keep running, but now Reevie had trapped us in a confined space with only one exit. The inside of the shop was crowded with rows of tall shelves crammed with books.

"Quick, in here!" an older man said as he flipped back a tasseled rug near the front desk, revealing a trapdoor underneath.

I desperately tugged at the metal ring. It creaked open. I half-expected to see a set of stairs leading down to a cellar, but it was nothing more than a pocket beneath the floorboards. I tossed Reevie inside and practically jumped on top of him. The old man closed the door, and I could hear the rug thump back into place.

What little light there had been between the cracks in the floor-boards disappeared as a cloud of dust rained down on our heads. I grabbed my mouth and pinched my nose, willing myself not to sneeze. I could hear my heart pounding as we lay on our backs and listened to heavy footfalls fill the shop above us.

CHAPTER
8

"**H**OW WELL DO you trust this old man?" I kept my mouth pressed close to Reevie's ear so my words wouldn't carry beyond the floor above us.

"With my life."

I nodded. It wasn't like I had much choice either way. I closed my eyes and prayed Reevie's faith in the man hadn't been misplaced.

I could hear raised voices, but the rug dampened the sound so much I had to strain to hear.

"Two boys. One about yea high . . . the other about so."

"Boys, you say? My boys are all grown up."

"Not you, you old fool. Two street kids just came through here. Did you see them?"

"Did I see who?"

There was an impatient groan. "Two boys. The taller one had dark hair to his shoulder. The shorter one had light brown, maybe half as long. Walked with a limp."

"Of course I have a limp," the old man said. "That's why I have this cane, you brainless lout. Now if you are quite through, I've got orders to fill."

"Search the place. They've got to be in here somewhere."

Books began to hit the floor, covering us with dislodged dust. I covered my face as best I could.

"Hey! What do you think you're doing?" the old man hollered. I could hear him strike something, probably his desk, with his cane. "Get out of my shop! You have no right to come in here and mess with my books!"

The patrollers didn't acknowledge him.

After what seemed a small eternity, all the boots reconvened right above us.

"Anything?"

No one spoke.

"If we find out you've been hiding street rats in here, you and your wife will spend the rest of your days chasing mice around your dungeon cell." Heavy boots clomped their way to the door, and the bell signaled their departure.

The dungeons? That seemed a harsh sentence for someone wanting to help hungry children. However, if most of the street rats were anything like Red and her gang, I could see why the patrollers were anxious to round them up. They were nothing more than a deranged group of thugs.

The rug finally rolled back and the trapdoor opened. I squinted at the light. I hopped out of the cramped space and helped Reevie out before dropping the door back into place. The shopkeeper flipped the green-and-gold tasseled rug back over the door, causing another puff of white dust to lift off the floor. The shop was in clear need of a good brooming.

"I'm sorry, Master Fentin," Reevie said. "I never meant for this to happen."

The book merchant locked the door and then pulled the shades. With a heavy sigh, he turned around. The shop was in shambles. Books covered the floor five or six volumes deep. It looked like the men had just walked down the aisles and swiped them from the shelves for no other reason than they'd wanted to.

"It's nothing for you to worry about," he said as he hobbled over to the first shelf for a better look. "Been meaning to re-alphabetize these things for years. Just hadn't had a good reason to until now." He looked at Reevie and chuckled. "So, what were they after you for this time?"

"It wasn't me," Reevie said with a nod in my direction. "It was Ayrion. He saved some kid from being run over by Lord Gerrick." Reevie spat the name out like a sour grape. "The horses got spooked and threw the lord and his lady from one side of the carriage to the other."

Master Fentin reared back and wheezed out a fit of high-pitched laughter hard enough that I thought he was going to end up on the floor. Surprisingly, he managed to keep his balance with the help of his cane. "That's the best news I've heard in weeks, my boy." He smacked the end of his stick across his desk. "What I would have given to see that." He thrust a wrinkled hand in my direction. "I'd like to shake hands with you, young sir. Any time you have need of a place to hide, I'm here."

Master Fentin had a firm grip for such an elderly man. I wanted to say I had done what anyone would, but after what we'd just been through, that hardly seemed true. "Thank you, sir. I'm new to the city. Reevie helped me out after I was mugged by a gang of cutthroats—"

"It was Wildfire," Reevie interjected.

Master Fentin took a deep breath and produced an all-too-knowing nod, then placed a hand on Reevie's shoulder. "Well, you can't find better than Reevie for rounding up lost strays, that's for sure. Now let me get a look at you." He grabbed a pair of spectacles from his jacket pocket and perched them on the edge of his nose. "Hmm, thought so. Upakan, am I right?"

I nodded.

"I've only come across one of your people before, and that was many years ago. But it was an experience I'll never forget. Killed five men, he did, with his bare hands. Most amazing thing I've ever seen. Are all your people taught to fight like that?"

"Most of them, sir, from birth. Upaka means *warrior* in the old tongue."

"Actually, *Upaka* is often mistranslated. Here." Master Fentin made his way to a shelf at the back of the shop that had somehow remained untouched by the patrollers. He pulled a large volume and started thumbing through the pages. "Ah, here we go." Walking back to the front, he laid it on the desk and traced a finger down the page, stopping on a passage written in a tight, cramped hand. "The word *Upaka* is a derivative of the ancient word *Upakora*. Its closest direct translation isn't *warrior*. It's . . . *protector*."

"*Protector?*" Reevie huffed. "That fits. It was your"—Reevie cleared his throat—"*protecting* that got us into this mess in the first place."

Master Fentin closed the book and plopped onto the stool next to his desk. He stared at me for an uncomfortable amount of time before speaking. "So, what is one of the Upaka doing so far from home?"

Reevie edged closer, trying—and failing—to not look eager to hear my answer. He'd never asked me about my past, and up until this point, I hadn't seen a need to share it, at least not much of it.

I thought about lying, spinning a tale so wild and exciting that whether you believed it or not, it was just plain fun to hear. My father was a master storyteller. He could make you believe, or at least want to believe, whatever he desired just from the way he talked about it. I didn't have the gift. My stories tended to be too rigid and detailed. By the time I got around to the make-believe part, no one would.

This probably wasn't the best time to try, anyway. Best to peel off the bandage nice and quick and hope the pain wasn't too excruciating. With that in mind, I took a deep breath. "I'm here because . . . because I killed someone."

Neither Reevie nor Master Fentin said a word. I think Reevie's eye twitched.

I'd been dreading this moment. Nothing like telling the person who saved your life and offered you a place to stay that they were in fact sheltering a murderer—great way to quickly lose your sleeping arrangements.

"Well, go on, son," Master Fentin said as he rested his elbow on the table and propped his chin on his hand. "I hope that's not the end of the story."

"No. It's just the most important part."

"I'll have to disagree with you there, my boy. For example, what if you were to tell us that the reason you killed this person was because you had some sort of malediction, that whenever you heard the name Reevie, you felt compelled to kill the owner of that name? That would tend to be the most important part, I think." He chuckled and poked Reevie in the arm. Reevie didn't look amused. "The motive behind the action is most often just as important as the action itself."

"I guess you have a point," I said with a shrug. "Where should I start?"

"Ah . . ." The old man gestured toward the open room. "Just like a book, every story has a beginning, a middle, and eventually an end. How about we start at the beginning?"

I took another deep breath and released the tension from my shoulders. I climbed up on a stool at the edge of the table and let my legs dangle over the end. "How much do you know about my people?"

Master Fentin and Reevie shared a blank look, so I went on to explain some of the finer points of being an Upakan. I told them of our training, of the contracts we took. I also told them of our highest laws, the Shal'Noran, and the principle of never killing another Upakan.

"What if they tried to kill you first?" Reevie asked.

"What if it was by accident?" Master Fentin chimed in.

"What if you killed someone's pet?" Reevie asked, obviously thinking he'd thought of a way to trip me up. "Like maybe their dog wouldn't stop barking and you fed it some milkweed or something."

I crossed my arms and sighed. "Unless the dog took the oath, then it isn't considered one of the Upaka."

"Then what if you killed a baby?"

"Why would I kill a baby?"

Reevie shrugged. "I don't know. But what if you did? They clearly haven't taken the oath—"

"Okay, okay." Master Fentin raised his hands to calm us down. "I think we get the picture."

I went on to tell them of my fight with Flon, and his accidental death, and the council's ruling to have me banished. From there, I regaled them with tales of my adventures from the Lost City to

Aramoor: my run-in with the highway bandits, my trip down the Shemoa, our rescue of the Cylmaran miners, and our standoff with Captain Owen. I ended the exciting tale with an accounting of my first full day in the capital city and the subsequent week and a half of bedrest. By the time I was finished, I was wondering how I'd survived this long.

"Must be the Creator's way of punishing me," I said, not realizing I had spoken out loud.

Master Fentin tapped his cane on the floor. "I hardly think the Creator's in the business of castigating little boys for defending themselves against bullies. It was clearly not your fault. Although I'm sure that doesn't ease the loss of your family." The merchant studied my face. "How long has it been, son?"

"Been for what?"

"Since you've seen them."

I tried to picture my family in front of me: my father with his strong arms and wise counsel; my mother with her warm embrace and unending kindness; my sister, Rianna, with her constant curiosity; and my brother, Jorn, who would follow me around wherever I went. My eyes began to burn.

"Since Sòl," I answered. "So, about seven months, I guess."

Master Fentin nodded.

The three of us sat there for an uncomfortable amount of time before Master Fentin finally broke the silence. "Well, I do believe my stomach is telling me it's time for lunch. What say I have Orilla whip us up some sandwiches before we start on this mess?"

"I'd say your stomach knows what it's talking about," Reevie said. "Mistress Orilla makes the best sandwiches in Aramoor. I just wish she'd tell me her secret."

"Ah, but the mystery is half the enjoyment," Master Fentin said with a cheeky smile.

I pulled myself away from my reminiscing and scanned the disarray across the floor of the shop. I sighed and hopped down from the stool. "Lunch sounds good to me."

CHAPTER 9

W E SPENT THE BETTER part of the following week
working in Master Fentin's shop. I actually found the routine of sorting through the mountains of books and arranging them
by title and content to be therapeutic. There was also the added
benefit of using my slowly healing muscles in gentle, repetitious
work.

Reevie had pledged our help in exchange for food and some
supplies we needed around the granary: fresh candles, another
broom, and cushions to make a second bed. We offered to do it for
nothing—we owed Master Fentin our freedom—but neither he

nor his wife would hear of it. I think they were looking for any excuse to help us out.

On Fifthday, Mistress Orilla took us shopping for some new clothes. It was Reevie's idea. He figured if he dressed me nicer than his too-small hand-me-downs, I would stand a better chance of being accepted by his tribe. I wasn't sure how my wearing a new set of clothes would persuade a gang of street kids to do anything more than try to take them from me. I hoped Reevie knew what he was doing.

I used the gold piece the lady in the market had given me for saving her son. In truth, I was actually excited by the whole ordeal. It was the first time I'd ever owned clothing not made by my mother.

We each got a new pair of trousers, a light-colored linen tunic, a sleeveless leather jerkin, and a couple of pairs of woolen socks to go along with our new shoes. I was most thankful for the shoes. I didn't know which was worse, walking around Aramoor with bare feet or trying to squish into an old pair of Reevie's.

Our new clothes were simple but well made, which was perfect for a couple of street kids not wanting to stick out in a crowd. More importantly, they were clean, comfortable, and actually fit.

I had a feeling Mistress Orilla supplemented the bill with her own coins. I couldn't see how a single gold piece could have purchased everything we walked out of the shop with. Instead of making a fuss, I spent as much free time as I could helping them around the shop.

The days passed quickly, and my body continued its slow journey back to health. By the third week, I felt well enough to begin the training regime I had grown up with. The exercises were rigorous, designed to push myself to the limit, creating a honed Upakan warrior.

I didn't jump into my exercises full force. I knew my limitations. The last thing that I wanted was to end up in bed again because of impatience.

The granary was the perfect place to train. It had lots of wide-open space and high ceilings with hefty rafters, perfect for climbing ropes. There were empty boxes and barrels and pallets to use as hurdles for a makeshift obstacle course. I even found an old pulley to use for weights.

Above all its other worthy attributes, the granary was void of unwanted guests. We were an island to ourselves in a sea of stone and plaster. Only the immensely brave or the immensely stupid chose to live this close to the old city.

"Have you lost your mind?" Reevie practically fell out of the open hatch when he saw me hanging from the rafters by my legs. "I didn't spend the last few weeks putting you back together so you could kill yourself in front of me!"

"Don't worry. I do this all the time—or did, back home." I waved it off. "It's nothing. Helps with blood flow."

"Tick fever it does! Now get down here before I feed your supper to the cats since you seem too stupid to eat it!"

The threat of losing supper was all it took. I repositioned my legs around the beam and began to rock myself back and forth. A rope hung from another beam about six feet away. I needed to reach enough momentum to swing myself over to it before I let go of the beam. It was a difficult move, but I had done really well in my training today and I felt up to it.

I slowed my breathing and concentrated, letting go of everything around me and focusing on just the rope. The rope was the only thing that existed in that moment.

"You're not about to . . ." Reevie didn't finish. I figured he was too afraid he'd break my focus and cause me to fall. Knowing him, he was probably thinking up some really nasty diseases to swear at me as soon as I landed.

I kept my eyes on the target. My body was moving swiftly now, back and forth, swinging me a little farther out each time. I could feel my heartbeat. I didn't look down. All that existed were me, the rope, and the beam. Nothing else mattered. I pictured the rope in my hands and held on to the image as I counted down on the forward swings. *Three . . . Two . . . One . . . Release!*

I let go of the beam and sailed forward. I was a leaf on the wind. For one blissful moment, I was free. I opened my hands and grabbed hold of the rope and swung outward. It was a wonderful feeling. I let the rope pull me along as I flew through the air. I hit the apex and—

It snapped.

My heart leaped into my throat.

I vaguely heard Reevie cry out as I continued forward, the frayed piece of rope still clutched in my hands. I threw it and grabbed at another. I missed. The concrete was coming fast. My fingers managed to wrap around the last of the five climbing ropes, and I yanked with all my might. My body did a complete flip, and I landed on my back, but not with enough force to do anything more than knock the wind out of me.

Before I could make it to a seated position, Reevie had his arms around me, squeezing me to death. I could have sworn there were tears in his eyes. After an uncomfortable amount of time, he finally pulled away and punched me as hard as he could before limping back downstairs. No horrific diseases were cursed my way, no threats of a lost meal, only silence.

I would have preferred the diseases.

Reevie didn't say anything about my training after that. I think he resigned himself to the fact that I was going to do what I was going to do, and if I ended up getting myself killed doing it, then he'd simply have to clean up the mess and look for another crazy roommate with whom to share his meals.

I found some newer, stronger rope and continued to train. With no one around to see, I'd strip to my underpants in order to spare my new clothes the wear and tear of a hard workout. By the time I was through each day, I was thoroughly soaked, winded, and in need of a good bathing. And Reevie would let me know it.

We found an old washbasin in one of the abandoned buildings nearby. With some brilliant ingenuity on Reevie's part, we managed to move it into one of the smaller rooms at the back of the granary.

There were times during my training that I'd catch Reevie watching me as I moved through my combat routines: punching, kicking, spinning, rolling. My body's natural responses were coming back. I was barely getting winded now. The burning ache after a grueling session of drills felt wonderful. It told me I was making progress.

I was even able to talk Reevie into joining me during some of my simpler exercises. There was only so much he could do with his bad leg, but I was able to devise some helpful exercises that allowed him to build his endurance and strengthen his upper body.

"No, move your foot here," I said, pointing at a spot on the floor with my bare toes. Reevie slid his foot forward to the place I indicated. "See? That will give you more balance." I placed my hands on his shoulders and rocked him slightly. "When your feet are spread farther apart, it makes you less likely to fall."

I wanted to give him some amount of ability to stand up for himself since he couldn't exactly run from a fight, so I taught him some of the basics. In truth, it was all I really knew to offer. "Good. Now block with this arm, and punch with that fist. Like this." I demonstrated and Reevie copied. "Yeah, that's it."

The more we practiced, the more proficient Reevie became. At the very least, it gave him some much-needed self-confidence, which was very important for someone in his shoes. The way things were shaping up for me here in Aramoor, I had a feeling we were going to need all the help we could get.

Red and her gang were still out there.

CHAPTER

10

"ARE YOU READY?" Reevie shifted his feet with eager anticipation as he waited for me to step out the front door of
the granary and into the gray-fingered light of an early dawn. The
ship bells in the harbor rang out the change of watch. Their tones
echoed through the empty streets, heralding a new day.

The fresh, salty tang to the air outside our warehouse was in-
vigorating. I slid my fingers down the edge of my leather jerkin.
The still-new smell of my clothing gave me confidence. Maybe today—unlike most of the other times I'd set foot on the streets of
Aramoor—wouldn't go horribly wrong.

It had been at least three weeks since I'd last left our cozy hideout on the south side of town, three weeks since I had visited Master Fentin's shop or eaten one of Mistress Orilla's mystery-meat sandwiches. I felt guilty about my lack of attention, but I had spent every free moment working to get my body back into shape so I'd be ready for today.

I took a deep breath and exhaled with determination. "Yes."

Reevie looked skeptical, but he nodded and shut the granary door.

"Where is your tribe located?"

"At the heart of the Maze."

"Maze?"

"Another name for Cheapside."

"Why's that?"

"You'll see." He handed me his sack of herbs, and we started up the street. "Now, remember, don't speak unless spoken to." He glanced in my direction. "Better yet . . . don't speak at all."

"Thanks for the vote of confidence."

"I'm just looking out for you. You've only got one shot at this. Don't waste it with an ill-timed comment. You might be some super-deadly assassin-warrior, but in my world, a pair of swift hands and fast feet is no match for a cool head and a sharp tongue."

I almost laughed. That sounded like something my instructors would have said. Well, maybe not the bit about a "sharp tongue," but definitely the need for a cool head. *One who is swift to emotion is swift to defeat*, my father would say.

Reevie even reminded me of my father sometimes: same inflections in his voice, same serious tone, same scrutinizing glare. It made me feel appreciated for the same reason it did when my father used to scold me. Because I knew he cared.

"All right," Reevie said as we started into the Maze. "There are some things you need to know. First of all, the head of our tribe is Spats. And before you go asking, I've got no idea why he's called Spats.

"Hurricane isn't the largest tribe in Aramoor, but they aren't the smallest, either. They are one of the poorest, however."

"So, why did you choose to join them?"

"Necessity, mostly. They were the first tribe to contact me, and because of my small skill as a healer, they were happy to let me join."

Reevie didn't seem all that proud of his association with Hurricane. It seemed a relationship of convenience. This was foreign to me. Upakans were proud of their families.

"Hurricane has been around for nearly two decades," Reevie said, "which is quite the accomplishment, considering the conflict between tribes, especially over picking grounds."

"Picking grounds?"

Reevie passed me a sheepish look. "A picking ground is a . . . a . . . Blisters! It's not really important what a picking ground is. We need to focus on getting you on Spats's good side and keeping you there."

"How do I do that?"

"For starters, by not asking so many questions."

"How am I supposed to learn anything if I can't ask any questions?"

"By keeping your mouth shut and your eyes and ears open."

"Why haven't you told me all this before? Why'd you wait until now?"

Reevie shrugged. "Guess I didn't figure you'd actually stick around as long as you did. I figured once you healed, you'd have moved on."

That was a sad sort of revelation. Guess I couldn't fault him for it. Everything else in his life had let him down; why not me? "I'm not going anywhere."

Reevie didn't look at me. His smile said it all.

"So, tell me more about this Spats character."

"Spats surrounds himself with bootlickers. Being willing to do anything he says gets you attention—and a promotion more often than not. He likes winners, as long as they acknowledge their success results from his exceptional leadership. So, keep your mouth shut and your head down. With your skills, you don't want to be seen as a threat. Exceptional people tend to catch fatal diseases, like acute metal poisoning in the back."

I grimaced. The more Reevie talked about this Spats, the less I liked him. I wanted to ask him again why he was a part of this group, but I didn't push. I got the sense that he wasn't thrilled that his survival depended on his standing with a rough group of kids. I wasn't thrilled with the idea of teaming up with them myself, but apparently, I wouldn't last long in Aramoor if I didn't.

The streets slowly filled the farther north we walked as the rest of the Maze began to wake. Men kissed their wives good-bye while mothers called their children in for breakfast. I found myself longing once more to hear my own mother telling me it was time to eat.

The houses in Cheapside were crammed together like stacked shipping crates on a dock waiting to be loaded. There was hardly room enough to breathe. Families were stuffed into tiny, barely affordable spaces. Lines of clothing ran like spider webs between buildings. The air was rife with the stench of overpopulation. I tried holding my nose, but it didn't help. How could anyone live here?

Reevie noticed my expression. "You get used to it."

I found that hard to believe.

We crossed out of a residential district and into a cluster of small shops. The buildings, though much nicer than the residential area we had just left, were in desperate need of repair.

"This used to be the main shopping district for Aramoor centuries ago," Reevie said as he stopped long enough for me to have a brief look around.

Even decayed with age, the buildings were ornate. Instead of flat stone, the walls had definable layers. The builders had done a lot of work chiseling out each block, some with elegant designs. Intricate trimming around the windows and doors added a unique flare.

I could almost imagine what they must have originally looked like. But, much like the Warrens, these buildings had been left to rot as the city grew and expanded. The decay had begun to chip away at the walls, leaving entire sections looking as though a good wind would bring them down.

I understood all too well the effects of time. The Lost City had at one time been the capital of all Keldor, but after the eruption of Mount Ash and the tremors that followed, the city was swallowed, burying its once-regal beauty under a mountain of rock.

"We need to prove to Spats that you're valuable," Reevie said, diverting my attention from the surrounding buildings. "We need to give him a reason to keep you around, something that doesn't make you stick out."

"I'm sure I can think of something," I said with a mischievous grin.

"Yeah, that's what worries me."

"I can handle it."

"I hope so. 'Cause . . . we're here."

We rounded the corner of the last shop. A brick path wound its way through a small grove of trees, ending at a large, ornate wall. It was at least twelve feet in height. Chiseled into the lower half of the stone were strange creatures, with unfamiliar glyphs at the top.

"Interesting place for a street tribe," I said, gawking at the wall's decorations. I had never seen or heard of any of the animals carved there.

"We call it the Temple."

"Why's that?"

Reevie scratched at his mop of light brown hair. "I guess because it used to be a temple."

"Temple to what?" Several heads peeked over the top of the

wall as we neared the front gates.

"To Egla."

"Who's that?"

Reevie looked at me funny. "She was one of the faerie overlords defeated during the Faerie Wars. Don't you know your history?"

I shook my head.

Reevie shrugged. "Anyway. I heard her subjects captured her with one of those durma collars and fed her to her own pets. Guess that's what you get when you make yourself out to be like the Creator."

I glanced at the wall of strange creatures and shuddered.

The faces of the lookouts began to take shape as we approached. "Who goes there?" a squeaky voice called out.

"You know who," Reevie hollered back. "You're looking right at me, Toots."

"You know I've got to ask, Healer."

Reevie sighed. "This is why I prefer to live on my own." He looked back up at the top of the wall where three or four new heads had popped up to see what was going on.

"Give us the password," one of the heads said.

"Oh, for pity's sake. This is embarrassing." Reevie shook his head and recited,

There is no chief as brave as Spats.
All other chiefs are as dumb as rats.
If any wish to enter here,
Stick out your tongue and then draw near.

"Bet you'll never guess who wrote that little ditty," Reevie muttered under his breath. "Just follow my lead." He stuck out his tongue and then took two steps toward the iron gate. I grudgingly did the same. I couldn't believe we were standing there with our tongues sticking out at a metal gate while kids above us snickered down their approval. I guess, from their perspective, we did look pretty ridiculous. I would have chuckled myself if my tongue hadn't already been preoccupied.

The metal gate creaked as the bar swung upward and released the lock. As soon as it opened, a number of boys and a couple of girls rushed out to get a look at me. I pulled my tongue back inside my mouth and straightened my back. I wanted to look as formidable as possible.

"One more thing," Reevie said under his breath as the gates ground to a stop. "Whatever you do . . . don't embarrass me."

CHAPTER 11

"WHO'S THIS, HEALER?" an older boy asked, looking me over. He was at least a foot taller than I and skinny as a broom handle. His arms and legs were thin, easy to break if the need arose.

"This is Ayrion," Reevie said to the growing crowd. "He's new to the city and wants to petition a place in Hurricane."

"Not much to him," one of the girls in front said as she stepped forward and stared at my colorless irises. "Those are some strange-looking eyes." She was taller than I was but not by much. Her sandy-blond hair had been pulled back into a partial braid.

I smiled. Not much else I could do.

"I'm Sapphire," she said. It was easy to see where she had gotten her name. She had the deepest blue eyes I'd ever seen. She took a step back and crossed her arms. "Ayrion. Hmmm. That's a pretty name."

I winced. It wasn't exactly how I wanted to be remembered.

"Where's Spats?" Reevie asked.

Sapphire glanced at the main building. "He's meeting with some runners in his study. Doesn't look good." She wore a strange, almost-eager grin.

Reevie grunted. "When does it ever?"

"All right, break it up," one of the larger boys said. "You've all seen the new kid; now get back to work before Spats catches you sitting around doing nothing and puts you in the hole."

The kids scattered. The threat of the hole—whatever that was—put wings to their feet.

"Sounds like Spats will be busy for a while," Reevie said. "Come on, I'll show you around."

Metal screeched, and I whirled to see the gate swing shut and the bar clang back into place. Around the wall, scaffolding had been erected at different intervals for the lookouts.

"They're called *watchers*," Reevie said as he caught me studying the haphazard stations scattered around the Temple's wall. Each station had a brass bell.

"Watchers?"

"They watch from the wall and sound the alarm if they see a threat. Everyone in Hurricane has a job. For some, it's based on their skills, or their size." I caught Reevie rubbing his bad leg. "But typically, it's wherever they're most needed at that time."

Reevie led us along a stone path that ran the perimeter of the Temple. Smaller walkways crisscrossed the yard in front of the Temple buildings. The yard looked like it had been a garden at one time, complete with small pools and flowing streams. There was nothing now but dried-up holes and empty ditches that followed the walkways.

Statues, fountains, half-fallen arches, and benches dotted the landscape, speaking to the beauty this place had once held. The only surviving plants were a couple of stubborn old white oaks. Their limbs, thick with leaves, stretched out over the walkways and provided shade to those mingling beneath. If I closed my eyes, I could almost imagine what the courtyard had looked like.

Whoever Egla had been, she had built a small oasis there in the middle of this hardened section of Aramoor. Of course, for all I knew, before she became animal fodder, this might have been the aristocracy's side of town. The ornate buildings in the old shopping community supported my theory.

"Those are part of the guard," Reevie said, pointing to a small group of older boys lounging beside one of the buildings. Each wore a black vest like Sapphire's. "They're the tribe's best fighters, the ones picked to be Spats's personal sentries. You can't see him without first going through them."

I studied the guards' movements, the way their hands never strayed too far from the weapons they carried, the way their eyes were constantly watching, darting about at any small noise or movement. I doubted these boys—though few of them could be considered boys anymore with their size and the sporadic patches of growth on their faces—were anywhere near on the level of what I had been raised with, but I wasn't going to dismiss them as possible threats. Their matching black vests had me wondering if a certain red vest I had recently come in contact with had been worn for more than just its aesthetics.

"Next are the beaters. They're our fighters. They aren't the brightest lot, but they're big and they follow orders. It's a pretty easy job, mostly sitting around all day, waiting for some action. Unlike the others, they don't have to scrounge for food or supplies." Reevie smirked. "They're like the Elondrian Lancers but without all the protective armor, or shields . . . or weapons, for that matter. Come to think of it," he said, scratching his head. "I guess they aren't like the Lancers at all—"

"More like a group of kids running around with bare feet and clubs," I said, earning me a raised brow and eventually a shrug and nod from Reevie.

We stopped at one of the empty pools where a fountain had been. The inside of the dry hole was lined with a collage of once brightly painted stones, and at its center sat a statue of a beautiful woman with long hair down to her feet, playing what looked like a large harp. I nearly choked when I walked around to the front and realized she didn't have a stitch of clothing on.

Reevie laughed at my reaction to the naked, harp-playing faerie. "That's Egla for you. There's hardly a mural or statue of her that doesn't depict her in all her glory."

I peeked once more when Reevie wasn't looking. I'd never seen anything so beautiful in my life. I couldn't understand why Egla wasn't embarrassed at having everyone see her like that. I certainly would have been.

"Next are the pickers. They are the breadwinners of our little society. Keep the wheels turning."

"What do you mean by *pickers*? Do they have something to do with the picking grounds you mentioned earlier?"

Reevie nibbled on a nail. "Remember Lord Gerrick?" I nodded. "Aramoor doesn't like street rats. Every now and then, you'll come across someone like Master Fentin and Mistress Orilla who are willing to help us out, but as a rule, we are shunned. It's next to impossible to find work that doesn't end with us being shipped off to one of the mining colonies. And since we have to eat, we acquire food any way we can, which generally means . . ."

"You steal it."

Reevie hung his head. "We call it *picking*. We see something we need, and we pick it up, usually followed by a lot of running and hiding, as you saw with those patrollers who chased us a few weeks back."

I didn't like the idea that I'd been nourishing myself over the last few weeks on pilfered food. Upakans didn't steal. It was beneath us, and the Shal'Noran forbade it. I guess if I really thought about it, this was an odd sense of morality, considering what we did for a living.

Could I still keep the Shal'Noran if I had no way to earn food? I shoved the question aside for another time.

"So, we steal everything we need?"

"Well, not everything. On occasion, we do actually find legitimate employment by hiring out our fixers. However, because of where we're located, most people don't have a lot of extra coin for fixing things."

"So, what do the fixers do?" I asked.

"Fixers are kids who've had some professional experience, like apprenticing in a smithy or with a carpenter or tailor, some type of skill that the tribe can use to their benefit. I guess I'd fall under that category. The medical training I received under my father was my entry into the tribe. No one else has the extensive knowledge that I do when it comes to applying herbs and treating illnesses."

We climbed the steps leading up to one of the Temple's side buildings. "I'm a high commodity around here, which is why I have some leeway when it comes to the rules. Real healers are almost impossible to find. Anyone can claim to be one, but few have the skill."

We stepped inside the kitchen area, which looked out over a room full of tables and benches. "That's Cook," Reevie said, gesturing to a heavyset kid on the left who was wearing a dirty apron and stirring something in a very large pot. The coals underneath glowed, and the steam wafting over the rim filled the room with the scent of pepper and garlic. It reminded me of my time spent helping Kettle on the *Wind Binder*. I smiled at the boy when he looked up from his work to wipe the sweat from his face with his sleeve.

"Finally, you have the cleaners." Reevie pointed to the back of the room where a couple of smaller kids were busy swishing a pair of brooms around the tables. "They are a greatly undervalued bunch, quiet but busy. Their job is to—"

"Wait. Let me guess. Keep the place clean."

"Good, you're listening."

We stepped back out into the sunlight and started down the steps. Before we had reached the bottom, a squirt of a boy dashed over. "Spats said that he can see you now, Healer. Be quick. There's trouble with Avalanche. Talk is, Cutter's making threats again."

Reevie grunted and dismissed the boy, and the two of us walked over to the main building. "I don't know if trouble with Avalanche will be good or bad for you. He could be in a foul mood and deny you entrance out of spite, or he might see this as a way to grow the ranks." Reevie shrugged. "You never know with Spats."

I already wasn't thrilled with the situation, and Reevie's words didn't help. Once inside the main building, we walked down a couple of rounded passageways, each with its own built-in skylight that bathed the corridors with warm afternoon sunlight. The inside of the Temple was much like the gardens outside: once beautiful, but now rough with age.

We stopped outside the doors to Spats's office. Each had been masterfully carved with a breathtaking view of the former gardens.

My fists tightened at the sight of the two boys standing on either side of the doors. Their black vests labeled them as members of the Guard, though their stature was proof enough. They looked me over, assessing my potential threat. Their gaze was painfully brief. Still, they kept a close eye on me. One of them actually growled, which made me wonder what was waiting for me on the other side.

CHAPTER 12

"COME IN!"

I looked at Reevie. His face did little to hide the dread he felt. I swallowed and waited for him to open the doors, but his hand seemed to have gotten stuck somewhere between his pocket and the handle.

The guards chuckled.

"Reevie," I said softly, snapping him out of it. He shook his head, took a small step forward, and turned the knob. The door swung open and we stepped inside.

The room surprised me. From the way Reevie had described

Hurricane's leader, I'd expected to see walls lined with swords and staves, grisly paintings of hard-won battles, and the heads of Spats's enemies mounted on spears. Instead, I found an exquisitely organized chamber with shelves, a desk, and chairs, all in the same rich wood as the doors we had just walked through.

Rays of sunlight fell through stunningly crafted amber panes, giving the room an ethereal feel. Spats sat at his desk, busy poring over some loose papers. Spats was even further from what I had imagined. By the size of his guards and the way Reevie shook at the thought of being in his presence, I was half-expecting a monstrous brute or some enormous misshapen creature with three arms and five legs. Instead, I found a thin, angular kid with bulging eyes and an explosion of red hair. He wasn't much taller than I. He had to sit on a stack of books just to see over his desk, which had been built for a grown man. Hurricane's chief spared us a brief glance before returning to his papers. His face reminded me of a weasel with his high cheekbones, slightly offset eyes, and nose that came to a point.

"Ah, Healer. Perfect timing. Come in." He even sounded like a weasel. His high-pitched voice was rather nasal, as though he'd made it halfway through puberty and instead of dropping, his voice had decided to stay where it was.

I bit my tongue to keep from snickering. I had a feeling the kid in front of me hadn't climbed to chieftain thanks to a cheerful disposition.

The guards behind us stepped into the room and shut the doors. I could feel their eyes on the back of my head.

"Chief." Reevie bowed. He glanced my way and cleared his throat. I got the hint and bowed as well. Reevie waited for Spats to acknowledge him with a slight wave before straightening. "This is Ayrion. He's new to the city, and I—"

"What's wrong with his eyes?"

"What?" Reevie turned his head. "His eyes?"

Spats hopped down from his seat and stepped around his desk. He snatched my chin and twisted my head back and forth, studying one eye and then the other. It took everything I had not to punch him in the face.

"Why do his eyes look like that?"

I wanted to ask him why his head was so small and why his voice sounded like a girl who'd just had her backside pinched, but I thought better of it.

"Is he diseased?" Spats let go of my chin and wiped his hands down the front of his trousers as if touching me would suddenly change his eye color as well.

"He's not diseased," Reevie said. "He's Upakan."

Spats leaned back against his desk. "Upakan, you say? Hmm." He scanned me from head to toe. "So, are the stories true? Can you kill me with a single look?" There was a smile on Spats's face, but his eyes held a spark of wary caution. "Well, do you speak, boy?"

"He's a bit shy, Chief," Reevie said, clearly not happy with the direction the conversation was heading. "He's a healer. I think he'll make a good asset to our tribe. I can definitely use all the help I can—"

"Quiet."

Reevie shut his mouth; his hands were shaking.

"Is that true? Are you a healer?"

I nodded. It wasn't exactly a lie, since I had been trained in the appropriate herbs and tonics used to treat wounds and basic illnesses, things a warrior should know. If I were to be accepted as a healer, that should place me in high standing within the tribe, like Reevie. Hopefully, it would allow me to move about as freely as he did.

"Are you mute, boy?" Spats looked at me with a growing annoyance before turning to Reevie. "Can he speak?"

"Yes, sir," I finally said, keeping my eyes in what Spats would assume was proper deference. I needed Spats to believe that I was just as fearful of him as Reevie was, that they would have no reason to keep an eye on me.

Upaka were trained to fit in, to do whatever it took to meet the goal, which was usually getting close to our next target. To do this, we had to learn to let go of our identity and become someone else. It was a talent I hadn't quite mastered, especially if it required me to cower to bullies.

"So, not mute after all." Spats studied me for a moment and then walked back around to the other side of his desk and perched on his stack of books. "Normally, we test all applicants to Hurricane. It lets us know where to put them in the tribe—or if we want them at all. I have strict guidelines here," he said, snatching his quill and pointing it at me. "However, as it happens, you've come at an opportune time. We just received word that one of our warehouses was raided last night by a rival tribe." There was an edge to his voice that matched the embers building in his eyes. "I will not allow this to go unanswered. There will be blood in the streets by tonight, or my name isn't Spats. And where there is blood, we will need healers." He pursed his lips and leaned back in his chair, studying me again. "If our healer vouches for you, that's good enough for me, provided you can answer one question."

I tensed, hoping Spats wouldn't ask me something beyond the basics of my field training.

"If, in this battle, I and the Healer were wounded, who would you tend to first?"

"You, of course, Great Chief," I lied with a flamboyant bow.

Spats folded his hands and smiled. "Excellent. You're in."

CHAPTER

13

WE LEFT SPATS'S office, and Reevie took me on a quick tour of the rest of the Temple. It consisted of beautifully framed rooms and hallways trimmed with richly colored wood that had been shaped in a rather fluid-like fashion. Unlike the usual squared-off designs normally seen, the rooms and even the doors and frames had a sleek curvature to them. There was a soft beauty to the design that reminded me of the puzzle pieces I used to work on with my sister, each part blended perfectly together to make the whole. Outside, there were covered walkways connecting one building to the next, each open to the once lush gardens that had surrounded the entire complex.

"Oh, I almost forgot," Reevie said as he left the walkway and headed across the yard to a small shed near the perimeter wall.

I followed closely behind.

The shed was nothing more than a basic square frame and roof. I could see straight through the wire mesh that had been tacked on for its walls. Inside, stood rows of shelves, each holding what appeared to be a number of birds. A couple of holes had been cut into the mesh with a small landing for the birds to walk in and out of. "Our pigeons," Reevie said with a proud grin. "What do you think?"

I looked at Reevie, then at the birds, then back to Reevie. "I think there's not much meat on them."

Reevie looked disgusted. "They're not for eating, you nitwit. They're for sending messages."

"Huh?"

"They're messenger pigeons. We strap a small, rolled-up piece of parchment to their feet, and they carry it between one place and another. It's how Spats can reach me at the granary."

"How do they know where to go?"

Reevie shrugged. "I don't know. They always seem to know where home is."

"Is this considered their home?"

"For some of them, yes."

"Then how do they know how to fly to the granary?"

Reevie smiled. "Good question. We learned that if we kept their food separate from their home, they would fly back and forth each day. I have another cage on the roof back at the granary. That's where I keep the food for a couple of them."

"That's pretty ingenious." I was surprised he hadn't shown me this before.

We left the birds to their cooing and headed back inside, ending the tour in a small, brightly lit room, not that far from Spats's office. Reevie had claimed the space for his healing. A brass chandelier hung from the ceiling, its candles providing a warm addition to the light streaming through the octagonal windows at the back. Shelves built into the walls held marked jars of herbs and medicines. There were also a number of oddly shaped and colored decanters holding a variety of tonics and tinctures. Some of the labels I recognized, but many I was unfamiliar with. The side wall was lined with a number of cots for Reevie's patients.

Reevie grabbed a couple of knapsacks and handed me one of the them. "Here, fill that with as many bandages as you can. Whenever Spats gets that look in his eyes, I can count on burning through half of my supply."

He pointed to a large chest near the back of the room. I opened it to find layers of bleached wrapping already cut into strips. Reevie was clearly prepared. The way things seemed to work around there, you'd need to be in order to survive.

"When you're done with that, start loading the jars from those shelves over there." He pointed at one of the two cabinets on the other side of the room.

We spent the rest of the morning packing supplies for whatever retaliation Spats had in mind. At the sound of my stomach growling for the third time, Reevie had us stop for lunch. We left the supplies sitting near the door and headed for the dining hall.

The entire Temple was alive with excitement. Those in black vests looked eager; others—not so much. A few looked determined, but most looked worried, and some—like me—just looked confused. What weapons they carried consisted mostly of wooden clubs. Some had small pocketknives, perfect for chores but woefully inadequate for armed combat. I spotted a few daggers haphazardly tucked into belts and boots. Each of the guards wore a shortsword, and by the way they carried themselves, they knew how to use them. Unfortunately, the way the rest of the tribe's soldiers—*beaters,* Reevie had called them—appeared to be fumbling over each other just trying to get from one end of the hall to the other; they looked like they'd be more of a danger to themselves than to anyone else.

We reached the dining hall, and Reevie found us an empty spot at one of the back tables. We sat down to whatever Cook had been working on that morning. The broth was hot, but the single piece of meat I found in mine was chewy at best. Regardless of the quality, I found it remarkable that they were able to scrounge up enough food to keep everyone fed.

I studied the faces around us. The tension was building. Everyone was on edge. It showed in the nervous glances passed between tables, the stiff way the kids slurped their lunches. It was all too familiar, and I found my thoughts drifting to home.

I remembered how I used to be before a competition: the shake in my hands, the rush of adrenaline, the time spent pondering all the ways things could go wrong.

". . . has been coming for some time."

I lowered my spoon. "I'm sorry. What were you saying?"

He sighed and pushed his bowl away. "I see the madness has spread to you, too. I said that Avalanche has been sending their spies into our territories for months, trying to determine where our food stores are hidden. Obviously, they must have found one last night. Spats has been threatening to retaliate for some time, but up until now, he hasn't had a strong-enough reason to justify an all-out attack against another tribe. And he'll need a reason to justify it once the Guild finds out."

"The Guild. That's where the heads of all the tribes meet, correct?"

"Yes. They set the rules and the punishment for breaking them."

"Then why doesn't Spats just tell them what Avalanche is doing?"

"'Cause," Reevie said with a tone that let me know I must be asking another stupid question, "it would be our word against theirs. Spats ain't stupid. Trust me. He's already working on a way to get Avalanche back."

It was hard for me to reconcile Reevie's confidence with that redheaded weasel of a kid I'd met earlier. He didn't look like a mastermind of mayhem.

I drained what was left of the heavily peppered broth, and the two of us made our way back to the healer's quarters. I closed the door. "Will we be expected to fight? How will we stay out of the battle so we can tend to the wounded?"

Reevie made a face. "Do I look like I could do any sort of fighting?"

I shook my head.

"Spats likes to keep me with him. Don't worry. The Guard will protect us."

"The Guard? If the Guard and the chief stay out of the fight, then who's leading it?"

"Leading it? Why do you need someone leading it? Spats tells the beaters where to attack, and they attack. Just stay with me and we'll be fine. Now, where did I put that liniment?" With that, he turned and began rummaging through one of the large satchels.

Reevie's words flew in the face of everything I'd been taught about strategic warfare, but then again, this wasn't exactly what I would call a true war. Maybe things were different here on the streets. This tribe had been around for some time, as Reevie had pointed out, so maybe they knew what they were doing. As long as I could make sure that Reevie was safe, the rest didn't matter.

"Where's the armory?" I was growing bored of watching Reevie double-check our supplies.

"Why do you need to know? I just told you healers aren't expected to fight."

"When it comes to fighting, what's expected isn't always what comes to pass. What would happen if the Avalanche beaters managed to break through the ranks? Do healers have immunity?"

Reevie stopped his packing. There was a concerned look on his face. "Well, I guess it couldn't hurt to be prepared. Grab me something, too."

Red and her tribe had taken my weapons when they robbed me and left me for dead. Other than a small belt knife I had found lying around our quarters at the granary, I was nakedly unprepared.

My head shot up as something dawned on me. "Who's Avalanche's chief?" I asked, trying not to sound overly eager. The thought of getting my father's ring back and dishing out some much-deserved retribution had my mouth salivating.

"Cutter," Reevie said. "He's a right nasty piece of work, too. Avalanche has been our enemy since before I came here. It's because our two tribes share the same border. They have the region northeast of us. They're not as big as Hurricane, but ever since the patrollers added another station to Cheapside, their pickings have been difficult to come by."

I sighed and started for the door. "Which way to the armory?"

"It's in the next building over." He turned around and pointed. "Make a left out the door. Then at the end of the corridor, make a right, and then another left, and that will take you outside to the connecting walk on the back. Once you reach the next building, go inside and take the hallway on the right. The armory will be the second . . . no, third room on the left."

I nodded as though what he had said made perfect sense. I left Reevie to his work and shut the door on my way out. I figured I'd just follow everyone else. If I got lost, someone would point me in the right direction.

It didn't take long to wind my way through the open passageways and out to the covered walkway between buildings. Crossing the walkway, I stepped inside the next structure. There was a group of kids coming in behind me, so I moved to the side as they rushed past. I wondered if they were going to the armory as well, so I followed them.

Sure enough, they entered the third room on the left. Before I made it to the entrance, I could hear complaints wafting from the open door.

"Ah, man, all the good ones have been taken . . ."

"I told you we should have come here first . . ."

". . . I was hungry."

They passed me on the way out, shoulders slumped. I guessed they must have pilfered what was left of the weapons cache, which wasn't much, since they only carried a couple of small clubs no larger than Cook's ladle, a leather slingshot, and a wooden mallet.

The room was in shambles. I stepped over a couple of the smaller weapon racks that had been tossed to the ground after their contents were confiscated. The pegs dotting the walls were bare, and one of the racks at the back had been torn apart. It seemed someone thought a nice stick of wood was better than nothing. It was a depressing sight.

"Hello, Gray Eyes."

The voice behind me caused me to jump.

I turned to find Sapphire standing there with a cheeky grin on her face. At least, I thought it was a grin. Along with her black vest and sword, she had rubbed some kind of dark paint across her face.

She looked scary, which I guessed was the point. It reminded me of Bones and the white paint he had used on his face before our battle with the Cylmaran slavers.

I was surprised at how close Sapphire had gotten without me knowing.

"Guess I should have gotten here earlier," I said as I took another look around the empty room.

"Don't you worry, Gray Eyes. I'll watch out for you," she said as she tapped the sword at her waist. She slowly circled my position, studying my hands, the position of my feet, the balance of my stance. I felt like a new trinket in a shop window she was deciding whether to buy.

"I take it you're one of the Guard," I said, trying to break the awkwardness of her stare. "I noticed your vest, but I haven't seen any other . . . uh—"

"Girls?" she offered with a wink. "I'm the only *girl* in the Guard. Those blockheads would be lost without me. They're pretty good in a brawl, but when it comes to finesse, I'm in a whole different league."

I believed her. She reminded me of some of the Upakan girls back home, though they were a bit less boastful.

"So, I hear you're going to be joining us on our little adventure this evening. I guess you can't have too many healers around, especially ones that can keep up. Don't get me wrong. Reevie's a sweetheart and all, but his condition . . ." She shrugged. "It makes him a liability."

My fists clenched. I couldn't tell if she was trying to goad me because of my previous comment or if she really meant it. "Reevie's worth more than a hundred of you. What he has up here," I said, pointing to my head, "is far more valuable than anything else. Anyone can swing a sword or a club and call themselves a guard, but no one here can do what he can."

Sapphire studied my face for a moment without saying anything. Then she smiled. "You care for the cripple. That's good. That means you'll be willing to protect him." She turned and left the room, leaving me to scratch my head. She stopped in the hall and cast a glance back over her shoulder. "I'm watching you, Gray Eyes. There's more to you than you let on." She smiled with another wink and then disappeared down the hall.

I had a feeling she was going to be a handful.

CHAPTER

14

PATIENCE WAS IN short supply. After my futile trip to the armory, there wasn't much left to do but sit around and wait for something to happen. A deathly calm lay like a thick fog across the Temple as the tribe went about their tasks in silence. Even Reevie, who was normally bursting at the seams to show me some new herb he had acquired or disgusting sickness he'd come across, was unusually quiet.

The sky had begun to color as we made our way back to the dining hall. Supper consisted of cold leftovers from lunch, along with a small slice of dark rye for dipping. No one seemed all that bothered. They were all too busy waiting for Spats to give the signal.

When word finally came, it was like a heavy weight had been lifted. It broke through the Temple like a whirlwind. Kids crowded around the front gate, waiting for their orders. They wore simple strips of blue cloth on their arms to make it easier to tell which kids to bash once the fighting started. Reevie knotted one on my arm just below the armpit.

Anxious chatter spread through the ranks as they waited to hear how their fearless leader was going to march them to victory. The Guard, in circle formation, pushed to the front, knocking aside anyone stupid enough to get in their way. At the center of the small procession was Spats. His weasel eyes were fixed straight ahead.

Even I was feeling a certain level of anticipation for the looming battle. I was curious as to the tactics Spats would use. I kept Reevie close as we pushed our way to the front. Reevie was carrying one of the satchels we had prepared earlier that morning, and I had the other two. Each one was bursting with the supplies we anticipated would be needed to treat the wounded.

"Hurricane!" Spats called out as he raised his hands to gather everyone's attention. "The time has come!" Shouts went up from all around the gatehouse as the kids raised their makeshift bludgeons, staves, and spears into the air and cheered.

What are they all cheering about? All he said was "The time has come."

Sapphire stood off to the right side of the Guard. She seemed to be looking in my direction. It was hard to tell with the paint on her face and the fading light. The torches on the perimeter wall were lit, casting elongated shadows on the faces of those gathered around.

"I have a plan," Spats said. He stood on a stool between the same two boys who had been guarding his door earlier that day. It was the only way he could be seen and heard by everyone.

"He has a plan," I said to Reevie with a slight hint of cynicism. "I'm glad someone does."

"Shhh, I'm trying to listen."

"Do you want me to stick you on my shoulders so you can see him too?"

He answered me with a swift elbow to the ribs.

"Tonight, we are going to teach Avalanche what happens to anyone who steals from us! By the time we're through with them, they'll wish they'd never set foot in our territory! After tonight, they never will again!" The crowd roared. Spats started hopping up and down on his stool, working the crowd into mass frenzy. "We're going to cut their feet!"

Everything went silent.

Confused looks passed through the ranks. Finally, someone in the back hollered, "Cut their feet!" One by one, others joined in until the entire assembly was shouting, "Cut their feet! Cut their feet!" They jumped up and down, pumping weapons and fists into the air. "Cut their feet! Cut their feet!"

I felt like I was watching the beginning of a mass hysteria, a deadly outbreak of complete insanity. Reevie nearly punched me in the nose with his own fist as he joined in. "Cut their feet! Cut their feet!"

"Cut their feet? Cut whose feet?" *And with what? This is madness.*

There were maybe eight good blades in the bunch. What were they going to cut people's feet with? What was wrong with these kids? I understood the concept of rousing your fighters before a battle, but this was ridiculous. So far, I hadn't heard a single shred of evidence that spoke of an actual plan. What was the goal? How were they going to accomplish it? I figured Spats was saving the details until the end, so I listened.

Spats raised his hands for silence. "They took something from us." The kids around me nodded in agreement. "So, we are going to take something from them." Shouts rose from the crowd. "Tonight, we will let them know that if they hit us, we will hit them back. And we won't stop hitting until they are no longer able to steal from us again!"

The beaters went wild, chanting all over again. "Hit them back! Hit them back!"

I shook my head and sighed. This was not going to end well.

The firelight from the torches had Spats's red hair glowing. He sneered, and the shadows across his face made him look positively evil. "Tonight, we are going to raid their warehouses and burn them to the ground!" Spats raised his hands, anxiously awaiting the triumphant praise of his tribe, but none came.

"Burn them?" Reevie's expression changed. "That's not smart," he said under his breath. "You set a fire in Cheapside and it could wipe out a quarter of the tenements before they ever put it out."

"What if the fire spreads?" someone asked from farther back in the crowd.

Spats looked shocked that his great plan was being questioned. "Then it will spread on them! And we will finally be rid of our enemies once and for all! Their territories will become ours! And to make sure they cannot run away like the cowards we know they are, we will cut their feet!" He brandished his shortsword and sliced at the air like a drunken sailor. "Cut their feet! Cut their feet!"

Slowly, the crowd began to join in. "Cut their feet! Cut their feet!" Pretty soon, the madness had once again spread through the entire ranks, until all the kids were shouting and jumping and striking out with their sticks and staves as if fighting an invisible army. "Cut their feet! Cut their feet!"

Apart from ducking and weaving to keep from getting my own head bludgeoned, I stood there wondering how anyone could be so stupid as to follow someone into battle whose sole strategy was nothing more than to *cut their feet*. From the way Reevie had spoken of Spats, I had believed Hurricane's chief to be, well . . . smarter. But this utterly ridiculous plan demonstrated how dangerous this kid really was—to his own tribe.

The chanting continued.

If it hadn't been for Reevie, I would have slipped out and left these idiots to their lunacy. I glanced at the little healer beside me. He wasn't nearly as caught up in the chaos as he had been earlier.

"Am I the only one who thinks this plan is going to get us all killed?"

Reevie turned. "Why do you say that?"

"Well, for starters, I'm talking about the fact that *there is no plan.*"

"Yes, there is. You heard Spats. We're going to cut their feet and burn them out."

"Reevie, that's not a plan; that's the outcome, which, quite frankly, looks about as feasible as catching a fart in the wind." It seemed as though Reevie, out of his own desperate need to belong, was willing to blindly follow the rest of his tribe. I was surprised, considering he had always struck me as having a good head on his shoulders. Then again, I wasn't a cripple living on my own for the last few years. I guess I couldn't blame him for wanting to fit in. I waved it off. "Never mind." No matter what I said, it wasn't going to make a difference at this point. Most of these kids had been trained not to think for themselves.

For once, I was thankful that Reevie and I were going to be kept out of the battle. I could only hope that Avalanche's plan was just as absurd as Spats's.

The journey through the Maze and into Avalanche territory took longer than I would have thought. I guessed marching a troop of poorly armed and poorly trained street kids across the city in the dead of night was bound to take some time, especially while attempting to remain unseen. For the most part, the city was eerily quiet. We passed some stragglers on their way home from the evening shift, a few who had clearly stopped off at one of the local taverns, judging by the diagonal way they stumbled to get off the road when they saw us coming.

The evening air was sticky as usual, causing me to sweat straight through my new shirt. The occasional streetlamp on either side of the cobblestone walkways helped light the way through the enormous maze of small roads, side streets, and back alleys. The sounds of boots, slippers, and bare feet filled the stone-and-plaster corridors as our small army marched its way toward its destination.

We were near the back of the line, just behind Spats and the Guard.

"How close are we?" I asked Reevie, who was struggling to keep up as he dragged his gimpy leg along. He kept one arm around my shoulder and I supported him with an arm around the back.

"Too close," he said with a frustrated huff. "We passed into Cutter's territory some time back." His eyes darted back and forth as if expecting Cutter to come jumping out of the shadows and grab him. "We should be getting close to the eastern wall. They live in a bunch of old warehouses south of the metalworks. We're coming in from the southwest side."

"What's on those streets?"

"Houses, I think."

We turned the corner onto Barrel Street, and sure enough, I could see the white stone of Aramoor's wall in the distance and the warehouses in front of it. Reevie was correct. It was a direct line of sight to the Avalanche compound.

The warehouses didn't appear to have any protection. The

Temple at least had its wall, but this place was surrounded by nothing but homes. We followed Spats down the narrow lane. The three- and four-story housing on either side of the street gave the impression of a mountain pass. The evening breeze moving through whistled, rattling shutters and rustling loose clothing still hanging on the lines.

The hair on the back of my neck stiffened. Something was wrong. "Why are there no lights on this street?" I could see the warehouses ahead were well lit, but there wasn't so much as a single torch between them and us. The entirety of Barrel Street lay in darkness.

"Not sure," Reevie said. "Maybe they forgot to light them or haven't gotten around to it yet."

I couldn't tell if he was asking a question or making a statement.

"We need to pull back," I said.

"What's going on back there?" Spats demanded as he stopped and turned around.

"This doesn't feel right." Up ahead, our beaters began to slow when they saw their chief had stopped. "We're walking down a blind alley. Do you see any guards, any lookouts? I don't."

Spats took a moment to look around. "That's because Cutter's a moron. They're probably all asleep. The last thing they expect is for us to attack their main compound in the middle of the night. Now shut up and stick to your healing duties and leave the fighting to those of us who know what we're doing!" With that, Spats raised his blade in the air and motioned the beaters to keep moving. "If you can't keep up, then move out of the way."

The look on Sapphire's face let me know I wasn't the only one worried. She clearly didn't like the situation any more than I did. But, as one of the Guard, she had to go where Spats led.

"Come on," Reevie said, trying to push us forward. "We need to catch up."

"No, that's about the last thing we need to do."

"What are you talking about? We need to move. They're going to need our help."

"That's for flaming certain."

The windows in the second and third floors on both sides of the street hung open. In weather as warm as this, that was fairly typical, but as I studied the shadows, I could see movement inside. I didn't care what Spats thought. I raised my hands to my mouth and shouted.

"Look out! It's a trap!"

CHAPTER 15

N O SOONER HAD the words escaped my lips than doors on both sides of the street burst open, and kids with white bands on their arms came pouring out. The wave of armed fighters crashed against either side of our tribe like a human manifestation of their namesake—Avalanche.

"Bloody stool!" Reevie shouted as I yanked him sideways off the street.

I pulled him into the shadow of a nearby alcove and stuffed him behind a stack of crates. "Don't move! I don't care if Spats is being clubbed to death and eaten alive in front of you. You better not leave this spot."

Reevie nodded without saying a word.

I grabbed the knife from my jerkin and ran down the street, the cries of the wounded and dying fueling my determination. All the training in the world couldn't have prepared me for what I saw.

Chunks of rock and wood rained down from the windows above. I could hear bones snapping as the Hurricane beaters frantically tried protecting their heads. Kids were lying dead and bleeding in the streets, many knocked unconscious from the debris.

At the tail end of the procession, the Guard fought to hold the Avalanche fighters back from Spats. Sapphire was a cat. She danced from side to side, her braid whipping back and forth. She was never in the same place for long. Spats was screaming orders from the center of their formation. "Kill them! Stab them! Cut their feet!" If I had been close enough, I would've been tempted to cut *his* feet.

It was clear that Cutter had been hoping to draw Hurricane farther in before engaging so his fighters could close behind us and cut off our retreat. My warning had prevented that. Now those same fighters were taking the Guard head on. The Guard was ferocious, throwing back the Avalanche beaters as they fought to reach Hurricane's chief.

"Get me out of here!" Spats screamed.

The Guard tried to obey, but kids with white armbands continued pouring in from every side. We were about to be overrun.

Sapphire cut down one assailant after another with her shortsword.

Unlike the Guard, I had no concern for Spats's safety. Anyone who blatantly led their fighters into battle without the first care for their safety didn't deserve to live. But I didn't want Sapphire to die because of Spats's idiocy, and I knew she wasn't going to leave her chief behind.

The Guard was almost completely surrounded.

I stepped out from the shadows on the left side of the street. Most of the fighting was happening on the other side of the Guard as most of the Avalanche beaters were focused on Sapphire. A couple of Avalanche kids on my side were fighting to break through the line. I slipped my knife back in my jerkin and scanned the ground for some loose cobble. I grabbed a piece and hurled it at the closest kid with a white armband.

The rock hit the boy in the back of the head. By the time his unconscious body struck the ground, I had kicked the legs out from under the second boy and broken the arm of the third. The boy with the broken arm dropped his sword. I snatched the fallen weapon and stuck it in his thigh before spinning back around to strike the other boy in the throat with the side of my hand, completely closing off his airway.

All three were down without a single use of magic. I was feeling pretty good about that when one of my visions hit me and I ducked. I could feel the wind in my hair as the club flew over my head. I spun and swept the kid's feet out from under him, cutting the muscles in his shoulder with my newly acquired sword.

By the time I had cleared a path to the Guard, two Avalanche beaters had pinned Sapphire's arms behind her back and were pulling her away from the others. The look in the third beater's eyes left no question as to his intentions.

"You touch me and I'll kill you!" she said, and spat on the large boy in front. She bit one of the other boy's hands and he backhanded her across the face. Her head lashed to the right, blood dripping from the corner of her mouth.

I needed to get to her, but Spats and the rest of the Guard were in my way.

Another vision struck and I raised my sword, deflecting a blade meant to cut me down while my back was turned. I kicked the boy in the knee and it gave with a *pop*. Ignoring his screams, I looked for a way to reach Sapphire. The boy I had punched in the throat earlier was now on his hands and knees and only a foot or two from Hurricane's Guard.

I took a deep breath and charged. By the time I kicked off my human footstool, I had enough speed to vault myself over the Guard. Miraculously, the boy's knees didn't give way, but his curses followed me as I flew over the fighting.

I landed on top of a group of beaters on the far side. With a sword in one hand and knife in the other, I began cutting a path to Sapphire, stabbing and slicing arms and legs as I went.

The two boys holding her never saw me coming. A swift blow to the head of one and a deep stab to the thigh of the other had them writhing on the cobbles. As soon as they let go, Sapphire kicked her knee straight up between the remaining beater's legs. The boy sang like a troubadour as he grabbed his lower parts and doubled over. She finished him off with a knee to his face.

Sapphire grabbed her sword from one of the boys and was

about to kill all three if I hadn't pulled her back. "We need to get our people out of here."

Reluctantly, she turned, and the two of us cut a hole through the Avalanche forces back in the direction we'd come. Sapphire had no problem keeping up. Her ability to parry and block and move was impressive.

The Guard retreat was slow, but once Sapphire and I had cleared an opening, their pace quickened. Spats, like the coward he was, continued squawking orders for his beaters to keep fighting, even as he made his fast exit.

Behind us, the screams of the injured and dying turned my stomach. I couldn't just leave the rest of Hurricane to die. I had to do something. I laid the blame on Master Fentin. If he hadn't told me that Upaka meant *protector* and not *warrior*, I probably wouldn't have felt so determined.

"Stay with the Guard," I told Sapphire. "I'm going to see what I can do for our beaters."

I retreated into the cover of the buildings on the left side of the street and started working my way up the lines. It was utter pandemonium. A kid to my right, no bigger than Reevie, was clubbed in the head and crumpled. Another was stuck three or four times with an ice pick. A couple of girls were going at each other with broken bottles, their faces barely recognizable under the blood.

In all the confusion, beaters from our own tribe were attacking each other, not seeming to care whom they fought just so long as they pressed the attack.

MICHAEL
WISEHART

In front of me, a very large kid with an even larger cudgel spotted me creeping up the sidewalk. His white armband was easy to spot. He took one look at my blue band, grunted, and charged. His club was raised, expecting a good swing. That was his mistake. I didn't need magic, but it came nonetheless. I could see it all: the direction of his approach, the number of steps, even the angle of the swing. It was all there for me to use.

I lowered my sword and opted for something a little subtler. I waited a moment and then kicked an empty crate out in front of the boy's foot just before it landed. His foot went straight through, sending him forward. The surprised expression on his face as he hit the sidewalk and slid to a stop in front of me was reward enough. I kicked the bludgeon from his hand and then kicked the side of his head. He didn't move. The boy stank like he hadn't had a bath in weeks, and his mop of sandy blond hair was matted to his face.

"That was sneaky," a voice behind me called out. I spun to strike. Sapphire's blue eyes reflected the moonlight, but her painted face still made me uneasy. "I knew there was more to you than you were letting on."

"What are you doing here? I told you to protect Spats."

"I couldn't let you have all the fun. Besides," she said with a smirk, "I figured I owed you one." She playfully nudged my shoulder and then punched an Avalanche beater in the face before he had a chance to swing his club.

The debris that had been raining down from the second-floor windows had ceased. The brunt of the battle was now in the streets, and Hurricane was not winning. If we didn't do something now, there wasn't going to be anyone left to save.

I raised my hands to my mouth and shouted. "Retreat!"

Chapter 16

MY SHOUT ONLY added to the chaos.

Our beaters were not only surrounded, they were outnumbered. Any chance of escape was going to require an overwhelming distraction, and I could only think of one. I almost wished I hadn't.

I grabbed Sapphire and yanked her to the side as a large chunk of rock smashed into the street where she had been standing.

Sapphire looked up at the windows. "How did you—"

My magic warned me again, and I ducked to the side as someone behind me swung a long piece of wood at my head. He was wearing a blue armband just like me. He swung again, and I cut his club in half with my sword.

"What are you doing, you imbecile? I'm on your side!" I pointed frantically at the blue piece of material on my right arm. Blood was flowing down both sides of the boy's face. I recognized him. It was one of the kids who'd complained about not getting to the armory in time.

I grabbed him by the shoulders. "Fall back! And take as many with you as you can." I turned to Sapphire. "Force them back. They'll listen to you."

"What are you going to do?"

"Something stupid," I said, and pushed the wounded kid into her arms. "Now get them out of here!"

Sapphire started yelling orders.

Before I could turn around, three Avalanche beaters came at me at once. I leaped out of the way of the first kid's sword, and with a quick flick of my wrist, I deflected the second's long pole with my own blade. I retreated far enough to circle the three—two boys and a girl. The boys growled, and the girl actually barked. I was so surprised by her response that I nearly missed the second boy's chain as it whipped overhead in my direction. I jumped to the side just in time, and it clanged against the cobbles on my left.

The boy yanked the chain back and tried again. This time, I used my sword to block the swing, letting the links wrap around it. With a hard pull, I jerked the boy forward and right into the path of the girl's pole as she swung with all her might. The wood caught him in the mouth and sent him tumbling. I flung the chain around her legs and pulled. She hit the cobbles with a sharp cry.

The third boy dropped his sword and ran.

Behind them, more Avalanche fighters were on their way, so I grabbed one of the downed kid's white armbands and made a run for it. As dark as it was, it wasn't hard to disappear within the shadows, especially when I was heading *away* from the battle. I replaced my blue armband with the white one and started for the Avalanche compound.

It's amazing what a simple armband and a barely lit night could accomplish. The members of Avalanche I passed never gave me a second look.

The street ended just in front of the compound. It was too well lit for me to attempt a direct assault there. There had to be another way. I scanned the buildings and found a clothesline hanging low enough to reach—just what I was looking for. I crossed the street and fished a small tinderbox from my trousers, but I found myself having a difficult time striking the flame. It wasn't the flame that was the problem; it was the fact that I was even considering it. This wasn't the same as setting the grasslands on fire during my battle with the razorbacks. If I did this, it would be deliberate and possibly deadly.

The only reason I was even considering it was out of sheer desperation. I almost put the box back in my pocket, but if I did, would I be able to live with the deaths of all those Hurricane kids? Taking a deep breath, I struck the flint and watched the sparks ignite one of the tunics. With the warm breeze coming off the bay, it didn't take long for the fire to spread.

I left the growing blaze and ran toward the battle. As soon as I came within shouting distance, I raised my arm with its white band and started yelling at the top of my lungs. "Fire! Fire! Avalanche, fall back! Fire!"

The beaters close enough to hear me turned. One look at the fire and they joined in the shouting. Pretty soon, the entire Avalanche force was in a panicked retreat, all thoughts of wiping out their enemies replaced by the desperate need to stop the spread of the flames. By now, all the garments between the two buildings had ignited, and the fire was quickly spreading toward the buildings themselves. Smoke filled the street.

I moved to the side to get out of the way of the stampede, tripping over bodies as I went. I didn't have time to check on the injured. I needed to get to Reevie.

The wind coming in off the bay forced smoke up the street after me. I couldn't believe how fast the fire had spread. I could barely see where I was going. By the time I finally found the stack of crates where I had hidden my crippled friend, my eyes were burning and my lungs ached.

Reevie jumped out from his hiding place and threw a bottle of something at me. It hit me in the face and broke. Whatever was inside had me gagging, then everything went black and I fell. Suddenly, I was back on my feet and Reevie was jumping up from behind the crates once again. I loved my magic. I dodged the bottle and heard it bust on the street behind me. The stench of ether mixed with the overpowering smell of smoke was enough to turn my stomach.

"Are you trying to kill me?" I asked, getting ready to duck in case he decided to hurl anything else.

"You came back," he said, coughing through the smoke. He sounded surprised. "I thought you were one of them." He handed me two of the medical packs and then slung the third over his shoulder. "We need to get out of here." Reevie tied some of the cloth bandages around his face to cover his nose and mouth, using them as a filter for the fumes.

I grabbed a wrap from one of the bags and did the same. "No need to tell me twice." I put my arm around him, and we hurried down the side of Barrel Street, stumbling as we went. "Which way?" I asked, coming to a crossroads I didn't recognize. We had already passed the original street we had come in on due to the smoke.

"That way," he said, pointing to the right.

I could see why they called it the Maze.

It didn't take us long to catch up with the rest of Hurricane, even with Reevie's limp. With that many wounded and frightened kids trying to get from one side of Cheapside to the other, it was going to be slow. Many needed immediate attention.

"I'm glad to see you made it," Sapphire said, noticing us walking into the small, deserted park where our beaters had stopped to rest. She handed Reevie a bloody cloth she had been holding on a kid's head. "Here. We need help."

"Get the bandage wrapping out," Reevie said, pointing at the bag I was toting. I opened the satchel and started pulling out folds of clean cloth. "We don't have time to treat everyone," he said, "at least not here. We need to work on those who won't make it back to the Temple otherwise. The rest will have to wait till we get home."

I followed Reevie around the small grassy area nearest the streetlamps as he inspected the wounded, applying bandages where he told me and pulling out vials of strangely colored liquid for him to pour down the throats of the injured, whether they wanted it or not. After a while, I left him to his work and went to find Sapphire. She stood at the entrance to the park, watching the street out front.

"How are they doing?" she asked when she saw me coming.

"Some won't make it through the night," I said, stopping alongside her to stare out at the empty street. "Others will be lucky to reach the end of the week."

She shook her head and clicked her tongue. "Spats is an idiot." She passed a quick glance my way and then looked back to the street. "I didn't think I'd see you again. But when I saw the smoke rising above the buildings, I figured that had to be you."

I smiled.

"You were right," she said. "That was a stupid thing to do."

My smile melted.

"I'm glad you're all right, though," she said, her hand resting on the hilt of her blade.

"So, where did you learn to fight like that?"

She turned and looked at me. I don't think she was expecting the question. "My father's a sergeant in the Lancer corps. Taught me everything he knows."

"You have a father? Why are you living here and not with him?"

She turned back around to face the street. There was a strange look on her face that warned me not to push. When she didn't answer, I decided to try something else. "Where's your mother?"

"Dead," she replied, no remorse in her tone.

"Oh, I'm sorry."

"I'm not," she hissed. "She was weak."

My mouth hung open slightly.

"My father wanted a boy, and when he didn't get one, he figured he'd do his best to turn me into one. He used to shave my head and wrap my chest in order to hide who I was. Now I grow it as long as I want." She tugged on her blond braid to emphasize the point.

I wondered why she was telling me all of this. She didn't even know me, or maybe that was why she was.

"But as bad as he was," Sapphire continued, "my mother was worse." She turned and looked at me, her bright azure eyes a stark contrast against the dark markings on her face. "You want to know why?"

I didn't think I did, but I was too afraid to say no, so I offered a quick nod.

"Because she did nothing. She was my mother. She was supposed to protect me. Instead, she left us in the middle of the night and never came back." Sapphire sneered and turned back to the street. "Once my skills grew to the point that my father was no longer able to beat me, I ran away."

"I ran away from home as well," I said, hoping to find some common ground. "Although, truth be told, I wasn't given much of a choice."

"Well, I say the only person you can depend on in life is yourself."

"Sounds like something my father would have said." I glanced over my shoulder toward the injured. "I better get back to Reevie." I left her there watching the empty street, still surprised by how much she had decided to share. Even though I felt closer to her for it, it also left me feeling a little awkward.

Once the direst of the injured had been seen to, we broke camp and started back down the road toward home.

It was nearly morning when the Temple's gates came into view. By then, the stars had winked out of sight and the sky had shifted from black to dull gray. The watchers on the wall didn't bother with the password. One look at Sapphire's face and the gates swung open.

Apparently, Spats and what was left of the Guard had made it back without incident. Before heading for his sleeping quarters, Spats had ordered a double watch posted. He didn't care if they had to wake the cleaners and the kitchen staff to do it, which explained why Cook's bleary-eyed face was the one to greet us on our arrival.

Our return was anything but triumphant. Those still carrying weapons dragged them behind as they passed through. Many had dropped or discarded theirs along the way. It was a clear trail of breadcrumbs. If there was ever to be an investigation into tonight's events, it would certainly lead them to the gates of the Temple.

Reevie commandeered the dining hall for triage since it was the largest room available. The little healer barked out orders, and those of us who were still capable of standing on our own jumped to obey, laying out sheets and blankets for the wounded.

We stripped the clothing from injuries and organized the kids into sections, putting the most serious near the front. By the time Reevie had made a single pass of every patient to determine their status, dawn had come and gone and Cook was busy lighting up the hearth.

The cries and groans from those who weren't going to make it, or at the very least were going to lose a limb or two, were heart-breaking. What had it all been for? Were a few stolen items from a warehouse worth all of this? What would the repercussions be? Anyone capable of pulling off tonight's decimating ruse was hardly someone who would let this attack go unanswered.

CHAPTER

17

WITH THE HELP of the Guard, Sapphire organized rescue
parties to return for the beaters we had been forced to leave
behind. She led an army of stretchers and handcarts back to the
battlefield. Apparently, there was some unspoken rule by the Guild
that allowed for safe retrieval of the dead and wounded. Breaking
that rule, according to Reevie, would have incurred the wrath of
the other tribes.

From what Sapphire had seen, Avalanche had finally managed
to contain the fire I'd set to a couple of the surrounding buildings.
I was thankful it hadn't spread farther.

The worst of the injured beaters were slowly fighting their way back under Reevie's supervision. Those with amputations or deep wounds were looking at a long, painful road ahead. But as long as the pickers were able to keep us stocked with medicinal supplies, they stood a good chance of recovering. Many would never be able to hold a weapon again and would mostly likely be reassigned to a position on the watch or as cleaners.

Nearly a week had passed since our battle with Avalanche, and life at the Temple was slowly returning to normal, which had me worried. Not a peep had been heard from Spats. No retaliation had come from Avalanche. There was nothing. The unexpected calm had me more nervous than the initial battle.

By the time Secondday rolled around, I was going stir crazy. I knew Reevie wouldn't leave his patients, but I needed to get outside the walls.

"I'm going to go see Master Fentin and Mistress Orilla," I said, rising from my seat in the corner, where I'd been watching Reevie categorize what was left of his supplies.

"Fine, fine," he said, not looking up from his calculating.

I didn't think he'd really heard me. And before he had a chance to say no, I took off out the door. The thought of one of Mistress Orilla's mystery-meat sandwiches had my legs moving all the faster as I headed for the front gate. I was nearly there when someone called out behind me.

"Ayrion. Ayrion!" Whoever it was sounded anxious. I ignored them, watching the gate, willing the heavy crossbeam to move faster. If I didn't turn around, maybe the caller wouldn't see me.

The large metal doors creaked open, a sliver of freedom showing from the other side. I could almost taste the bread and cheese melting in my mouth. *Hurry up and open the flaming gate!*

"Ayrion!"

"He's over here!" one of the watchers on the wall shouted. I bit my tongue. If I'd had a rock within reach, he wouldn't have been up there much longer.

"There you are."

I took a deep, irritated breath and forced myself to loosen my clenched fists before turning around. One of the cleaners was running toward me. She was tiny and had a white sheet tied around her waist that hung all the way to her feet. She tripped on it halfway across the yard and fell face-first into the dirt. Served her right for cutting off my escape.

I released the breath I'd been holding and tried not to look like I wanted to choke her as she dusted herself off. Maybe whatever she needed wasn't anything serious. Maybe Reevie wanted me to bring him back a sandwich.

"Spats wants to see you."

I groaned, not bothering to hide my displeasure. She had hardly finished speaking before she was off again. It was a good thing, too, because I nearly changed my mind about the choking.

What could Spats possibly need to see me about? If he wanted to know about the beater's progress, he could have just asked Reevie.

Behind me, the gate boomed shut and the crossbar dropped back into place with a scraping thud. It appeared I was doomed to waste away inside these walls. With slumped shoulders, I made my way across the former gardens to the main building.

My stomach growled at having been denied its sandwich as I waited outside Spats's office. The same two boys were standing in front, blocking my way. They weren't sneering as they had before; they simply stood there staring at the wall in front of them.

The door finally opened, and Sapphire was there to greet me. Her blue eyes were determined.

"Are you just going to stand there?" Spats called from the other side of the room. "Come in, and close the door behind you." He sounded eager, which was worrisome. The two guards didn't bother following me inside.

The chief's study was in shambles. There were papers scattered everywhere, weapons within quick reach from any location in the room, and even a large cot at the back. How was he going to lead an entire tribe when he could barely lead himself from one side of his study to the other?

Around the perimeter of the room, a couple of members of the Guard stood watch. I felt like a prisoner about to stand trial with my executioners ready to carry out the sentence. I started running through scenarios of how I was going to fight my way out in case Spats decided I was too much of a risk to have around.

"I've never done this before," Spats said in his annoyingly high-pitched voice. His face was solemn, like a judge about to pass sentence. He had a shortsword strapped to one hip and a dagger on the other. After the battle we'd just survived, I wouldn't be surprised if he had a brace of knives tucked into his boots and a hatchet sticking out the back of his long underwear. "I don't think any chief has done this before."

My palms started to sweat. I glanced at the guards. They were armed to the teeth. Attempting to fight my way back to the door would be a mistake, especially considering Sapphire standing there. Although I didn't think she would stand in my way. From her reaction to Spats's decision to attack Avalanche, she'd probably end up helping. Still, my best chance would be grabbing Spats. I could probably use him as leverage to get myself outside the Temple's gates.

Spats opened a large chest in front of his desk. His back was to me, blocking my view of what was inside. I tried shifting to my other foot to get a better look, but it didn't help.

I hadn't received any visions, but ever since my magic had failed me during my melee with Red and her tribe, I'd been a bit leery about its effectiveness. My fingers slipped inside my jerkin as I reached for my knife when Spats turned and threw a piece of heavy black material at me. I ducked and the guard behind me caught the material in the face. He growled but handed the object to me.

There was a wide, almost mischievous grin on Spats's face when I held up the material and realized what I was holding was a black leather vest.

Sapphire was beaming.

"I don't understand," I said as I lowered the vest.

"You're getting promoted, you buffoon," Spats said, looking a little perplexed at my lack of enthusiasm. "I just made you one of the Guard, and without having gone through the Soren Challenge, no less."

I wasn't sure what to say. I'd never heard of the Soren Challenge.

Spats waited for my excitement to kick in, but it never came. "It's a great honor," he continued, as if feeling the need to explain his actions. "Every kid out there dreams of being on the Guard, and I'm just handing it to you."

"Why?"

"Oh, I don't know," Spats said, his voice dripping with sarcasm. "Hmmm, let me think." He fingered his chin. "Maybe because you singlehandedly took out a dozen Avalanche beaters without them landing a single blow. I've never seen anyone fight like that." Spats raised his arms and acted out a mock battle. "You were like, hah, take that, and that. And then you punched left and kicked right and flew over our heads like some crazy winged monkey. It was like . . . like . . ." Spats stared at me with a curious look and then waved it off. "Oh, never mind."

It was like *magic*.

"You're my new good luck charm," Spats said. "And I have the perfect way to test you out. The Guild has called for an assembly, no doubt to address our confrontation with that pig Cutter and his tribe of thieving bullies. And I've chosen you and Sapphire to be my official escort."

I offered a halfhearted smile. "Lucky me."

"Yes, I thought you'd like that." Spats apparently couldn't tell the difference between me being serious or sarcastic. Sapphire could, and she gave me a harsh look.

"I've given you a great privilege. I hope you don't embarrass me."

I wanted to laugh. Those had been Reevie's exact words before ushering me into the Temple for the first time. "Wouldn't dream of it, my chief," I said with a deferential bow. I even threw in a sweep of my hand for flair.

Spats clearly appreciated the gesture, as he straightened his back. "Pack whatever weapons you might need. You will have free pick of whatever we have."

"Right now?"

"Yes. We leave after lunch. Now go." He waved everyone out of the room.

There should have been a thousand different thoughts running through my head, but all I could think as I left Spats's office was that I would finally get the opportunity to look Red in the eyes once again. And this time, I would take back my father's ring. That was, until a more urgent thought replaced it.

How in the name of Aldor am I going to break the news to Reevie?

CHAPTER 18

"**I** GUESS THIS MEANS we'll be spending a lot more time together, Gray Eyes," Sapphire said as we left Spats's office and headed for the armory. The room was nearly as bare as when I'd last seen it. Most of our weapons—if you could call cracked table legs, cloth-wrapped shards of metal, or stone mauls *weapons*—hadn't returned from the battle. Not that I was surprised. I didn't think a single member of this tribe had ever been trained to use one.

I gave the room a quick sweep but saw nothing worth picking up, so I turned to leave.

"Aren't you going to get a weapon?" Sapphire asked, playing

with the end of her braid. "Walking into a Guild meeting without one is foolish. Each of the chiefs is bringing their biggest, toughest, meanest fighters with them." She did her best to look down at me, which took some effort, considering she was only a half-head taller. "If someone like you were to walk in there without a weapon, it might just give one of the other chiefs the push they need to attempt to put a quick end to us right there."

I wished they would, and that Red would be the one to attempt it. "Trust me," I said. "I'm armed. Everything in here is extra weight I don't need."

Sapphire took a step back and scanned me from head to toe, obviously trying to determine what weapons I spoke of.

"Besides, isn't there a rule against violence at the Guild meetings? It wouldn't make much sense to attend a meeting if the other heads of the tribes could assassinate you right there."

"There is," she said, giving up on her attempt to determine what sort of weapon I had stashed away under my clothing. "But *accidents* have been known to happen."

I stepped around her to leave, but she grabbed my arm.

"I, uh . . . I just wanted to say thanks."

"For what?"

"For what you did during the fight, for . . . coming after me."

"That's what friends do."

She stared at me for an uncomfortable amount of time. "Not around here," she said, then walked out the door.

I took a moment to let what she had said seep in before following her down the hall. Sapphire had almost made me forget about the conversation I was about to have with Reevie. Almost.

The closer we got to the kitchens, the more hesitant I became, especially since everyone had noticed my new black vest. Hushed whispers followed us. I stopped outside the dining hall and looked for Reevie. He was at the back, spoon-feeding some of the wounded.

"I need to talk to Reevie."

"I'll save you a seat," she said, walking over to get in line. "But hurry. We need to be ready whenever Spats decides to leave."

I nodded and waited for another group of kids to enter before following them in. I was hoping to sneak up behind him and see how long it took for him to notice, but he was so busy helping one of the amputees with their stew that he never even turned around to look.

"It's been a while since you fed me like that," I said, hoping to put him in a good mood.

Reevie turned. "If you miss it so much, then go get your arm chopped—" He looked at me, then my vest. "Black vomit!"

You could have heard a spoon drop. In fact, there were a few that did. Everyone's eyes were fixed on us. When your healer starts hollering about black vomit in the middle of the dining hall, it tends to put everyone on edge.

"Sorry," Reevie said, waving his hand in the air. "Misdiagnosis. Nothing to worry about. Go back to your eating." He grabbed me by the arm and marched me out the back door and onto the covered walkway that led to the sleeping quarters.

"What's this?" Reevie said, grabbing and tugging at my new

outerwear. "I thought I told you to stay out of trouble, not jump in feet-first." His eyes were bloodshot. I couldn't tell if it was from the sudden outburst or the lack of sleep over the last week. "Now you've gone and done it! How are you going to get back to the granary now? You're stuck here. You're Spats's little protector. You'll be at his beck and call night and day from now—"

"Look," I said, calmly, but still firmly, "I didn't have a choice. What was I going to do, leave everyone there to die?" I glanced around to make sure no one was close enough to listen. "Would you rather I had let them all get slaughtered?"

Reevie sighed. "I suppose not." His words almost seemed forced.

"And what was I supposed to do when Spats handed me the vest and told me he was going to promote me without me having to undergo the Sor . . . Sor—"

"Soren Challenge."

"Right, the Soren Challenge. What was I supposed to do, toss the vest back in his face and tell him that Reevie wouldn't let me take it?"

Reevie coughed.

"What's this Soren Challenge, anyway?"

"It's a test of skill, bravery, and downright madness, if you ask me. You have to pass it to join the Guard. It's one of the reasons so many of the other kids fear and respect the Guard. The fact that Spats is breaking with tradition and simply handing you your vest means there must have been more to that battle than what you told me." He studied my face, looking for confirmation.

"Okay, I might have put up more of a fight than what I let on, but like I said, I didn't have much of a choice." Since we were already having such a pleasant conversation, I figured I might as well tell him the rest. "Oh, and Spats just picked me to escort him to a guild meeting this afternoon."

"He did what?" Reevie looked like he was about to punch me. His face had turned a nice shade of plum. "The Guild? Are you insane! Those meetings can be dangerous!"

"Which is why Spats said he wants me by his side when he goes. Don't worry. It's not like I'll be going alone. Sapphire will be there."

"Sapphire?" Reevie was having a hard time catching his breath. "Well, at least one of you will have a lick of common sense." He opened the door. "You've got either the best or worst luck of anyone I've ever known. And don't ask me which. I'll let you know, if you make it back from the Guild in one piece." Reevie shook his head and stepped inside.

I definitely couldn't argue with that.

CHAPTER

19

AFTER A VERY COLD BATH in one of the hardly ever used washrooms in the Temple, I grabbed my sword and black vest from Reevie's chambers and met Sapphire at the front gate.

"You smell nice," she said with a mock grin as she took a whiff in my direction.

"Water was cold as ice," I said, my teeth still chattering.

"Spats wants us to look our best when going to the Guild." She looked me over. "Not that dunking in some water is going to help you much."

"Let's be on our way," Spats said, heading in our direction. He was wearing a pair of tan trousers, a white top, and a blue silk vest with a white cravat. The lace was flat, as though it had been slept on, and the once–dark blue brocade had begun to lighten with age. He probably only wore it on special occasions, like a meeting with the Guild.

Spats waved at the watch on the wall, and they removed the bracer and opened the gate. He stopped only long enough to inspect our dress. After a quick nod of satisfaction, he headed through the gate and started for town.

Like Sapphire, I was wearing my best outfit, which in my case was my *only* outfit. The mostly clean clothes and washed bodies helped us to blend in as we moved through the busy streets. The way we looked, we could have passed for a group of merchant's children.

The sun was warm on my face. It would have been a beautiful day for a stroll if my head hadn't been pounding. Like my visions, it seemed to be warning me of what was coming. Throbbing pain in my head didn't exactly have anything to do with my magic, but knowing where we were heading, I couldn't help but take notice.

The farther we wandered into the city, the more anxious I became. My thoughts were of Red. I would once again have the opportunity to look my enemy in the eyes. Unfortunately, looking her in the eyes was the only thing I would be able to do. It wasn't like I could attack a tribal chief right in the middle of the Guild assembly. Could I?

I took a deep breath to calm my nerves.

The warm breeze blowing in off the bay kept the clouds moving at a steady pace, casting fleeting shadows across the flowing tide of people around us. The shade, when it came, was appreciated. I could already feel sweat running down my back as we crossed one of the Tansian River's many bridges. The heavy black vest pressing my shirt to my skin didn't help.

I had been excited to find that my vest had a number of small straps sewn into the lining, much like the pockets I had sewn on my jerkin. I used them to hide one of the small daggers I'd collected during our battle with Avalanche. I found myself daydreaming about using it on a certain black-haired girl, but I quickly pushed it aside. Attacking Red at the meeting would be foolish. I needed to be patient. I would wait until I was reasonably sure I could not only hit my target but also manage a safe escape, just as I'd been trained to do.

A gust of wind blew several strands of hair into my eyes, so I tucked them behind my ears. Unlike Sapphire's, my hair wasn't long enough to tie behind my head. I passed a quick glance her way. She looked focused. The determination in her march and stern look on her face let those around her know that she was not someone you wanted to mess with. It was clear why Spats had chosen her as his first. I had no idea what the duties of the Guard entailed other than the obvious, protecting Spats, so all I could do was follow along, since I had no idea where the Guild Hall was located.

The streets of Aramoor were laden with the sounds of commerce. Costermongers lined both sides of South Avis as we headed into the merchant district. Their calls blended together into a single chorus as they worked to draw customers to their wares. Watching the vendors sell from their carts, I was reminded of Neelan—the farmer—and his wife and son. I wondered if they were here, somewhere among the crowd. I studied the faces of those we passed, hoping to catch a glimpse that never came.

There was a noticeable difference between the glamor of the merchant district and the hovels found in Cheapside. For one, the streets were cleaner. The buildings were of such grand design and magnitude that even the largest of the shops operating in the lower district would have fit into a single one of these buildings' cellars.

Carriages and carts moved slowly up and down the South Avis like boats on the Tansian River, transporting goods and passengers. The air smelled of new leather, perfumed bodies, and fresh-baked goods, a sharp contrast to the hard sweat, urine, and sour ale found in the lower regions.

Like King's Way East and West, North and South Avis ran from one end of Aramoor to the other. Both of these streets met at King's Square, which was at the heart of the merchant district. And at the center of the square was a large park.

We followed Spats across the main thoroughfare, dodging carriages as we went, and headed into a partially wooded section of the park. The path we took ended at a huge fountain, much bigger than the one of Egla back at the Temple. At the center of the fountain was an enormous statue of a man sitting atop a powerful steed. He wore a beautiful crown and held a sword overhead as if signaling a battle charge.

"Is that the king?" I asked Sapphire as we kept a couple of paces back from Spats.

Sapphire nodded.

In front of us, Spats pulled out a small pouch of coins and walked over to the edge of the fountain. He dug through it until he found a single copper piece. Lifting the coin to his lips, he kissed it and tossed it into the water.

"For luck," Sapphire said when she saw my confusion.

I wasn't sure how kissing a piece of copper and tossing it into a pool of water was going to bring good luck, but under the circumstances, we needed all the help we could get. In fact, if I had owned a copper piece myself, I might have been tempted to do the same.

The coin barely had time to hit the bottom before Spats was off again.

We left the fountain and took the north trail out of the park. From there we followed King's Way West, which was crowded with carriages, horses, and pedestrians. The wonderful smells of roast pheasant and freshly baked bread coming from some of the nearby eateries set my stomach to grumbling.

Once outside the main shopping district, Spats turned right on North Avis and we headed into a new section of the city, one I hadn't seen before, except from a distance. The buildings in this part of the city were even grander than those in King's Square. Five in particular towered over the rest. They were round, like giant pillars, with a network of enclosed walkways stringing them together. I could only imagine something like that being built with magic.

Some of the walkways rose hundreds of feet in the air. Others were low enough for me to see the people walking through them. I pointed at one of the lower walkways, where a group of excited children had their faces against the glass, waving at the crowds below.

Sapphire smiled and waved back.

I hoped that the Guild Hall was in one of those five buildings, just for the chance to walk across one of the elevated walkways. As if he'd heard my unspoken wish, Spats led us across the road, dodging carriages as we went. I could barely contain my excitement when we entered the first building on the left. We were standing in an open foyer that rose all the way to the top. I couldn't count the floors. It seemed to reach to the clouds. At the center was a circular stairwell filled with bodies, their heads bobbing up and down as they ascended and descended in an orderly fashion.

Both the floors and the walls were made of a soft gray marble with dark red veins that gently reflected the light from the windows above. All the pillars, railings, and archways were trimmed in gold leaf. Life-size murals filled the empty spaces between windows, and long tapestries hung from each floor. In a way, it reminded me of the Temple. While it didn't have the delicate features and smooth curvature of the Temple's architecture, it definitely had the rich coloring.

Spats and Sapphire had already started up the stairs before I realized I was still standing in the entrance, mouth open. I ran to catch up. More than one person cast a scrutinizing glare our way. Even wearing our best outfits, we still stuck out. The looks didn't seem to bother Spats or Sapphire, and no one tried to stop us, so I tried not to notice. I found that the stares ceased if I walked close enough to one of the women heading in the same direction.

I had lost count of how many times we had rounded the stairwell going up when Spats finally stepped off and headed for one of the connecting passageways between buildings. My heart raced. Spats and Sapphire made it a few steps in before turning around to look at me. The expression on my face as I cautiously made my way out onto the covered bridge must have been what they were hoping for as they shared a satisfied grin.

"Bet you've never seen anything like this before," Spats said.

That was an understatement, I thought as I walked over to one of the windows and looked out. I was standing on a walkway that was probably a hundred feet in the air and yet lacked any kind of truss or crossbeam support. My stomach turned when I looked down. This was embarrassing. I'd hung over Howling Gorge with nothing but my fingers ,and yet somehow this single narrow walkway had my knees quivering. I had to tell myself that people had been using these things for years, so they must be safe.

"Wizards built this over a thousand years ago," Spats said, as if reading my thoughts.

A thousand years? He could have kept that little tidbit to himself. *A thousand-year-old walkway . . . what could be safer?* With all the fear and hate of magic and its uses, I was surprised these buildings were still allowed to stand—or be used.

Sapphire smiled and reached for my hand as we stared out the window at the ant-size people below.

"Come on," Spats said, pushing off from the glass. "I don't want to be late."

Sapphire released my hand and we fell into place behind him, neither of us saying a word.

Once inside the next building, we took the stairs up two levels and started down another set of corridors. Each floor seemed to have its own color scheme. This particular hallway was lined by a thick woven runner of dark teal with gold tasseling. Even the decorative vases on the tables were teal and gold, complete with meticulous flower arrangements of the same colors.

The last two passageways were empty. Apart from our footsteps and the flickering hiss of the torches that lined the walls on either side, there was very little noise. Up ahead I could see a small gathering outside a set of open double doors.

Two well-dressed boys, who looked more like young men, judging by their sizes, talked off to the side. It was easy to spot them as being the heads of their tribes, since each boy had two guards standing directly behind them, far enough not to appear to be eavesdropping but close enough to react if the need arose. Spats's lack of reaction let me know that neither of the two boys was Cutter.

"The one on the left is Kore," Sapphire whispered as we drew closer. "He's the head of Rockslide. The one on the right is Noph, head of Sandstorm."

One look at the cut of their chief's clothing compared to ours, and I could see I had joined the wrong tribe. Even their guards were better dressed. Along with their newish-looking outfits, they wore actual sheaths for their swords, unlike me and Sapphire, who carried ours in our belts.

The other two chiefs wore suede waistcoats with decorative stitching. One of the coats was a deep purple to match Sandstorm's colors, and the other hunter green for Rockslide. I wondered how it was that these two had managed to procure such expensive-looking clothing. Were the pickings on this side of town that much richer than ours?

Spats pushed out his chest and straightened his back as we approached. In his flat lace and worn brocade, he looked more like an underpaid street performer than the head of his own tribe.

The other two didn't so much as glance his way. I felt sorry for the little redheaded weasel.

The four guards kept a close eye on us as we passed. They nodded at Sapphire but took one look at me and chuckled. We moved through the open doors and into a very large sitting room.

"Wait here," Spats said. He walked over to an older gentleman sitting at a small desk just left of a set of closed doors. The greeter wore a pale green suit with a fluffy sort of hat that kept falling forward every time he moved his head. There was a large book in front of him along with a goose quill and a jar of ink.

"The chiefs have to sign in before entering," Sapphire said, moving alongside me.

I looked around the room, noting the ornate furnishing. I had to wonder if we were in the right place. "How are we even allowed up here? Why aren't the patrollers rushing in here to have us all thrown in the dungeons?"

Sapphire kept her eye on Spats as she answered. "One thing you'll learn really quickly in Aramoor is that the size of your purse speaks louder than anything else. It's amazing what people are willing to accept when gold is involved. The rooms up here are purchased by organizations and individuals who prefer their privacy, and those that rent them out are well compensated for their discretion."

"That still doesn't explain how *we* are able to afford them."

"Not every tribe is like Hurricane and Avalanche. Those that work the northern sections of the city tend to have much wealthier pickings, not to mention the occasional contract for the aristocracy."

Before I had a chance to ask what she meant, Spats motioned for us to join him. "We're the third to sign in. Avalanche and Wildfire haven't arrived yet."

"They'll be here soon enough," Noph of Sandstorm said as he and his guards moved past.

Spats moved to follow the Sandstorm delegates, but a strong arm shoved him out of the way. "Move aside, Hurricane," Kore said as he followed Noph into the next room. "You're the reason I had to get dressed up and come down here."

"Hey, watch it!" Spats shot back. "You try that again and I'll—"

Kore turned around and looked Spats in the eyes "You'll what, sic your girl and your"—he looked at me and, like everyone who noticed my eyes for the first time, flinched—"your pet on me?"

His laughter followed him into the next room, his guards close on his heels.

CHAPTER

20

I FOUND THE LUXURY of the Guild's council chambers hard to believe, considering some of us were struggling just to find enough food to make it through another day.

Unlike the beautiful but austere marble foyer and halls we had walked through on our way up, these rooms were fashioned with a dark cherrywood, giving the place a warm and inviting feel. The carpeting was the same teal and gold as the rest of the rooms on this level. Thick velvet drapes hung to either side of an enormous window at the back, giving us a clear view of the city.

There was a fire in the hearth and chandeliers overhead, supplementing the light coming from outside. I hadn't noticed until now, but the building seemed impervious to the summer heat. In fact, I was actually hoping Spats would move a little closer to the fire.

In front of the window was a circular table, crafted from the same cherry as the paneling, with five high-backed chairs evenly spaced around it. In front of each chair lay a colored marker, one for each of the five tribes. Around the room were five seating areas, each positioned a safe distance from the next. At each, cushioned chairs and sofas surrounded a covered table with pitchers of drink and trays of snacks. We followed Spats over to the sitting area farthest from the other two chiefs.

Spats poured himself a glass of something red from a decanter and grabbed a handful of sugar-covered scones from the plate. He plopped down on the nearest sofa and began stuffing the sweet bread into his mouth.

I wanted to sample one of the glazed tarts but decided against it since Sapphire hadn't touched anything. Instead, the two of us stood guard behind the sofa and kept an eye on the others.

"What do we do now?" I whispered, low enough so only she could hear.

Sapphire leaned in. "We wait."

"Then what?"

"Then, while they hold their meeting and discuss whatever it is they came to discuss, we wait some more."

"Wow. That sounds exciting." My voice dripped with all the

enthusiasm I wasn't feeling.

She smiled.

Raised voices from outside the room caught my attention.

"Sign it yourself, old man!"

"I'm sorry, sir. I cannot let you in if you won't sign first." The old attendee had left his desk and planted himself firmly between the open doors. He had lost his fluffy green hat in the process.

"And just how do you plan on stopping me?"

Our position against the far wall allowed us a clear view of the tall boy harassing the attendant. He was covered from head to toe in brown suede. A large-brimmed hat cast a long shadow across his scruffy face. The only colored accent to his outfit was a white sash he had tied around his waist. Even the falchion he wore had a dark hilt and sheath. From the way Spats was choking, it was safe to assume this must be Cutter.

"Oh, just sign the flaming book, for pity's sake, Cutter, so we can get on with this meeting," Kore barked, nursing a glass of his own from the sitting area closest to the hearth.

Cutter growled and then grabbed the quill and scratched what looked like a large *X* across half the page.

"He's just embarrassed that he can't write his name," Noph said with a chuckle, having already assumed his seat at the meeting table.

The old attendant reached for his fallen hat, but Cutter kicked it back out into the hallway.

Spats's shoulders were quivering. I wasn't sure if it was from fear or rage or both. One look at the Avalanche chief and I was ready to make him eat the old man's hat myself . . . his own too, for that matter. Cutter scowled at Spats as he headed for the meeting table. When he saw me, a flicker of something crossed his face but was quickly replaced with a sneer.

Sapphire saw it as well. "I wonder what that was about."

I shrugged. "No idea."

"Where's Red?" Cutter asked as he pulled out his seat and sat down.

"Late as usual," Noph said. He twirled the liquid in his glass and took a sniff before upending it.

"No doubt still preening," Kore added as he moved to the window and looked at the streets below.

Cutter pulled his sword from its sheath and let it clang across the table in front of him. "That's what you get when you let a girl take over as chief of a tribe. Girls should know their place in the world—"

"And where would that be?" a warm, sultry voice called from the doorway. "Serving your dinner while patting you gently on that flat backside of yours?"

Spats laughed out loud. Kore stood there with a scowl on his face while Noph tried to hide his amusement by taking another drink from his cup.

One look at Red and my fists clenched on reflex. All those emotions I had tried to bury fought to break free. Her long, raven hair hung all the way down her back, and her lips had been painted the same bright red as her vest, which she wore over a pair of black trousers and a white silk top. Her boots, like Sapphire's, widened at the knee. Removing her wide-brimmed hat, she shook out her thick mane, making sure to take her time as she combed her hands through the waves.

Sapphire huffed at the display. Cutter, too, sneered, but he didn't avert his eyes. I couldn't blame him. I hated her, and even I couldn't tear my eyes away. There was something about the Wildfire chief that simply drew you in. Other than Spats, she was probably the youngest of the chiefs. The others all appeared to be somewhere between eighteen and nineteen.

Red's two guards fell in step behind her as she moved across the room. I recognized Toothless right away. I wondered how he was enjoying his soup. The other guard was a short, pudgy kid with black hair who, like me, didn't appear to belong.

Something was off. I felt . . . different. Like a part of me was missing. The feeling was similar to dreams I used to have where I would find myself strolling down a busy street in my best shirt and shoes, only to realize I was lacking my pants. The numbness that crept over me was the same as the last time I had faced her. Except the last time, she'd had a couple dozen of her beaters there to keep me company.

She tossed a quick glance at Spats before prancing over to an empty sitting area and pouring a tall glass of whatever the red stuff was. I thought it ironic that those of us who probably needed it most were the only ones not drinking it.

"Let's get this over with, shall we?" Noph said as he leaned forward and rested the purple sleeves of his coat on the table. "I've got

a dinner party tonight, pheasant with spinach-stuffed mushrooms."

Pheasant? With spinach-stuffed mushrooms? Where did they get
the gold to hold dinner parties? My stomach growled, and Sapphire
rewarded me with a sharp elbow to the ribs. I gave her an apolo-
getic look. It wasn't like I could help it.

Spats reluctantly left the sofa and joined the others around the
table. I was thankful that Hurricane's seating was on the opposite
side from Avalanche. The last thing we needed was for Spats and
Cutter to be placed within reach of each other.

Spats found his seat, and Sapphire and I assumed our places
behind it.

I stared at Red. She hadn't caught me looking yet. I wondered
if she would recognize me if she did. The last time she'd seen my
face, it was swollen to the size of a ripe honeymelon. She might
have recognized my eyes, so I quickly lowered my head.

Kore was the last to take his seat, to Spats's right. Next to Kore
were Cutter, then Red, followed lastly by Noph—quite the merry
little band of street thugs. With all the harsh looks and deadly stares
being tossed around, I wondered how long it would be before one
or two of those seats were vacant.

Chapter 21

"**O**KAY," NOPH SAID, straightening his sleeve cuffs. "To business. We've been informed that there was an unwarranted incursion into the Avalanche's territories last week, and—"

"Unwarranted? The Defiler it was!" Spats screeched, shooting out of his seat. He splashed part of his drink on the table as he pointed at Cutter. "He raided our food stores!"

Cutter feigned a startled look. "What? Steal your food? We did no such thing. Your attack was completely unprovoked. We were just minding our own business when *you* sent *your* beaters sneaking into our home, at night, to murder us in our sleep."

"That's a lie! You . . . you liar!" Spats's face was as red as his hair. "Why else would you and your beaters have been lying in wait for us? You knew we were coming because you attacked first. You knew we would retaliate."

"Where's your proof?" Cutter asked. "Where's your evidence that condemns me and my tribe of this heinous act?"

"Our warehouse is empty. That's my proof. We all know your territories have yielded little food this season. Every time the Guild meets, all you gripe: 'Avalanche has no food, boohoo, we need more picking grounds.' I know it was you. And you know it was you."

"I know it was me? That's the most ridiculous logic I've ever heard. That's your proof? That I know it was me?" Cutter turned to the other members, who had remained surprisingly quiet during the near shouting match. "This is why I questioned the decision to let someone so young lead."

"Just a moment ago, Cutter, you were busy lecturing us on why I shouldn't be allowed to head my own tribe either," Red said as she flipped a small jeweled dagger between her fingers. "By your logic, age and sex play a pivotal role in whether someone is worthy to be leader or not." She pointed her blade at the Avalanche chief. "I say that someone too stupid to write his own name should be stricken from that list as well."

Spats laughed. Noph held his in, but there was a grin on his face. Cutter's cheeks nearly matched the paint on Red's lips. She had ripped the legs right out from under him without even leaving her seat. I almost wished I didn't loathe her so much.

"Enough of this," Kore said, taking another sip of his drink. "You're giving me a headache. On one hand, we have Hurricane claiming their warehouse and food storage was raided by Avalanche, and on the other, we have Avalanche claiming that Hurricane executed an attack against them without provocation. The fact is, we know there was a battle, and it was bad enough to get the attention of the patrollers." Kore turned to Spats. "Did Hurricane attack Avalanche?"

"Only because they raided our warehouse and stole a large portion of our—"

"I didn't ask you why. I asked you if you did."

Spats reluctantly nodded.

Kore turned to Cutter. "Where did this aggression take place?"

"Barrel Street. Just outside our compound."

"So, it was clearly in Avalanche's territories?"

"You could have hit my bedroom window with a rock," Cutter said as he slid back in his seat, sensing justice swinging in his direction.

"And did you or any of your people raid the Hurricane warehouse?"

"Of course not."

"Well, there you have it," Kore said. "Hurricane is clearly in the wrong."

Spats slammed his fist on the table. "And how do you figure that?"

"'Cause you just admitted taking your beaters on a clear aggression against Avalanche. And as far as the raiding of your warehouse,

all we have is your word against his." Kore took another swallow
of his drink and glanced around the table with a proud smile as
though he had just mediated a truce between Elondria and Cylmar.
"That was easy. Now let's declare punishment and go home."

"Yes, let's," Cutter said with a wicked grin.

"Not so fast," Noph interjected. "As keen as I am to make it
back in time for my pheasant, I can't help but think that something
seems amiss. First of all, the animosity between these two is no
secret."

Red grunted her agreement.

Noph waited to see if she was going to say more before turning
to Cutter. "Let me get this straight. You're saying that this was a
completely unprovoked attack, correct? And that you had absolutely no idea that Spats was going to bring his beaters into your
territory looking for a fight?"

"Absolutely. That's exactly what I'm saying. We had no idea
Hurricane would ever do such a thing, and against their neighbors,
no less. If we had only known that they were having such difficul-
ties, we could have lent aid. All they needed to have done was ask.
We might be a poor community, but we are more than willing to
share what we have with those in need." I actually thought Cutter
was going to wipe a tear from his eye by the end of his speech.

"Hmm." Noph pinched his chin. "Then I guess what I don't
quite understand is that if this had been as unexpected as you
claim, and you had been taken completely unawares, how was
Hurricane nearly annihilated that night instead of Avalanche?
From what I've heard, Avalanche came away with hardly a scratch

while Hurricane is still burying their dead?"

"That's right!" Spats said, slamming his fist against the table, clearly too stupid to have thought of that evidence himself. "That proves Cutter's a liar right there."

I breathed a small sigh of relief, glad to see someone in the Guild had a lick of common sense. Cutter glanced at the other members as they waited for an answer. "It's obvious why we came out on top. Because . . . because we have a more superior fighting force."

"You lying spawn of a faerie!" Spats interjected. "They were waiting for us. The entire thing was an ambush. They tried to trap us."

I could see a smirk creeping across Cutter's face from across the table.

"All the streetlamps had been extinguished," Spats roared. "They had people shooting at us from every window. If it wasn't for my quick thinking, we'd all be dead right now."

Sapphire shifted from one foot to the other. She must not have been happy with Spats taking credit for himself.

"Thankfully," Spats said, "I have a gift for strategy—"

"Strategy?" Cutter leaned forward, resting the sleeves of his brown leather jacket on the table. "If it had been up to you, you all would most certainly be dead! All that screaming about cutting people's feet." He started to laugh. "The only reason you managed to escape was because one of your people decided to light a fire in the middle of the Maze!" Cutter turned and pointed right at me. "And he's the one who done it!"

The others leaned forward in their seats.

I felt a chill run down my back. *How could he have known it was Hurricane that set the fire? I had one of Avalanche's white armbands on.*

I kept my head down. I could feel Cutter's gaze boring into the top of my skull like a hot poker. I started running through possible scenarios in case they tried to subdue me. Cutter's falchion was still sitting on the table in front of him, but I could plant a knife in his chest before he had a chance to grab it.

"It's those eyes. Never seen eyes like that on anyone. Faerie eyes, if you ask me. I was standing in the building across the street when he set the flame, and even from there, the light reflecting off those eyes was unmistakable." Cutter sneered. "Now it all makes sense. I couldn't figure out for the life of me why one of my own people would be setting fire to our homes, but now I see that cowardice is how Spats runs his tribe."

Spats was speechless, probably for the first time in his life.

The others at the table shifted in their seats to get a better look at me.

"Now you tell me," Cutter said. "What sort of coward sets fire to a building in the Maze in the middle of a summer drought?"

Our *fearless* chief never said a word. In fact, he was uncharacteristically silent.

"The kind that is trying to keep his tribe from being completely exterminated," Sapphire said under her breath, but loud enough that everyone in the room must have heard.

Cutter hopped to his feet, his chair tipping backward and land-ing with a thump on the teal carpet. "How dare you address us without permission!"

Spats's face had gone from red to purple. He looked like he was about to explode. I only hoped he didn't do anything stupid, like go for his blade. I could sense the movement of the other guards around the table, their hands slowly sliding toward their waists. If this thing turned ugly, Spats was on his own. I was going straight for Red.

Spats sat forward slowly. I readied myself. *Here it comes.* But instead of letting Cutter have it, he turned in his seat and looked at Sapphire. "Know your place! Keep your mouth shut!"

I blinked. *What just happened?* I had half a mind to toss the weasel out the window and see how long it took him to hit the ground.

There was movement to my left. From the corner of my eye, I caught a flash of red heading in my direction.

I was standing close enough to Sapphire to feel her trembling. Her hand was on the hilt of her sword.

"Look at me, boy," Red said with that low, seductive voice of hers. She took a step closer. "Did you not hear me? I said look this way."

I raised my head and our eyes met.

Red's lips parted into a smile. "It *is* you." She turned to the short, pudgy guard on her left. "Po, look who we have here."

"That's him, sure enough," Toothless said as he reached for his sword and growled. I half-expected him to attack, but to his credit, he didn't draw. By now, both Sapphire and Spats had turned to see what they were talking about. The befuddled look on Spats's face was nothing new. Sapphire's eyes were smoldering.

Red took a step back to get a better look at me. "It's our little tourist from the Lost City. I thought for sure we'd seen the end of you after that embarrassing performance the last time we met."

I balled my fists, took a deep breath, and counted to ten.

"You do have a way of getting around, don't you? First you try taking on Wildfire, now you're humiliating Avalanche—"

"Watch your mouth, girl," Cutter said, in the middle of picking up his chair. "It was Hurricane who was running for their lives, not Avalanche."

"Yes, but as it's already been established, it was only because this pretty-eyed tourist set your shorts ablaze."

"Hah! Just another reason why Hurricane should be punished for all of this," Cutter said, taking his seat.

Red moved a little closer, staring into my eyes. "Such beautiful eyes. Ayr . . . Ayrion, am I right?"

I bit my tongue and nodded.

"I always thought that was a pretty name." She took a step back. "I have an idea," she said as she sauntered back to her seat. "It's been a while since we've had some decent entertainment around here, and since we can't seem to come to an agreement on who was in the right or who was in the wrong, I vote we settle this in the Pit."

Sapphire tensed, and her fingers found mine.

Red gestured to Cutter. "The best from Avalanche against"—

she pointed at me—"our little tourist over here. The winner deter-
mines whose tribe is right." She reclined in her seat with a wickedly
satisfied grin.

Kore straightened the lapel of his green waistcoat and leaned
forward. "I like it. This argument will finally be put to rest, and we
will have the opportunity to make a little coin on the side with
some much-needed sport. I second the motion."

"Aye," Cutter said as he rubbed his hands together in a greedy
sort of way, "and I've got just the fighter for the job: Flesh Eater."

Flesh Eater? What sort of a name was that for a kid? It sounded
more like a name given to one of the rabid pigmies in the deep
jungles near Cylmar.

"I'll add my vote," Noph said, "so long as it allows us to call an
end to this meeting. Portabellas are no good cold."

All eyes were on Spats. I don't know if they needed a unani-
mous vote or if it was because half the challenge was put on his
tribe, but they seemed to be waiting on him to officially confirm
the resolution. Spats finally nodded. He never turned to ask for my
opinion, never even hesitated to think it through. He just bobbed
his head in silence.

"Well, that's that," Red said as she stood from her seat. "Do we
call this meeting adjourned?"

The members all agreed with a single "Aye."

Red and her party left the table and started for the double
doors. Halfway across the room, she stopped and turned around.
"By the way," she said as she slowly unbuttoned the top of her shirt,
provocatively sliding her hand down the middle and pulling out a

gold chain with something dangling from it.

My eyes widened. I could feel the blood in my veins start to boil. My father's ring.

"Thanks for the jewelry," she said with a wink. "You definitely know how to treat a girl." I could hear her laughing all the way out the door.

I started after her, but Sapphire grabbed my arm and yanked me back. "You'll get your chance soon enough."

As soon as Red and her entourage had left the Guild, my magic returned. Spats waited for everyone else to leave before finally standing. His entire body shook as he turned and looked me in the eyes. "You better be as good as you think you are." Without saying another word, he turned and left.

Sapphire leaned forward and squeezed my hand. "Don't worry. You are."

CHAPTER 22

"THE PIT? I leave you alone for one afternoon and the next thing I hear is you're being sent to the Pit! Sweet spreading fungus! Why is this always happening?" Reevie turned his hard glare on Sapphire. "And you! I thought you had something besides potato mash in that thick skull of yours. How could you have let this happen?"

"Hey! It wasn't my fault," she said, tugging on her braid. "You're the one supposed to be watching him."

Reevie turned to me with a crazed looked in his eyes. "You're cursed!" he finally said, tossing the empty satchel he was holding into the trunk beside his desk before slamming the lid shut. "You have to be. No one's this unlucky." He walked around to the other side and picked up a quill, jabbing it in my direction. "Whatever you've done, you'd better start asking the Creator for forgiveness." He paused. "And a little common sense." He paused again. "And while you're at it, maybe a couple more feet in height and a hundred pounds of muscle." He glanced at Sapphire. "Who's the challenger?"

She gulped. "Flesh Eater."

"Flesh Eater! Oh, hanging toenails! The Creator hates me." Reevie threw his arms up in frustration. "I should have left you on the streets, but no, I had to save you." He finally dropped into his chair, placed two fingers on the side of his neck, and started counting. "You're going to be the death of me."

"Who's this Flesh Eater?" I asked.

Reevie lifted his head. "He's only the biggest, meanest, ugliest piece of infected scum to ever enter the Pit. No one's ever beaten him."

"Why is he called Flesh Eater? It's not because . . ."

Sapphire nodded.

I grimaced. "Then what's the Pit?"

Reevie leaned forward and crossed his arms over the neatly stacked vellum scrolls on his desk. He didn't seem all that concerned about flattening them. "The Pit is where the Guild holds their games. It's also where the chiefs send the members of their tribe stupid enough to want to join the Guard."

Sapphire glared at him, but Reevie paid her no mind. "Originally, it was a depository for raw ore. It was eventually swallowed up by Cheapside, so the owners sold it to the Guild and moved north."

"And where does the Guild get all this gold for repositories, lavish meeting rooms, and dinner parties with stuffed mushrooms?"

"Stuffed mushrooms?" Reevie looked at me like I'd lost my mind. "Who said anything about stuffed mushrooms? And what lavish meeting rooms are you talking about?"

"Haven't you ever been to the Guild Hall?"

Reevie snorted. "Do I look like someone Spats would ever take to the Guild?"

He had a point. "You should have seen the place," I said. "It was like nothing I've ever seen." I spent the next few minutes describing it, from the overhead walkways to the marble floors, the teal and gold carpets, and red cedar paneling. I even told him about the special snacks and drinks, even though I never got the chance to try any. "How could a bunch of street kids afford such things?" I asked. "I doubt you could pick enough pockets in a lifetime to pay for what I saw up there."

Reevie sat in silence, absorbing it all. "So, what's all this about stuffed mushrooms?"

I huffed. "Forget the mushrooms. I want to know how the Guild is able to rent rooms like that, and purchase warehouses, and wear fancy clothes while we are barely able to feed ourselves." I looked down at my now scuffed shoes. "Apart from Spats, the three of us are probably the best-dressed members of our tribe, and that's only because some woman gave me a gold piece for saving her child."

"Ah, and there's your answer," Reevie said with a smug look.

Now it was my turn to look at him like he was crazy.

"Favors," he said. "The Guild might be looked down on by the aristocracy as nothing more than a nuisance, but secretly, they use our services in exchange for certain favors."

I tossed some books off a nearby seat and sat down. "Like what? What could a lord or lady possibly need from us that they couldn't pay anyone else in the city for?"

"Discretion," Sapphire said, butting into the conversation. She followed my lead and sat on the examination table. "They pay for our anonymity as well as our disposability—"

"Sure," Reevie said. "The aristocracy are politically motivated. Their currency of choice is secrets. If you want to get ahead of one of your rivals, then you blackmail them. But blackmail requires leverage, and that's where we come in. They hire us to follow their rivals around until we find some dirt on them. Our ability to procure certain items is also of particular value to the upper class."

"In other words, they hire us for spying and thieving."

"I wouldn't have put it quite that way," Sapphire said. "But yes."

The picture that Reevie and Sapphire painted was a corrupt and dangerous one.

"Clearly, Hurricane isn't landing many of those contracts. You should have seen the suits that Noph and Kore were wearing, not to mention Red—"

Reevie's head shot up. "I forgot she'd be there. How did that go?"

"I'm being thrown in the Pit. How do you think it went?"

"Fair point."

"So, why is it that those three tribes are in such better shape than we are?"

"That's easy," Sapphire said. "Location. Location is everything. For those of us in the Maze, pickings are pretty slim. The wealthier districts, where the pockets are bulging and the purses carry more than coppers, are out of our territory. The other three tribes, except for Avalanche, have been able to establish themselves around the more lucrative picking fields. Wildfire and Rockslide operate out of North Aramoor and Sandstorm out of the east."

I started to say something, but Reevie beat me to it. "The reason no one has managed to set up a territory on the west side, which I'm sure is what you were about to ask, is because it's too close to the palace. That district not only holds the largest patroller office in Aramoor but also the main branch of the Elondrian Lancer Corps. With our territories being predominantly in the Maze, we don't exactly attract a lot of those political jobs we were just discussing."

"Makes sense."

"We aren't the only ones holding the short end of the stick," Reevie said, leaning back in his seat. "Avalanche is even worse off than we are."

"You wouldn't know it by the cut of Cutter's jacket and

breeches, not to mention that ridiculous hat."

"Cutter isn't known for his generosity," Reevie continued. "He rules his tribe through fear. Whatever the tribe brings in, he deems as his and only disperses to the members what he believes they need in order to keep them working."

"And I thought Spats was bad," I said. "It's a wonder anyone stays with Cutter. Why don't the kids just leave, if he's so terrible?"

Sapphire shared a look with Reevie. "Cutter has a way of making examples out of those who try. It instills fear in the rest."

I sighed. "I know the type. The only thing they respect is someone bigger and meaner than they are." I didn't understand how Spats and Cutter ever came to be chieftains. Both were terrible leaders—though Cutter had Spats beat when it came to nastiness. "What does it take to become the head of a tribe? What makes them so privileged? Kore I could see. The kid's bigger than his own Guard. I doubt anyone wanted to fight him for the position. And Noph seems to have a pretty good head on his shoulders. Cutter's probably the meanest snake in his bunch, and Red, well, what can I say; she's Red." Sapphire shot me a dirty look. "But how in the name of Aldor did someone like Spats get placed as chief?"

Reevie chuckled, not sounding amused as he did. "It was given to him. Spats's older brother, Kerson, was the head of the tribe before being offered a position in the Warrens. When he left, he handed his title to Spats. No one dared challenge his decision, seeing as he was even bigger than Kore and twice as cruel." Reevie shrugged. "The monarchy has been doing it for thousands of years. The crown is passed from father to son."

"Or until someone kills the son," I said.

Reevie and Sapphire looked at each other.

"So, instead of his brother appointing someone who can actually do the job," I said, "we end up with Weasel Face."

"Shhh," Sapphire scolded, turning to look at the door. "Keep it down. Someone might hear you."

"It could have been worse," Reevie said. "We could have ended up with someone like Cutter."

I shuddered at the thought.

"When's this fight supposed to take place?" Reevie asked.

I looked at Sapphire.

"There's no telling." She hopped down from the table. "Arrangements will have to be made, schedules readjusted, security set up. It's very difficult—not to mention dangerous—to get all five tribes into the same building without massive casualties."

"What do you mean, *all five tribes*? I thought this was going to be a simple fight. You know, me versus this Flesh Eater person to determine who gets punished."

Reevie stood from his seat behind his desk. "You don't think the Guild is going to go through all the hassle of setting up a challenge for just a single fight, do you? Whenever the Pit is involved, it's a big deal."

I was almost afraid to ask. "What are we talking about, ten or fifteen from each tribe in attendance?"

Reevie and Sapphire looked at each other and started laughing.

I had my answer.

CHAPTER 23

A FTER A GRUELING discussion with Spats, I managed to convince him to free me of my imprisonment within the walls of the Temple. I needed to keep up with my training, and I couldn't do it there. Spats was surprisingly open to the idea once he realized it would help me win in the Pit. He had no intention of forking out his gold to pay as a fine to Cutter if I lost. I was even encouraged to take food and supplies from Spats's own table.

Reevie and I ate very well over the next week. Spats made sure I had only the best. We had pork, wild turkey, and smoked cheese, and not the hard stuff we were used to eating that tasted like it had been sitting in a dank cellar for too long. I was even afforded a bottle of spiced wine straight from Spats's personal stock. I was more than a little jealous of the quality of food Spats ate while the rest of the tribe barely had enough to get by.

Things were looking up, if you didn't count that at any time I could be marching off to the Pit to face off against Flesh Eater. I focused on running through my exercises and conditioning my body. I pushed myself harder than I'd ever pushed before.

I even took some time to go see Master Fentin and Miss Orilla. They were both doing well. They had heard about the street skirmish and, when we didn't come back by to visit, had grown concerned. But they were glad to hear that the two of us had made it through and were doing fine. Of course, I left out anything about how close we had come to dying during that battle or that I was being forced to fight for the honor of our tribe.

I was beginning to agree with Reevie. Maybe I *was* cursed. It seemed like my life was made up of one fight after another.

I helped tidy up the shop for Master Fentin the best I could. The constant ache in his back and knees kept him from being able to clean like he used to, and I wondered how much longer he and Miss Orilla would be able to keep it running. I was rewarded for my efforts with one of Miss Orilla's famous mystery-meat sandwiches. It was a good day.

I left the bookshop as the sun was beginning to set, and by the time I reached the Temple's gates, it was well after dark. Torchlight dotted the top of the wall, casting ugly shadows across the already ugly creatures engraved there. I could see a couple of heads peering out over the gate.

"Password!" one of the kids shouted from the top.

I rolled my eyes and wondered if it was too late to try joining another tribe.

There is no chief as brave as Spats.

All other chiefs are dumb as rats.

If any wish to enter here,

Stick out your tongue and then draw near.

I finished the childish quote by sticking out my tongue and walking toward the gate. Just like every other time, the watchers overhead started to giggle. Once I was within five paces, I could hear the heavy crossbar being lifted. The gates parted and I found myself facing an unexpected crowd.

Members of Hurricane lined either side of the walkway leading from the gate to the main building. There was a wide-enough space between for two people to pass through if they stood shoulder to shoulder. Some of the kids were holding torches.

I walked over to the front to look down the human corridor and spotted a group of kids hobbling through the crowd in my direction.

"What's going on?" I asked one of the watchers standing near the gate—Toots, I thought.

"They's Avalanche rejects," he said, spitting off to the side. "Trying to gain membership here in Hurricane. Like we'd ever let Avalanche rejects in here."

Most had scars and cuts that looked to still be healing, but the wounds were red and infected. Half were limping, while the others struggled to keep them on their feet and moving.

Where was Reevie? I glanced down the row as far as the limited torchlight would allow, but didn't see him.

There wasn't a single one of these kids that looked like they'd had a decent meal in weeks. The dark circles under their eyes said they weren't sleeping, either.

"They was wounded in the recent battle," Toots said. "And now they's no longer fit for use. If you can't perform your duties, then you's a burden on the tribe."

"Surely, we can find something for them to do here."

"We can barely feed our own. You gonna give up your rations for 'em? Besides, you think Spats is going to help the vermin who just tried to do him in?"

"I guess not."

As the Avalanche rejects neared the entrance, I realized one of the bigger kids looked familiar. I knew him. He was the blond kid I had tripped with the crate. He was still limping from it.

In fact, I realized there were quite a few faces I recognized. Two were part of the group that had tried breaking through the Guard to get their hands on Spats. One of them was the kid I had used as a stepstool in order to leap over the others.

The tall blond kid slowed as he neared me. He looked like he wanted to say something, but then he lowered his head and kept moving. The look of humiliation, hunger, and desperation in his eyes turned my stomach.

"What's going to happen to them?" I asked.

"Who cares," Toots said. "No one's gonna take 'em in. Probably just go off and die, or end up in the dungeons or salt mines."

"Salt mines?"

Toots looked at me funny. "The salt mines is where they send prisoners to work off their sentences. They pack 'em up and ship 'em over to the Isle of Delga."

I took a hard look at the faces of the Hurricane members as they watched the small parade of injured, starving kids pass. I saw no empathy, no remorse, no concern in any way, not even guilt. If there was a hint of emotion, it was revulsion. These castaway kids had become like the leper colonies on the Isle of the Forgotten. Once deemed unfit to work, or rejected from another tribe, it seemed their use to anyone else was permanently marred.

The injured rejects passed through the gates and struggled up the stone path in the direction of the merchant shops. I followed Toots and the other watchers back to the gate. "Have you seen Reevie?"

"He left before supper. Said he wanted to make it home before dark."

"Mind if I borrow that?" I asked, pointing at the torch in Toots's hand. "I've got a long walk. Don't want to break my leg falling in a pothole. Spats might be a bit upset if his prize fighter was injured before he ever stepped into the ring." I smiled.

Toots started to laugh. "You's got a point there," he said, then handed me his torch. "I don't envy you none going to the Pit, but I don't mind tellin' ya I'm right excited about the prospect. I heard this Flesh Eater is quite the beast." He cast a wary glance at those still mingling around the gate before taking a step closer and leaning in. "I wouldn't go spreadin' this around, but I put half my earnings this month down for you to win."

I placed my hand on his shoulder with a reaffirming squeeze. "You're probably the only one."

Toots's smile seemed to slide a little. "You better watch your step," he said as I started down the path. I doubted it was my safety he was concerned about.

I could hear the gates shut behind me. The heavy thud of the crossbeam echoed into the night. Once I reached the end of the stone, I raised my torch to see which direction to take.

There was something I needed to do before going home, something I was sure would land me a nice scolding from Reevie.

CHAPTER 24

"WHAT THE FLAMING bunions are you bringing them here for?"

Reevie stood in the granary's doorway with his nightshirt hanging clear down to his ankles, not the most intimidating presence I'd ever seen. In his hand, he threatened the small group of outcasts with the cudgel he normally kept stashed under his pillow.

"They need help, Reevie."

"What they need is to get back on the road and keep walking until they reach the bay." He waved his nightstick in a circle over his head. "And then keep going."

I stood there in silence for a moment, completely taken back by his response. "What sort of thing is that for a healer to say? Just look at them," I said, lowering my voice so the others wouldn't hear. "They'd be lucky to make it to the street corner without keeling over." Three or four of the kids were sitting on the ground, unable to stand on their own, and those that had been carrying them were too exhausted to move.

"Can I see you inside a moment?" Reevie motioned with his head for me to follow. He kept a close eye on the rejects, making sure they didn't try anything. Once inside the warehouse, Reevie turned and pointed his stick at me. "What do you think you're doing? Do you know who they are? Avalanche's rejects. I bet even Hurricane wouldn't be willing to take them in. No one wants Cutter's rejects. He makes life difficult for anyone who tries to help those he considers unfit to survive. How'd you end up with them in the first place?"

"I stopped by the Temple looking for you, and when I got there, they were . . . well, being kicked out."

"There! You see?" Reevie said, bringing his cudgel up once more. "Hurricane won't even take them, and they have the most lax policy of all the tribes when it comes to accepting members."

"They've got nowhere else to go," I said, hoping to find some way to reach Reevie's normally compassionate nature. I had thought one look at the sad state of these kids and the healer in him would have taken over.

"What's that got to do with us?"

I sighed and shook my head. In a way, I was just as much an

outcast as these injured kids. "It should have everything to do with us. What happened to that boy with the gimpy leg who decided to help a poor wounded kid lying in the middle of the street? The boy who took me in, dressed my wounds, fed me, and spent countless hours nursing me back to health? Where's that boy? 'Cause from what I can remember, he didn't know me from a piece of loose cobble."

Reevie lowered his stick and let it bump against the side of his leg. "That was different."

"Oh? How so?"

"Well, for starters, you weren't a former member of Avalanche."

"Yeah, but you didn't know that."

"One look at you and anyone would have known that," he said with a smirk. "Besides, there was only one of you. There's nearly two dozen of them out there."

"It's not like we don't have the room," I said with a quick gesture to the empty building. I could see he was starting to crumble. "You're a healer, for pity's sake. Don't you have some healer code about helping those in need?"

Reevie chewed on his lower lip.

"Look, it will only be for a couple of days, and who knows; they might be of some use."

Reevie raised a single brow and gave me a hard glare. "They're rejects, Ayrion. Worse, they're injured rejects. What sort of value could they possibly have?"

"I don't know. I'm sure we'll think of something. Every life is worth something."

"That's ironic, coming from a would-be assassin."

I ignored his jab, true or not. "The problem with the other tribes is that they place their value on the needs of the whole and not the individual. It seems to me that any society that holds this type of a mindset is doomed to eventually follow the path of only the strong surviving. I should know. That's the way of the Upaka.

"That's the real reason why I was banished. It wasn't so much that I had killed the Primary's son, anyone who witnessed the fight could see it had been an accident, but what they really couldn't stand was that I was different from everyone else. It was the *excuse* they needed to get rid of someone who stuck out. When you're raised from birth to believe in the unit, it's hard to see the value of the individual."

Reevie fiddled with his cudgel. "I suppose we could put them in some of the empty rooms in back. But only for a couple of days, mind you. We aren't running some charity house here. I don't want to see you bringing home strays for me to take care of every time I turn around. The point of being on this side of the Maze was to get away from the tribes, not so we could start our own."

My head lifted. "Why not?"

"Why not what?"

"Why not start our own tribe? I'm sure there are plenty of other rejects looking for a home. We could bring them here."

Reevie stared at me in dumb silence, no doubt trying to think of an appropriate curse. "Have you gone completely mad?" His cudgel was back in the air and swinging wildly. "Just the very thought of starting our own tribe would bring the others down on us faster than you could say *Ayrion the Idiot.*"

"They wouldn't have to know. We can keep it a secret."

Reevie started to laugh. "And how long do you think that will last? In order to survive, we need food and clothing, medicines, bedding, warm blankets for winter, lanterns, not to mention weapons for defense. Where do you suppose we're going to get these things? A benevolent faerie?" Reevie turned and headed for the front door. "Come on, let's get them inside before someone sees them. You've already got me out of my bed; might as well be doing something useful."

I decided not to push the matter further, at least for the moment. I needed more time to consider the ideas now racing through my mind.

CHAPTER

25

OVER THE NEXT couple of days, Reevie and I stayed
around the granary as much as possible while he treated the
rejects. He had me make a few runs to the Temple to get supplies
from the stash in his office. I didn't complain, since it gave me a
chance to see Sapphire and report to Spats on the condition of my
training. Mostly, he just wanted reassurances that I was going to
beat Flesh Eater. He needed someone to hold his hand and tell him
everything was going to be all right.

Even with the influx of injured rejects, Reevie still made sure
to check in on his Hurricane patients as well. Their injuries were

healing nicely, having been treated much sooner than those at the granary. Even the worst of Hurricane's injured, those unable to wield a weapon again, were almost well enough to join the ranks of the watchers or the cleaners. So far, to Hurricane's credit, they hadn't turned out any of their fallen comrades. However, I didn't believe for a moment that Spats would have thought twice about evicting the wounded if he deemed them of no further use.

The Guild had yet to set a date for the fight. According to Sapphire, there were already significant wagers being dealt between the tribes. No one bet on who would win or lose but on how long I would last before Flesh Eater devoured me. Some were even betting on which parts he'd chew on first; others, what parts he'd leave behind. So, naturally, I took what was left of the money Spats had given me in order to purchase supplies for my training and placed a wager on myself *to win*. The boy handling the bets laughed. Looking at the odds, if I did manage to beat Flesh Eater, I'd have enough coin from my winnings to keep the granary stocked for some time, long enough for those living there to get back on their feet. And if the worst happened and I lost, then I figured I wouldn't be around long enough to worry about it.

"Ayrion." Sapphire's voice had the boy with the betting ledger scurrying off in the opposite direction. She skirted Egla's fountain, drawing my attention once again to the life-sized image of the naked faerie. One of these days, I was going to find a warm coat for her to wear.

"Spats wants to see you," she said, stopping in front of me.

I had just taken the first bite of my apple. "What for?"

"I didn't ask. But I bet it has something to do with the head of Sandstorm arriving while you were helping Reevie with the wounded."

"Noph is here? I didn't know tribal heads made house calls."

"They don't. At least not usually. Must be important."

"Then I wonder why they want to see me."

She thought for a moment, then smiled. "'Cause they just can't get enough of those gray eyes."

I grunted as I stood.

"So, how's it going with the new houseguests?" she asked as we slowly made our way back to the main building. "Reevie told me you've gotten in the habit of bringing home strays."

I gave her a befuddled look. "I don't know what you're talking about."

"Well, I think it's great. No one's ever been brave enough to do anything about them before."

I colored at the compliment but quickly regained my composure and filled her in on what Reevie and I had been up to.

We passed Reevie as he exited the dining hall and I tossed him my half-eaten piece of fruit. "Noph just arrived, and Spats is demanding to see me." I gave him my most sarcastic smile.

"Great! What've you gone and done this time? Cursed, Ayrion," he said, pointing at me with my apple. "You hear me? Cursed!"

There were four guards outside Spats's door, two of ours and two from Sandstorm. The two from Sandstorm wore purple sashes around their waists. I wished I had taken the time to stop by

Reevie's room and grab my black vest.

Forehead, one of Spats's guards, best known for his ferocious head-butting technique, not to mention the large permanent knot that had grown there because of it, knocked on the door when he saw us coming. Spats's high-pitched voice answered and Forehead opened the door for us to enter.

The door clicked shut behind us, but the guards remained in the corridor. Spats sat in a large high-back chair off to the right, and Noph was reclining comfortably on the small sofa in front of him. The same two guards who had accompanied Noph during our meeting at the Guild Hall stood like sentinels on either side of the sofa. They reminded me of the bronze statues I'd seen in the park at King's Square—silent and unmoving.

"Ah, and there's our little scrapper now," Noph said as he leaned forward and placed his weight on his silver-tipped cane. He wore another richly clad waistcoat. It was shorter than the one I had seen him in before, but it still bore the same deep purple hue. His pants matched his coat in design, and his hat curled slightly on the sides with a black leather band around the small top-bowl, complete with a purple plume. He looked quite the dandy.

"You wished to see me?" I asked with a slight bow to Spats, a show of courtesy since Noph was present. Spats had dusted off his faded blue vest for the occasion. He had, however, forgone the silk cravat, which I thought was a wise choice. It made him look like a complete buffoon instead of merely the half-wit he was.

"Yes," Spats said. "We were just discussing your upcoming competition. I was telling Noph that you were sure to win."

Noph remained silent. He seemed to be studying me. He might have dressed like a fop, but I believed my earlier assessment of him was correct—he was smarter than he let on. "Yes, there is quite the talk floating around about the upcoming event," he said. "Not much in your favor, I'm afraid."

I offered a polite smile.

"But the Pit is the least of our worries at the moment." The Sandstorm chief lifted his black cane and let it thump on the woven rug at his feet. "I've been watching you. I notice your lips hardly ever move, but your eyes seem to say quite a bit. For instance, they tell me you have a keen perception of your surroundings.

"I watched as you entered the room. You took notice of who was here, where they were positioned, and what weapons they carried. You looked for the nearest exits, and right now you're judging whether the hollow sound of my cane is being made from the rug, or if there is something hidden inside." Noph smiled and dropped his cane again. "How am I doing?"

"Actually, I was deciding which of your guards I would take down first in order to get to you."

"Ayrion!" Spats hopped to his feet, looking mortified.

Noph leaned back and laughed. "Sit down, Spats, before you give yourself a palpitation." He undid the buttons on his waistcoat and stretched one arm over the back of the sofa as he studied me. I couldn't help but wonder if I was being weighed for a different purpose altogether. Noph was clearly a tactician. He wouldn't have come if he didn't have something specific in mind. I bet he was a tough person to beat in a game of batmyth. "I'm here because we seem to have a common problem. I wonder, Ayrion, if you could tell me what that problem would be?"

"Cutter."

Noph smiled. "And that is why I requested you be here for this meeting. Please"—Noph gestured to a couple of chairs in front of the two of them—"take a seat."

I glanced at Spats so as not to make him feel like he'd lost authority in his own house. Spats nodded, and I walked over and took one of the two empty chairs.

"You too, Miss Sapphire," Noph said.

Spats nodded again, and Sapphire took her seat next to mine.

"I wanted to start by saying I have no doubt that what you said during the Guild assembly was correct and that Cutter sent his thugs in to raid your warehouse specifically to draw you out. That is how he thinks. He craves power and isn't afraid to take risks to get it. Like Hurricane, Sandstorm borders the Avalanche territories, and with each passing month, his tribe pushes further into our region. I believe he's testing the waters, wanting to see how far he can go before we push back.

"Unfortunately for you, he anticipated your attack or, better yet, orchestrated it."

"He just got lucky," Spats said, refusing to admit his own incompetence. Noph didn't argue.

"You're not the only tribe that Cutter has been testing. Just last month, we caught a small party from Avalanche near our compound. We stopped them about three streets over. Their excuse was they'd gotten lost. But, with a little well-placed persuasion, they admitted they had been ordered to see how close they could get before being discovered. They proceeded to beg us not to send them back. They said Cutter had sent them out after deeming them no longer useful. The fresh stripes on their backs seemed to testify to the fact. But the last thing we had room for was Avalanche's rejects."

"If you don't mind me asking," I said, leaning forward in my seat, "if Cutter is such a tyrant, then why does his tribe continue to grow? I'd think his members would be leaving en masse."

Noph tapped the end of his cane with a shiny black shoe. "Those that are already there are too afraid to leave, and those that continue to join do so looking for power. And Cutter's promise of making them all rich is a strong incentive for their decision to join Avalanche. Anxious ears will generally hear only what they want. Doesn't matter how ridiculous the lie; as long as it's presented in such a way that it aligns with their desires, they'll blindly follow it all the way to their own destruction."

I liked the way this kid thought. If there was ever any doubt before, it was gone now. Noph had a good head on his silk-covered shoulders.

"What I don't want to see happen," he said, "is Cutter using the Pit to bolster the image of his tribe by claiming another victory—"

"You don't have to worry about that," Spats interjected, "'cause Ayrion's going to win." He shifted in his seat to look at me. "Isn't that right?" he asked, not giving me a chance to answer. "He's been training every day."

"That's good to hear," Noph said. "You might be Upakan, but the Pit isn't for the faint of heart, especially when facing something like Flesh Eater."

I noticed he had said some*thing* and not some*one*. "What's to stop Cutter from carrying out an attack at the Pit? If his lust for power is as strong as you say, what better opportunity than when everyone is assembled?"

"You make a good point," Noph said, crossing one leg over the other. "It's the reason all members are required to disarm before entering."

"All but the chief's immediate guards, of course," Spats added.

"There is the occasional brawl that breaks out when one tribe's champion beats another," Sapphire said, "but without weapons, it doesn't get far, and is usually snuffed out by the rest of the tribes. The last thing anyone wants is an open bloodbath."

"Or maybe that's exactly what Cutter wants," I said.

"I don't believe he would take it that far," Noph said. "He's a greedy son of a faerie, but he's not stupid. If he were to incite something now, he'd only be ensuring a quick alliance between the other tribes. And Avalanche, although growing, is nowhere near large enough to withstand that." Noph leaned back in his seat. "No, I don't foresee anything quite so dramatic as an all-out attack. Cutter's goal will be to win the Pit, and in doing so, he'll not only wiggle out of any repercussion for his unlawful raid, but he'll pass that punishment on to you, all while building Avalanche's reputation as a tribe worth joining."

"I see your point," Spats said with a worried frown.

Noph leaned forward and offered me a sly grin. "My question is, what did you do to Red to get her so riled up? I get the feeling it's personal somehow."

I didn't have to look to know that Sapphire's eyes were blazing. "I defended myself against her goons on my first day in Aramoor. They decided they wanted what was in my pack, and I decided they couldn't have it."

Noph impatiently tapped his cane with his fingertips. "And . . ."

"And she lost a large portion of her Guard and a few of her beaters before they managed to get it from me."

Noph leaned back in his seat. "Yep, that would do it." He smiled. "Red doesn't like to lose."

"Neither does Cutter," Spats mumbled from his seat.

CHAPTER 26

THE NEXT MORNING, I woke to the sound of Reevie rummaging around his collection of herbs and tonics at the far corner of our chambers under the granary.

"Why didn't you wake me sooner?" I asked, fighting back a deep yawn.

"Sorry." Reevie cast a quick glance over his shoulder before shuffling through some more half-empty jars. "I was trying to keep the noise down. You need all the rest you can get, what with your upcoming . . ." He didn't finish. "Anyway, those rejects up there are having a hard go of it. Infection has set in. They should have been treated a week ago. With my supplies as low as they are, we might not be able to save them all. We used most of my herbs on Hurricane's wounded. I'm going to need to get some more."

"Where?"

"Master Fentin has a small reserve that I've squirreled away. Any chance you'd be going over there?"

It didn't sound like a question.

"I can. It won't hurt to take one morning off from training." I crawled out of bed and stretched my arms as far as they would go, which triggered another extensive yawn. It did feel good to get a little extra sleep.

After a quick breakfast of bread, cheese, and some sliced fruit, washed down with some watered-down ale, I headed up to the main floor to see to our guests. They were all awake. Some were moving around, tending to the more injured while waiting on Reevie to make an appearance.

Bull, the leader of the small group, who also happened to be the large blond boy I had knocked unconscious during our battle with Avalanche, was busy moving from one cot to the next, making sure everyone was drinking enough water. He stopped as soon as we entered the room.

"Mouse isn't looking too good," Bull said, walking over to greet us. "Neither is Petal. She won't drink anything. Says her tummy hurts."

"I'll take a look." Reevie hefted his bag and made his way through the crude sleeping quarters, careful not to step on anyone. Most of the outcasts were still bedridden. The mattresses had come from one of the abandoned inns across the street. Some of the smaller kids slept two and three to a mattress.

Reevie moved from one bed to the next. Every now and then, the little healer would grunt, open his satchel, and pull out a small bottle of this or a pouch of that, applying the medication where it was needed.

"Why are you helping us?" Bull asked. He stood beside me in the doorway, watching Reevie work.

I looked at him kind of funny. "Because you needed it."

"But . . . we tried to hurt you."

"Then why did you agree to come here?"

Bull leaned against the edge of the doorframe as he weighed my question. "Because . . ." He paused to think some more. "Because you offered."

"But I hurt you. I injured your leg and left you unconscious."

There was another extended moment of silence. "I guess because I didn't see we had any other choice," he finally admitted.

I turned to look at him. "And neither did I. The way I see it, we have a duty to help those less fortunate."

"Don't know many of those."

"Those?"

"People less fortunate than us."

I laughed. "You have a point there." I turned my attention back to the injured. "This city would be a much better place if people spent their time helping each other instead of exploiting one another."

Bull snorted. "That's not going to happen."

"Maybe not, but can you imagine what we could accomplish if it did?"

There was another long moment of silence. I figured he'd had enough philosophy for one day. Maybe he hoped if he didn't answer, I'd shut up.

"If there were such a tribe," Bull said finally, pushing a tuft of dirty-blond hair back from his eyes, "I'd be proud to join."

I turned and looked at him, almost surprised by his words. *If there were such a tribe, I'd be proud to join.* My mind raced with possibilities, but I stamped them down. I couldn't let myself get swept up in daydreams. "Yes," I said, turning my attention back to the room of injured rejects, "if only there were such a tribe."

Reevie finished his initial walkthrough. After spending the last week or so helping him with the Temple's wounded, I knew his routine by heart.

"I'm going to need you to get those extra supplies after all," Reevie said, walking over to join us at the door. "Mouse requires more goldenseal, Petal and Squeaks need cranberry leaf oil, and I'm nearly out of both."

I nodded. "I'll take Bull with me and introduce him to Master Fentin in case you ever need him to get something and I'm not around."

Reevie pursed his lips and glanced at Bull. "Just promise me you won't do anything stupid like jump in front of a runaway carriage."

"Stupid? Me?" I offered Reevie a wide grin.

He shuddered and walked back to his patients.

I glanced at Bull. "Have you had any breakfast?"

"We had the rest of the porridge you gave us last night."

I nodded. "Good. It's quite the walk."

We left the makeshift sleeping quarters and headed across the open floor of the granary. The sun was just beginning to peek between a pair of tall buildings in front of us as we stepped outside. The harbor bells tolled the hour. My stomach grumbled, clearly looking forward to the possibility of one of Miss Orilla's sandwiches.

We made good time by avoiding the Maze. Instead, we headed west on Mora and then north along Bay Street. I took every chance I could to catch a glimpse of the bay. I never got tired of staring out at the blue horizon of seemingly endless water, something I never would have been able to imagine as a small boy living in an underground city.

Bull had difficulty keeping up, thanks to his injured leg, but he never complained. I kept the pace slow, something I was used to doing while following Reevie around the city.

"What can you tell me about Flesh Eater?" I asked. I figured if there was anyone who would be able to give me a straight answer, it would be someone who had actually lived with this potentially cannibalistic monster. I needed to find a weakness, something I could exploit.

Bull thumbed his chin. "Not much, I'm afraid."

I cast a sidelong look his way. "You lived with the kid. How do you not know anything about him? There's got to be something you can tell me. How big is he? Does he favor his right or left side?

How does he fight? Does he . . ." I gulped. "Does he really eat people?"

"I've only seen him fight twice, and I didn't really get a chance to see what type of fighting he prefers, or if he favors a side."

"Why not?"

"The fights didn't last long enough. As soon as Flesh Eater got his hands on them, the fight was over."

My heart sank. "At least tell me what he looks like."

"I can't tell you much except he's big." Bull waved his hand high over his head. "Really big."

I let out a sigh of exasperation. "Was this boy in your tribe or not?"

"He was, but he was never allowed out."

We stopped at one of the main streets leading into the merchant district and waited for a couple of carriages to pass. "What do you mean, *not allowed out*? Out of what? The compound?"

"No. Out of his cage."

"His cage?" If I hadn't been worried before, I was now. After glancing both ways to make sure we weren't going to get run over by some reckless aristocrat, we followed the crowd across the street.

"Yeah, Cutter keeps him locked in a cage in one of the buildings out back. Whenever he's in public, he wears a mask that covers his whole head." Bull pursed his lips. "You know, I don't believe I've ever seen his face."

I decided to drop the topic altogether. I doubted I was going to get anything more helpful out of Bull, and I didn't see any point in spending another moment thinking about my strange masked opponent.

"I'd forgotten how nice it is over here," Bull said as we headed into the lower merchant district. We followed the flow of the Tansian River northeast, slowly dodging around and weaving through the current of people as they passed from one shop to the next. "It's been at least five years since I've been over here. Cutter didn't let us get out except to work. Only certain members were allowed to move about the city, and that was only with his direct permission. We were assigned routes that we worked with half a dozen other pickers. If the pickings were good, everything was fine. But when the pickings were down, which they usually were a couple of months of the year, things weren't so good."

I waited for him to elaborate, but he didn't seem to want to talk about what *not so good* meant.

"I was assigned the wheat and barley quarters." Bull grunted. "That's all well and good during the harvest seasons, but what were we supposed to do during the rest? The only thing we could do was try picking outside of our area. We didn't have a choice. There's nothing worse than making Cutter mad, and measly pickings were about the fastest way to do that."

"It sounds to me like Cutter did you a favor by kicking you out." I tried to sound upbeat.

Bull grunted again. "At the time, we didn't think so." He limped off the walkway and over to a knee-high stone wall that ran along the front of the river. He winced as he sat down to give his injured leg a rest. "Getting labeled as a reject, especially an Avalanche reject, is pretty much a death sentence."

I joined him on the wall. The disgusting smell coming from the tannery across the way overpowered everything else, forcing me to breathe through my mouth.

"Do you really believe we're all important?" Bull took a moment to stare at the throngs of people rushing by, no one really stopping to notice each other. "Your granary's like a sanctuary. I'm sure if you looked hard enough, you'd find there's a lot more street rats out there looking for a place to belong."

"Let's not get carried away," I said with a nervous chuckle. "If I were to go gathering up any more lost strays, Reevie would probably throw me out."

Bull offered a half-smile. "It was just a thought."

We left the leather district and headed into the book district. The sun was high in the sky when we crossed onto the street that held Master Fentin's shop. Master Fentin was busy helping some customers at the front when we stepped inside. As soon as he spotted me, he waved us on to the back.

"I'll be with you in just a moment," he said with a bright smile.

Bull began to wander around the back part of the shop, scanning each row as he went. "I've never seen so many books. I wonder what they're all about."

"A great many things, my young friend," Master Fentin said as he poked his head around the aisle.

"Makes me wish I knew how to read." He ran his finger across the gold-embossed title on a thick volume about three rows up. "What does this one talk about?"

Master Fentin hobbled over with his cane and adjusted the

spectacles on the bridge of his nose. "Ah, that book discusses the various temperatures used for tempering iron-based alloys, and the effect they have on durability. It also tells how to determine a metal's processing temperature. Did you know that steel, for instance, can be identified by its color?"

Bull whistled, and looked back at the book.

"Yes, well." Master Fentin cleared his throat. "I suppose you didn't come all this way to discuss metallurgy." He stood there for a moment studying Bull before turning to me. "Would you mind introducing me to your large friend?"

"Oh, sorry, Master Fentin. I don't know where my manners have run off to. Master Fentin, this is Bull, gatherer and protector of street rejects. Bull, this is Master Fentin, collector of rare books and purveyor of even rarer stories."

Master Fentin performed a sweeping bow, at least as far as his back would allow. "Ah, Master . . . Bull. Indeed a strong name. I am delighted to make your acquaintance."

Bull turned a tad red in the cheeks at all the show and attempted a bow himself. It was a bit clumsy, but we got the point. Just then, the bell over the front door rang out as an older gentleman and what looked to be his grandson stepped into the shop.

"Be right with you," Master Fentin called out. The gentleman smiled and went about his perusing.

"Reevie sent us to get his herb stash. We have a number of injured kids we're treating at the granary."

"Ah, well, they'd be upstairs. Just go on in. The missus is just doing a spot of cleaning at the moment. Tell her what you're looking for and she'll get it for you. And tell her that I said to make sure you didn't leave without something to eat. It's a long walk back."

My eyes widened. I could feel the saliva building at the corners of my mouth. "Yes, sir, thank you."

It didn't take Ms. Orilla long to gather up the supplies, nor for us to gobble down a couple of her mystery-meat sandwiches. I thanked her with a firm hug and a small peck on the cheek, while Bull offered another one of his awkward bows.

Master Fentin was busy with some more customers, so we merely waved our goodbyes before heading on our way. By the time we made it back to the granary, the sun was just reaching the top of the Sandrethin Mountains, leaving the sky very beautiful shades of purple, pink, and peach.

Reevie was sitting outside the front door when we arrived.

"Took you long enough," he said.

"Sorry. You know how Mistress Orilla is, wouldn't let us leave without making us a plate of something to eat."

Reevie frowned.

"Don't worry. She didn't forget about you." I pulled a wrapped sandwich from the satchel and handed it to him.

His face brightened.

"And we got the herbs." I handed Reevie the satchel, and we headed back inside.

"A pigeon just flew in not an hour ago," Reevie said, part of his last bite still hanging from his mouth. He stopped, and I could see it in his eyes. "They've set a date."

CHAPTER 27

THREE DAYS.

I had exactly three days before the tribes were to assemble at the Pit. Three days would have normally seemed like a long time, but knowing what awaited me, three *weeks* wouldn't have been long enough.

I continued running through my exercises while Reevie continued to nurse the injured kids back to health. Up and down the ropes I went, building the strength in my arms and stomach. Over, under, around, and through the various obstacles of my course I plunged—spinning, punching, kicking, rolling. I pushed myself further than I'd gone before. I was in the best shape I'd been in since leaving the Lost City.

My audience grew. Reevie believed it was a great motivator for many of them to leave their beds and start walking around. I pushed them from my thoughts and focused on my training.

I didn't use weapons, since I'd been told that the match was to be openhand. That news had not only put a damper on my spirit but had forced me to rethink my entire strategy as well. I had been counting on the advantage I would have with a weapon. At the very least, it would have helped me keep Flesh Eater at a distance. Now I was being forced to meet this barbarian with nothing between us but the clothes on our backs.

Each night after a hot soak in the tub, Reevie would rub me down with liniment, and the soreness in my muscles would vanish. By morning, I was ready to go again. The night before the big fight, Reevie was uncharacteristically quiet as he poured the liniment in his hands and began to massage my shoulders, arms, and back.

Normally, Reevie had plenty to say. There was never a shortage of reprimands to dish out about things I'd done, things I hadn't done, things he was sure I was going to do that would land us in "another fine mess," as he would put it. I suspect it made him feel needed. As many times as I had told him that his crippled leg made no difference to me, he still overcompensated for it. I wished I could convince him that I wasn't going to just leave him behind one day and move on to bigger and better things.

"Are you worried?" Reevie asked as he ground his fingers into

new clusters of sore muscle on my back, trying to alleviate the stiff-
ness.

"Of course not." His fingers pressed a little harder, causing me to
squirm. "Fine. Maybe a little," I said between groans.

I could feel his hands quivering as he applied the cool balm. I tried
turning around. "What's wrong?"

"Nothing," he said, grabbing the sides of my head and forcing me
back around.

"I'm going to be okay," I said. "You don't have to worry about
me, you know."

"Who's worried?" Reevie pinched the back of my neck a little
harder than normal and I winced. "Now hold still, or I'll never get
this done."

There was another moment of silence.

"You can beat him, though, can't you?" he asked, his words
sounded unsure.

"Of course. I'm Upakan. It'll take more than some big, ugly cannibal to stop me."

Reevie's hands paused. "What if you can't? What if you make a
mistake? What if Flesh Eater—"

I twisted around. "Don't worry, he won't. I'm coming back, if for
no other reason than to make sure you have enough grief in your life.
I would hate to deprive you of your favorite reason to complain." I
attempted a weak grin.

I half-expected a witty comeback, but instead, he let his hands fall
to his lap, face serious. "You better. You're the only friend I've got."

I sat up, grabbed my shirt, and slid it over my head. "Don't worry.
Nothing's going to happen to me."

CHAPTER 28

SLEEP THAT NIGHT was slow in coming, and when it did, I was plagued with dreams.

Red and Sapphire bound me with my climbing rope while Spats stood off to the side with a butcher knife, ordering them to "cut my feet." Master Fentin and Miss Orilla were there as well, but instead of offering me one of their delicious sandwiches, they tried stuffing me between two large pieces of dark rye. I couldn't figure out where they had found an oven large enough to bake a loaf that size. Cutter stood behind the others, waving his wide-brimmed hat over his head; the top half of it was ablaze. He kept demanding to know why I'd set it on fire.

The ground shook and Spats fell to his knees and cried out in his high-pitched voice for Flesh Eater to take me as a sacrifice. A giant figure that looked closer to a mountain troll than a human stepped out of the darkness. Its head was covered except for a single hole at the mouth. Fangs, like the enormous stalactites found in the lower regions of the Lost City, jutted from the mask's opening.

I begged Sapphire to let me go, but she refused, explaining that Egla the Beautiful desired my life in payment for her freedom. I couldn't figure out what sort of freedom Egla desired, since she was nothing more than a naked statue standing in the middle of an empty fountain.

The giant reached down and grabbed the enormous pieces of bread with me in the middle and lifted me into the air. There was no mystery to this meat. My stomach reeled from the upward rush. I screamed at myself to break free. I was Upakan. We didn't give up. We fought to the end. And we certainly weren't eaten by giants, masked or otherwise.

I could feel the heat of the creature's breath as he lifted the sandwich up to the hole in the leather mask and spread his jaws. I gagged. The smell was enough to make me wish I was already dead.

I could hear Reevie screaming below me. "He's my friend! You can't eat my friend! He's the only one I've got!"

My bottom half went in first. I couldn't move, couldn't scream. I could hear the giant's garbled laugh as he bit down.

I flung myself out of bed, dragging my blanket to the floor with me as I fought to catch my breath. My heart was pounding in my chest. I must have cried out because Reevie nearly fell out of his bed grabbing for the bludgeon under his pillow. He hopped off his mattress and took a swing at the air.

"What's going on? Who's attacking?"

I was careful to respond in case he decided to try swinging his piece of wood in my direction. "No one's attacking," I said, taking another deep breath as I wiped the sweat from my forehead. "I had a bad dream. Sorry I woke you."

It took a moment for the cobwebs to clear.

Reevie plopped down on the end of his bed. "Bad dream? I thought maybe Avalanche was attacking." He dropped his beater on the bed and rubbed his hands down his face. "Not exactly a good omen, is it?" Leaving the bludgeon where it was, he yawned and crawled back under his covers.

I flipped the wet side of my pillow over before lying back down. "Let's have it, then."

"What?"

"Your dream, what was your dream?"

"It was nothing," I said, trying to sound casual. "Something about a giant and a sandwich."

"I love sandwiches." Reevie turned to face the wall. His words began to slur as he fell back to sleep. "Mistress Orilla makes the bes . . . san . . . ches." And just like that, he was snoring.

I lay there for a long time listening to the steady creaking of the building above, envious of Reevie's ability to drift off to sleep. Finally, I gave up, crawled out of bed, and made my way upstairs. The best way I knew to take my mind off things was to train. I was careful not to push myself. I was going to need everything I had for this evening. So, I spent most of the time, stretching and warming up.

The rest of the morning and afternoon came and went before I had time to realize they were gone. Reevie and I were already on our way back to the Temple to meet up with our tribe when it suddenly dawned on me what we were doing. It wasn't like the Pit hadn't been in my thoughts every waking moment since Red had suggested it to the Guild, but the rush of nerves hadn't caught up with me yet. It was like how a person behaves after a serious injury. Reevie called it shock. They don't feel the pain and sometimes their mind doesn't even register they're in danger until it's too late.

Our shoes clopped on the mismatched cobbles as we made our way northeast toward the Temple. Instead of the light brown jerkin Misses Orilla had helped me pick out, I wore my black vest, leaving no doubt as to my position within Hurricane. The warm afternoon breeze did little to stifle the humidity in the air. I could feel perspiration running down my back.

Reevie carried his healer's sack slung across his body. It bounced against his hip as he limped his way down the street.

The Temple gate was open when we arrived, and the tribe already assembled. Spats and the Guard joined us at the front. Sapphire spotted me and attempted a smile, but it came out lopsided, her worry tugging one corner of her mouth downward.

"Are you ready?" Spats asked, looking me over. He was once again wearing his blue brocade vest and white cravat.

"Yes, sir," I said with as much confidence as I could muster under the circumstances.

"Right! Let's be off."

I fell into step behind the rest of the Guard so I could lend support to Reevie. "How far away is the Pit?"

"We'll take Terrance south until we hit Mora," Reevie said, "and then straight east until we reach the depository." He shrugged. "A good hour at least, I reckon." Reevie reached inside his knapsack. "You want something to eat? I brought apples."

I was so nervous I didn't think I could stomach it, but I took one, knowing I would need the energy.

As rundown as the back of Cheapside was, it still felt almost new compared to the old stone and brick structures that made up the Warrens. It was an interesting experience walking down Mora, Cheapside on our left and the Warrens on our right. It was like walking between two different worlds.

The streetlamps of Cheapside gave dim illumination for residents on their way home after a hard day's work. In the Warrens, it was pitch black, nothing but silence. Even with my Upakan eyes, I could only see about twenty or thirty feet down each vacant lane before the thick gloom overshadowed my sight.

The sound of boots and bare feet echoed down the empty street. The lack of chatter from the other members made it clear they were feeling edgy. They didn't care to be marching a mere stone's throw from the Warrens.

It didn't take long, though, before the hairs on the back of my neck began to prickle. It felt as though there were eyes within the darkness peering out at me, but every time I looked, there was nothing there. I shook my head at the silliness of it all.

The march down Mora was slow and tedious. The brightest of the stars were just coming into view. It was a clear night, and I could taste the salt in the air.

After what seemed like hours of walking, a noise ahead caught my attention. It grew in volume the farther down the street we marched. I tried moving Reevie over a little so I could peek around the Guard, but the way ahead was too dark, and it looked like the road curved sharply to the left.

"We're almost there," Reevie said. I felt his small hand grip my arm like a vice. In front of us, Spats and the Guard followed the sharp curve until it reached its end. We appeared to be leaving the Warrens behind as we took the next street to the left. Unlike the others we had passed, this road was lit with torches on either side, directing us to our final destination—the old repository, better known as the Pit.

A block wall surrounded the grounds. It was nearly as tall as the one around the Temple but didn't look as solid or decorative. We passed underneath the open arches. Cooking fires dotted the area inside, casting wary shadows across the stone buildings and open yard.

Hundreds of kids sprawled out across the grounds, grouped by tribes. Each tribe was marked by an armband: white for Avalanche, purple for Sandstorm, red for Wildfire, and green for Rockslide. Distrustful glances passed from one fire to the next. All chatter ceased when we stepped through the gates.

Our procession was uncharacteristically silent as we made our way toward the large, stone-encased building that stood at the center of the compound. It was at least twice the size of the others, the front lit with torches as a steady stream of kids made their way in and out.

The silence was eerie. All eyes followed us across the open yard.

"This ain't at all creepy," Reevie whispered as he scanned the faces of the closest kids. There was a hunger in their eyes that sent a shiver up my back. I half-wondered if they were all planning to eat my flesh as well. Maybe that was the reason for the cooking fires.

Once we entered the building, the conversations outside started up again, but they were quickly drowned out by the noise ahead of us. The floor shook with the sheer volume of it.

The tiny foyer surprised me after having seen the size of the building from the outside. It was hardly larger than Master Fentin's bookshop. A stone wall separated us from whatever was on the other side.

"It sounds like they've already started," Reevie said. He had to lean in close just to be heard.

Two corridors led from the entryway back around to the other side of the wall—one on the left and one on the right. There was a set of armed sentries at each, checking the kids before they passed.

Our tribe split in two. Half went right, the other went left. I followed Spats and the Guard as we took the left entrance.

"What are they doing?" I asked Reevie as we approached the guards.

"They're making sure that no one is carrying weapons inside

the Pit."

The armed boys stationed at the entrance allowed those of us wearing black vests to pass unchecked, including me. One of the guards looked inside Reevie's bag while another patted him down.

The noise reverberating around the inside of the passageway was unnerving. Reevie clung to my arm as we headed in, the sound threatening to swallow us. In truth, I wanted to cling to his. The torches lining the stone corridor cast distorted shadows on the walls as we made our way down and around to the other side. If my heart hadn't been racing before, it certainly was now. I had no idea what to expect. I thought by the number of kids we had passed outside that there couldn't have been that many more inside.

I was wrong.

CHAPTER
29

WE STEPPED OUT of the narrow corridor and my jaw
dropped.

There had to be at least a thousand street rats gathered, all
screaming at the top of their lungs at a fight in the arena below.
Where had they all come from? Were there that many forgotten
children living within the walls of Aramoor? Sometimes, I failed to
remember how big the city really was.

The Pit was nothing more than a large hole dug out in the center of the warehouse—at least thirty feet in diameter with a floor
of packed soil and a layer of sand thrown on top. Wood planks

lined every inch of the walls to keep the dirt from eroding, much like the mining tunnels on the outskirts of the Lost City.

The fights had already started. Two boys were beating each other with their fists, and not very well. They swung their arms high and wide, as if trying to maneuver a ten-pound ball-and-chain flail. They were likely to do more damage to themselves than their opponent.

The warehouse was stifling. The smell of damp soil and old pine was all but drowned out by the stench of so many unwashed bodies. The Pit was completely surrounded by wooden stands divided into five sections. Each tribe's seating was divided from the others by colored markers painted on the back.

An open walkway ran directly behind the seating, allowing the tribes to get from one section to the next without having to mingle. It seemed the Guild was trying to prevent any unnecessary conflicts.

"This way!" Spats shouted over the crowd. I grabbed Reevie by the arm and helped him up the wooden steps toward the outer walkway. We met the other half of our tribe as they exited the opposite corridor farther down.

The first section of risers had been painted white. Before we were halfway to the next, we were met by a group of Avalanche Guards. I could see Cutter in the back, pushing his way forward. "There was a ten-to-one wager you wouldn't even show up," he said, stopping in front of Spats. "Too afraid to show your face outside your Temple."

"You're gonna wish I had stayed home," Spats shot back, "after we embarrass you in the Pit."

Cutter laughed. His guards laughed. Embarrassingly enough, some of our own members laughed.

Cutter eyeballed me, rubbing the scraggly patch of hair on his chin. "I believe we're going to set a record tonight. The shortest fight in the history of the Pit. You might want to have another champion lined up, just to make sure it's worth the crowd's time." He laughed again and patted Spats on the shoulder, then made his way back to his seat at the front with as much show as possible.

Spats's face was nearly the color of Red's vest.

Reevie passed me a sympathetic look as the tribe started forward once again.

I felt the Wildfire chief's presence before I saw her. It was the same empty feeling I got whenever she was around, like some part of me was missing, namely my magic. I only wished I knew what she was doing to cause it. She stood at the back of her tribe's seating and watched us pass.

Toothless was on her left. He looked at me and drew a line across his throat. He had quite the menacing presence if he didn't open his mouth. In complete contrast, the guard on her right was as short as Reevie and twice as wide. I wondered if he was in some way related to Red, since he had the same black hair. Or maybe she relied on him for advice, although I found the idea of Red taking advice from anyone rather hard to imagine.

My father's ring hung from her neck for all to see. She gently caressed it between her fingers, pouring salt on the wound whenever she had the opportunity. She winked, and I balled my fist. If

I could have reached her without starting an all-out war, I would have.

Sapphire snorted, obviously having seen Red's flirtatious gesture.

We passed Sandstorm's risers without incident. They seemed more focused on the fights in the pit than on us moving around to our seats.

Finally, we reached ours. Blue paint marked the backs of the empty tiers. Spats waved his hand, and kids rushed to find their seats. It was a mad dash to see who could get the closest. Eventually, the biggest of the lot claimed the better seating on the lower levels by throwing the smaller ones back. It was the perfect example of life on the streets—every kid for themselves.

"Spats, a word, if you don't mind," Noph said, circling his way around the back of Rockslide to get to us. His own escort of armed guards followed closely on his heels. "How are you feeling today?" he asked me after acknowledging Spats with a slight tilt of his head. "Hopefully fit."

I nodded. "I'm ready." I hoped my words sounded sincere, because my gut was telling me something completely different.

Noph studied my face. "Good, good." He glanced at Spats. "We don't want Avalanche walking away with another victory, do we? He's won the last three in a row. I don't intend to see a fourth."

This news did nothing to calm my already frayed nerves.

"Besides, I've got a lot of coin riding on you."

"Easiest gold I've ever made," Kore said as he joined the small gathering, his green vest showing off his intimidatingly muscular frame. "Like stealing coins from a blind beggar."

Noph simply smiled, but it was the smile of someone who appeared to be holding a few cards up his sleeve.

Kore rolled his eyes and turned to Spats. "A decision has been made as to the punishment that will be levied on the tribe that loses tonight. Restitution will be given in the amount of fifty gold pieces—"

"*Fifty* gold pieces?" Spats looked like he'd swallowed his own tongue. "We can't possibly afford that much gold! This . . . this is outrageous!"

Kore's grin dripped with sarcasm. "Then I guess you better win," he said and left.

Noph fiddled with his purple tie. "Don't worry. I have a good feeling about tonight." He spared a glance at me, nodded, and left as well.

Spats's cheeks had turned a pale green. It was an interesting contrast to his red hair. He looked like he was ready to order a quick march out of there, but to his credit, he didn't. Sapphire had to help him down one of the aisles toward the front.

Reevie leaned on me as we followed them to the front row of our section, which had been left open for Spats and the Guard. We started to take seats on the end when Spats waved us over to sit with him, forcing some of the guards to move down, a gesture they didn't appear happy with.

"You see that over there?" Spats said, pointing down to an alcove on the opposite side of the Pit. He had to raise his voice to be heard over the shouts and cheers from the kids watching the bloody match below. "That's where the fighters enter the ring. There's another one just below us."

I hadn't noticed the small door before. It had been blocked by the stands on our way in. "Where do they lead?" I asked.

"They go underneath the risers and come out on the other side of the walkway behind us."

A shriek of pain and a sudden roar from the crowd brought our attention back to the center as one of the boys wearing a green armband took a nasty kick to the side of his leg. He fell backward and started to crawl toward the door on the other side of the ring. His opponent, with a red band, kicked again, but the injured boy had managed to get his arms up in time to keep his attacker's foot from connecting with his face.

"You'll be fighting last," Spats said, his eyes glued to the fight below. "You are the main attraction, after all." He didn't say anything else as he watched the green fighter on the ground push himself up against the door and start banging on it with his fists.

"Let me in! Let me in!"

Parts of the crowd began to laugh while others shouted their displeasure at his cowardice. Most cheered on the red fighter with chants of "Fin—ish him! Fin—ish him!"

The red fighter charged, and the green dove to the side. But before he had a chance to get up, the red was on top of him. The green raised his arms to protect his face, so the red fighter went for the body. There was no finesse, no calculation, no forethought or purpose, nothing but the desire to inflict as much damage as possible. All that seemed to matter was that his fist connected with the other boy's body.

I glanced across the arena and caught Red staring at me. She was smiling. Suddenly, I was back on that empty street, held between two boys as she used my face as a punching bag. My heart began to race, so I looked away.

The red fighter pulled back and slowly circled the wounded green, raising his arms in the air to drive his audience into a frenzy. They didn't need much prodding. The kids in the stands were now stomping their feet to the rhythmic chant of "FIN—ISH HIM! FIN—ISH HIM! FIN—ISH HIM!"

Kore was leaning over the edge of the Pit, shouting down threats at his injured fighter, trying to force the kid to get back to his feet and keep fighting.

The injured boy tried crawling back toward the wall, while the other one played to the fans. It was plain to see the green fighter was through. He winced with every breath. Tears streamed down his face as he scuttled for the wall.

He had barely made it a few feet when the red fighter turned and kicked him in the head and sent him flailing on his back. This fight was over. The kick had muddled the boy's senses. Why weren't they calling the match?

The red fighter stood over the green. The injured kid was too busy crying to see what was happening. My stomach churned as I watched the fighter lift the other boy by the front of his tunic, then turn and raise his fist to the audience. The kids in the stands leapt to their feet. Reevie and I were the only ones still sitting as the fans shouted once more. "FIN—ISH HIM! FIN—ISH HIM! FIN—

ISH HIM!"

The red fighter smiled, then punched the kid in the face. Then he punched him again and again, and kept punching him until the boy was completely unconscious, his broken body limp and his face covered in blood.

The crowd cheered.

I shared a look with Reevie. No words were needed. The worried look on his face said it all.

As soon as the green fighter's unconscious body was dragged from the Pit, a tall, lanky boy with short brown hair and a rather distinguished yellow tie ran out to the center of the ring and grabbed the red fighter's hand, raising it in the air. "Thunder-Feet! With another win for Wildfire!" The announcer's voice carried quite the distance for someone so skinny. "Our next match will be between Bone Cutter from Avalanche and Iron Death from Sandstorm!"

I had to say this, they had quite the inventive names.

The rest of the evening followed the same pattern: another fight, another winner, another loser, and all the while, the audience ate up every bloody moment. The fighters from Avalanche and Rockslide seemed to be the most vicious, each one trying to come up with some new and creative way to shed blood.

The fights that brought about the most amusement from the crowd, however, were the bouts between the girls. There was something about watching two girls beating each other to a pulp that brought a smile to those watching above. It probably had more to do with the fact that occasionally one or both of the fighters would lose part of their tops in the struggle than it did with the impressiveness of their fights, although there was a dark-skinned fighter from Sandstorm who kicked the front teeth out of her opponent's face. She sent the girl flying at least four feet. They had to carry her out on a stretcher. I had to admit, it was a pretty impressive move. After that, no one else wanted to challenge the dark fighter.

Had Sapphire ever gotten into the ring? I remembered Reevie talking about the Soren Challenge and how it took place in the Pit. I wondered if this was how the tribes recruited their guards.

After the latest kid's body was removed from the arena, the announcer made his way to the center of the Pit and raised his hands to quiet the audience. "It's finally here! The fight you've all been waiting for. The winner-take-all battle between Avalanche"—the lanky boy pointed toward the white seating and the Avalanche kids stomped their feet in acknowledgment—"and Hurricane," he said, turning to point our way. My seat began to vibrate as our tribe did the same.

My pulse was racing. I still had no use of my magic. I could sense its presence but not control it. I looked across the ring and Red winked at me again. I wondered how far away I needed to be for it to return.

"It's time to go," Reevie said, his voice causing me to start. "I'll walk you down."

I broke off my staring contest with Red and stood. I was about to follow Reevie down the aisle when someone grabbed my hand. I turned. It was Sapphire.

"Be careful." She looked like she wanted to say more, but

didn't.

I offered an encouraging smile. "Always."

She released my hand. I left her there with the rest of the Guard and followed Reevie to the end of the row. The announcer continued working the crowd as we passed between the risers. Those on the outer edges stared down at us as we moved underneath, some with encouraging smiles, others with looks of mourning and regret.

"Wait just a moment!" the announcer said. "I believe we have some news."

The stands quieted down as they waited to see what was happening. I stopped near the end of the row and turned around. I couldn't see the Pit or the announcer from where we stood. *What's going on? Are they going to call it off?* I doubted I was that lucky.

"There has been a last-minute change to tonight's fight," the announcer finally said. "And it is sure to make the wait worthwhile. I've just been informed, and this is coming directly from the Guild, that tonight's final round will be . . ." He paused.

If my heart had been racing before, it was about to beat out of my chest now.

"A fight to the death!"

CHAPTER 30

THE STANDS ERUPTED, kids jumping up and down, shouting at the top of their lungs at the unexpected turn of events.

Reevie tripped over his own feet and went down. I was too stunned to do more than watch. My thoughts were on the fight, and the fact that I was going to be expected to kill someone or, worse, be killed myself. Flashes of Flon lying in the ring, staring up at me with those lifeless eyes, were enough to clench my stomach. By the time I gathered my thoughts, Reevie was nearly back to his feet, pulling himself up on a support post at the back of one of the stands. I rushed to help him the rest of the way.

"They haven't had a fight to the death since Skull Crusher."

"Skull Crusher?"

"They banned those fights years ago because of the effect it had on the tribes. Once they got a taste for death, it only grew. Pretty soon, they expected to see someone die with every fight."

"How was this a Guild decision? I was at the meeting. No one said anything about a fight to the death."

"It requires a majority vote," Reevie said. "Which means three chiefs had to have agreed. This must be Cutter's doing, and I don't see Kore turning an opportunity like this down. He's always enjoyed a good fight, which leaves—"

"Red!" I hissed. "I know it was her." The way she had been staring at me the entire evening made sense now. She'd known what was coming. This was her way to be rid of me once and for all.

Over my dead body. My back stiffened as I turned and marched straight for the entrance leading down to the ring. It would be a cold day in the Aran'gal before I'd let them win. They didn't know who they were messing with.

I started down the steps and into the dark passageway below. The smell of soil, blood, and vomit assaulted my nose. Light from the arena poured through a set of bars ahead.

"Ayrion, wait," Reevie called out, dragging himself after me. "Let's just get out of here. We can make it on our own. We don't need the tribes."

"He's right." Sapphire's voice was soft but firm as she ran to catch up. "You need to get out of here, Ayrion."

"If I leave, every tribe up there would brand me a coward and hunt me down."

"Then we hide," Reevie said.

"For how long?" I asked. "The rest of our lives? That's no way to live."

"Then . . . then we leave Aramoor." I could hear the desperation in Reevie's voice at the very mention of leaving his home. Aramoor was all he had ever known.

From the arena behind me, the announcer was continuing to drive his audience into total madness. The stadium overhead thundered with stomping feet as they demanded the fight to begin. Tiny clods of dirt rained down on us, and I shook them from my hair. "I'm an Upaka. I was born to fight. This is who I am."

"You were also born with some common sense," Reevie said. "Now let's get out of here while we still can." He grabbed my arm and started to pull, but I jerked away.

"I'm not about to go sneaking out of here like a coward and let Cutter and Red and the rest of them up there get away with this."

"Better to live a coward than to die a hero," Sapphire said.

"You don't believe that any more than I do."

She opened her mouth, but instead of saying something, she stepped forward and kissed me on the lips. My entire body flushed. I'd never been kissed before. It was the most wonderful feeling I'd ever felt, so wonderful I almost gave in. Would it have been that bad to just walk away? Who cared if people thought I was a coward? Who cared if it left Hurricane in Avalanche's debt? I didn't really want to be there in the first place.

But then I pictured Red's smug satisfaction and the way Cutter had dismissed me as trivial, not to mention the Guild and their decision to see me fight to the death. I pulled away from Sapphire's embrace and turned to face the Pit door. "I have to do this." I knew I couldn't look either of them in the eyes again or I'd never be able to go through with it.

"No, you don't." Reevie sounded like he was on the verge of tears. "You're talking about . . . killing someone—"

"What do you think I've been training for all my life?"

"All your life? In case it's escaped your attention . . . you're thirteen. What could you have possibly done at thirteen?"

I stared through the bars. "You'd be surprised."

Reevie huffed. "I'm more worried about him killing you. Please, Ayrion, let's just get out of here." He grabbed my arm and spun me around.

"If I were to leave in disgrace, how do you think that would affect the rest of Hurricane? You think Cutter won't see that as a clear sign of weakness? How long do you think he'll wait before he attacks the Temple?" I turned back toward the door as the announcer wound his spiel to its climax. "I don't want the blood of Hurricane on my conscience."

"You don't owe them anything," Reevie mumbled under his breath.

I didn't reply. My own pride wouldn't let me leave now. It was time I lived up to my heritage. I was Upakan, and we didn't back down from anyone.

". . . challenger, our mysterious newcomer and first-time fighter in the Pit . . ." The announcer quickly walked over to the door. "What's your name?"

"What?"

"What's your name? I've got to give them your name."

"Ayr . . ." I started to say and then shook my head. That wasn't going to work. I needed something . . . more. I couldn't very well face someone named Flesh Eater with a pretty name like Ayrion.

"Death's Shadow," Reevie called out behind me. "His name is Death's Shadow."

Death's Shadow? That's a strange name to pick, I thought. I liked it.

The skinny announcer stepped back out into the arena. "Death's Shadoooooow!"

There were a few claps and a couple of whistles as I opened the door and stepped into the amber light of the torches that lined the upper railing. The lackluster applause came from some of the Hurricane members behind me, probably just to encourage me to walk out there in the first place.

I didn't pay much attention. My eyes were focused on the closed gate across the Pit. From the other side, I could hear people yelling and what sounded like the crack of a whip. Was Flesh Eater a person or an animal?

The tall kid, having finished with my brief introduction, was busy talking with someone at the far door.

I glanced at my shoes, which had already seen some rough wear since I'd purchased them. They might have been comfortable enough to walk around town in, but they weren't exactly made for a fight. Not only were they extra weight, they were a little loose. Ms. Orilla had told me to purchase them a size or two larger so I wouldn't grow out of them too fast. I knelt and started untying the laces, listening to the snickers and taunts as I stripped down to my bare feet.

"Look at those lily-white toes!"

"You plan on stinking us to death?"

"He just wants to make sure Flesh Eater has something to chew on!"

The jeers and laughter continued to grow, then I took off my shirt. One look at my back and chest, and the catcalls ceased. I, of course, was used to it, but most kids don't have scars covering three-quarters of their body. I tried not to worry what Sapphire might think.

The earlier laughter had faded to hushed whispers by the time the announcer made his way back out to the center of the ring. I walked over to the door and handed my clothes to Reevie.

"Your back, Ayrion." Sapphire's eyes glistened in the torch-light. "What happened to your back?"

"It's nothing."

I motioned for Reevie to pull the door shut, then took a few steps to the right and started to stretch. The last thing I needed was to rip a tight muscle in the middle of the fight and end up getting chewed on by Flesh Eater. It didn't take long to run through my warm-up routine, building the blood flow, then stretching down from there. My muscles were fairly limber that evening, having had the entire day to warm.

I was very thankful for the one piece of clothing I had kept on: my pants. They were loose and lightweight, allowing me the use of my legs for kicking or running. I continued to focus on what was coming, not bothering to turn around when the announcer gave his opening introduction to my opponent. I knelt and thrust my hands deep into the layered sand until I hit the soil beneath. It was tacky, exactly what I was looking for. My hands needed a solid grip, so I made sure to cover them both.

". . . known for his voracious appetite! The Pit's reigning champion! Flesh Eaterrrrr!"

Unlike my entrance into the Pit, my opponent's was met with a standing ovation and a roar of "Flesh Eater! Flesh Eater! Flesh Eater!" The crowd's feet stomped in time. Some of the kids were so riled up, I thought they were going to jump into the Pit and start fighting themselves. No such luck.

I stopped my stretching and turned around when the gate on the other side finally opened. Like all the others, I waited to catch a first glimpse of my opponent.

From the shadows of the unlit corridor beyond, two large boys stepped out, their backs to the ring. In their hands were long wooden poles that were attached to something still inside the tunnel. Whatever it was, they were having a *bloody flux* of a time dragging it out. I shook my head. That was something Reevie would have said.

I heard a deep growl from somewhere in the blackness that sounded anything but human.

The two older boys gave a final tug on the poles as a crack of a whip drove my opponent out the door.

As soon as the torchlight hit him, my heart skipped a beat.

CHAPTER 31

$\mathcal{F}$ LESH EATER WASN'T just big for a boy. He was big for a man. I'd never seen anyone that tall. He was the closest thing to a true giant that I could imagine. He was covered in leather straps. I couldn't tell if they were being used as some sort of makeshift armor or just another way to add a bit of eeriness to his persona.

Bull was right. Flesh Eater's face was completely hidden underneath a hideous leather mask. Two holes had been cut for his eyes, and a larger one started at the bottom of his nose and ran down under his chin. The monstrous fangs I had seen in my dream might not have been present, but he was terrifying nonetheless. His arms were bigger than my legs. He looked like he could squash me with a single blow.

I barely had time to catch my breath when the skinny announcer nearly ran me over, trying to get to the door on my side. He offered a hasty "good luck" on his way by.

A third boy followed the other two through the door on the far side. He cracked a short whip across Flesh Eater's back to keep him moving in the right direction. The rods being held by the two boys had metal hooks on the ends that connected to Flesh Eater's harness. They used the poles the same way a sailor used a boathook to maneuver the mooring lines.

As soon as they had managed to drag Flesh Eater far enough into the arena, the boys unhooked their poles, and all three made a fast dash for the door. Flesh Eater was too quick for them. He released a deep barking growl and charged. The first two made it through, but the third tripped on his pole and skidded to a stop just shy of the entrance. He scrambled to his feet, but the other boys had already slammed the door shut.

"No! Let me in! Let me in!" he screamed, banging on the metal bars with both fists. Before the boy had a chance to turn around, Flesh Eater was on him. The kid shrieked as the masked behemoth grabbed his leg and dragged him to the center of the arena. The boy fought to break free as he cried for help.

The crowd roared with excitement.

Flesh Eater looked up at the kids surrounding him and cocked his head. He swiped at them with his free hand, the way an alley cat would at a stray dog. He looked back down at the boy whose leg he was holding and raised him up off the ground. The boy punched and kicked, but Flesh Eater seemed oblivious.

The leg of the boy's trousers slid down to his knee. Flesh Eater lifted him higher and sniffed his calf. The crowd started chanting, "Eat his flesh! Eat his flesh!" The giant looked down at the white leg and then back up at the crowd, who were now pumping their fists in the air and stomping their feet. "Eat His Flesh! Eat His Flesh! Eat His Flesh!"

The boy was weeping uncontrollably, pleading for someone to help him as Flesh Eater raised the leg to his mouth. The stands were going wild. Flesh Eater growled and bit down. The kid screamed, and the arena shook as the audience continued to chant at the top of their lungs: "EAT HIS FLESH! EAT HIS FLESH!"

Flesh Eater's mouth was covered in blood. It dripped from his chin. He spun in a circle and launched the kid across the ring. The boy screamed as his body flailed through the air and hit the sand, coming to a stop about ten feet from the far wall.

I carefully eased my way back to the door, my back pressed to the wall, making sure not to draw Flesh Eater's attention. Reevie and Sapphire were watching through the bars.

"Lock this," I said. "No matter what, don't open it for anyone."

"What about that boy over there?" Reevie asked, pointing to the bawling kid on the other side of the Pit. He'd somehow managed to make it to his hands and knees and was dragging himself to the far door.

"He's my distraction."

I scanned the Pit for anything I could use as a weapon. Luck—or possibly the Creator—smiled on me. Not only had they left this kid behind in their rush to get through the door, but they had left his pole hook as well.

This wasn't exactly the type of fight where a long wooden rod was going to be of much assistance, hook or not. If my only goal was to keep him off me, then a lengthier weapon would have been exactly what I needed. However, with this being a fight to the death, I was going to have to get close enough to inflict real damage.

So far, Flesh Eater hadn't noticed me. That was one good thing about his mask. While it was certainly effective at making him look frightening, it hindered his peripheral vision. As smoothly as possible, I skirted the walls of the Pit, making my way around to the other side, where the boy's pole hook lay half-buried in the sand.

Flesh Eater continued to growl and bark at the kids above, swatting at them as if they were pesky sweatflies. The injured boy howled as he tried to drag himself to the door, drawing Flesh Eater's attention back to the ring.

I was almost to the pole when Flesh Eater finally gave up trying to get his hands on the kids in the stands and started once more for the boy. While his back was to me, I lengthened my stride, keeping a close eye on the mask in case it turned. I grabbed the pole and tested its weight. It balanced like a javelin or halberd, minus the sharp tip at the end. If the pole had been tipped instead of hooked, ending this fight would have been as simple as walking up behind him and thrusting at an angle through his back.

As it was, the pole's thickness gave me an idea.

I could feel the tension in the crowd grow as I stepped out from the wall and slowly made my way up behind Flesh Eater. Kids screamed for the masked cannibal to turn around, to look behind him, to watch out, but their calls merely blended with the rest, a great cacophony reverberating off the thick stone walls.

As soon as he saw Flesh Eater coming his way, the injured boy stopped scuttling for the door and crawled as fast as he could back toward the nearest side of the Pit.

When Flesh Eater was within striking distance, the injured boy began kicking at him with his good leg. He landed a solid blow to his shin and Flesh Eater growled, stomping his feet in anger. He leaned over and grabbed one of the boy's arms and lifted him off the ground. A hard shake and the boy's shoulder dislocated.

How much longer can the kid withstand the pain? I wondered, using his suffering to get myself into place.

Desperation took over and the kid managed a solid punch to one of the mask's eyeholes. He was rewarded by a sharp cry from Flesh Eater and being dropped back to the ground. He landed with a thud and quickly pushed his way back against the wall, curling into a fetal position.

Flesh Eater shook his head and rubbed at his eye. It was the distraction I needed. Gripping the pole hook about a third of the way up, I bent my knees and focused. "Don't you move," I said, and then charged.

My bare feet padded noiselessly across the sand, kicking up debris with every step. The kids above me cheered and shouted, anxious to see some action, but I tuned them all out. Nothing existed but my target.

Everything faded away as I flew across the Pit. I could hear the beating of my heart, the breath forced from my lips, each step drawing me closer to my target. His back was still turned as he tugged at his mask. If I did this right, it would all be over in a matter of moments.

Three strides: I twisted my arms to get as much swing as possible. *Two strides*: I took a deep breath and aimed. *One stride*: I roared with everything in me and swung.

A loud crack echoed off the wood-slate walls as the end of the rod slammed into the side of Flesh Eater's skull. The audience, for the first time since I had stepped foot in the warehouse, went deathly quiet.

Instead of collapsing unconscious to the ground, Flesh Eater was thrown to the side. He stumbled to one knee. There was an awkward moment of silence, followed by the most hideously disturbing wail I'd ever heard. The giant boy raised his hands to his head and began to weep. I was so taken aback by the unexpected reaction that instead of rushing over to finish the job, I just stood there. Apparently, those watching from the stands were just as shocked. No one said a word.

The enormous boy in the mask stayed on his knees. His entire body shook with the force of his crying.

I needed to finish this while he was down. I lifted my pole and noticed it was split. It wouldn't withstand another strike. The hook at the end of the pole wasn't exactly sharp, but with enough force, it could do some real damage. If I could hit the large vein in the side of his neck, my opponent would bleed out in a matter of minutes.

Flesh Eater was only ten steps away. With my weapon at the ready, I started forward. His neck was completely unprotected. If I could just—

"Watch out!" an unexpected voice cried out from the audience above. It was a voice I recognized immediately, a voice that had brought no small amount of annoyance to my life over the last weeks. It was one of the last voices I would have expected to hear. It was the voice of a high-pitched weasel.

I froze for an instant, but that was all Flesh Eater needed; he spun around at the warning and grabbed the other end of the pole.

The crowd went wild.

I was so fixated on the fact that my own chief had just betrayed me that I didn't realize I was spinning in a circle until it was too late. My feet left the ground as I clung to my end of the rod. I watched the sides of the Pit's walls come and go as I continued to spin.

How did I get to this point? Was it chance or fate? Looking back, it was hard to reconcile everything that had happened to me as being the product of chance, some random sequence of happenings that had culminated in my eventual standoff with Flesh Eater inside the Pit. The odds of it were absurd.

On the other hand, if this was designed by fate, a master plan sent down from some all-powerful Creator, then what was the point? I definitely wasn't seeing it. To be honest, I wasn't seeing much of anything but a blur at that moment as my body swung around and around.

If there was a Creator and he did have a purpose for all of this, it would really be nice to have been given some sort of warning first. Finding myself stuck in the middle of this arena facing a cannibalistic monster without a real weapon was bad enough, but to also be deprived of my magic bordered on the cruel.

I was afraid to let go, but if I didn't, I was going to be too dizzy to put up any worthwhile defense, so I closed my eyes and released. It felt like I was still sailing through the air on the end of the pole hook when I finally hit the dirt. On instinct, I curled my body and rolled, coming back to my feet in one swift movement.

I'd barely had time to open my eyes and stop the world from spinning when Flesh Eater slammed into me. It was like being hit by a boulder—not one that had just wiggled free from its niche in the side of a mountain, but one that had traveled the entire length of Dragon Fang, building momentum to an absolute peak before plowing me over.

I was lifted clean off my feet and sent flying backward with a speed that took my breath away. The only sounds I could hear were the roar of the crowd and the wheeze of my own breath rushing from my lungs as I hit the wall behind me. I landed on my hands and knees and coughed blood. I couldn't breathe. No matter how hard I tried or how wide I opened my mouth, the air wouldn't come. For the first time in a long time, I was truly terrified.

CHAPTER

32

ALL THE TRAINING in the world could not have prepared me for the horror of watching Flesh Eater come for me. He howled like a person possessed, his mouth painted in blood. I could feel each vibrating step as he charged. His arms were outstretched, his teeth spread wide, ready to sink into my flesh. My training tried to flee like a frightened jack rabbit, but I fought back. I set my jaw. I wasn't going to be a victim. I was an Upaka.

I coughed, and my chest heaved as I sucked in breath. I scooted back against the wall, pulled myself to my feet, and waited. Three. Two. One.

Flesh Eater swung his elbow straight for my head, but I ducked and spun left. His elbow slammed into the wall with a loud crack. Bits of wood flew everywhere. The masked giant stared at the wall in confusion, then down at the ground, trying to figure out what had happened to me.

I circled behind him, trying to keep out of his sight as long as possible while I fought to regain my breath. Flesh Eater roared and ripped chunks of the timber framework from the wall as if I had somehow managed to crawl behind it.

My chest was on fire. He had cracked at least one rib. I spat blood, an all-too-familiar taste thanks to my Upakan training.

The injured boy on the far end of the Pit was attempting to drag himself over to *my* door this time, no doubt hoping Reevie would let him in. He'd better not.

Quickly, I searched for the pole and found it leaning ever so perfectly against the wall about fifteen feet away. Flesh Eater had apparently discarded it, concerned only with getting his hands on me. I slowly backed my way in its direction.

My strike to Flesh Eater's head seemed to have rattled his already-dubious mind. He was still ripping pieces of the wall from the Pit.

"Behind you! He's behind you, you stupid, ugly idiot! Turn around!" Somehow Spats's voice managed to break through the rest of the shouts and whistles and screams, and Flesh Eater turned.

I raced for the pole, the only weapon I had available. My chest felt like someone was thrusting a dull knife into it with every stride. I didn't need to turn around to know Flesh Eater was right behind me. I could feel his steps and hear his eerie barking growl.

I jumped and landed on the pole, feet first, hitting dead center. The wood split with a loud snap, and I grabbed the two pieces, hefting them like a set of wooden practice swords.

Digging my feet into the sand, I turned and with every ounce of strength I could muster, I struck his right leg. As big as he was, I still managed to sweep it out from under him, and he toppled, landing on me before I could dart out of the way.

The air whooshed from my lungs all over again, which was a small blessing because he stank worse than anything I'd ever smelled before. It wasn't like Bull, who smelled of week-old sweat. It was the smell of someone who had never bathed a day in his life, someone who had soiled himself repeatedly without washing.

I rammed the butt end of one of my sticks into his jaw and heard it pop. He rolled off me, releasing another one of his child-like wails as he clutched his face.

Stumbling back to my feet, I lifted one of my sticks to strike, but Flesh Eater recovered faster than I would have thought possible. He backhanded me and sent me into a cartwheel, and I landed with a bone-jarring thud about eight feet away. I rolled to my knees and used my sticks to push my way to my feet. This time, Flesh Eater didn't charge but circled cautiously, out of my sticks' reach.

The kids overhead continued shouting, thrilled with someone lasting this long. Some had even begun to chant, "Death's Shadow! Death's Shadow!" The tribes seemed to be at odds with each other as they fought to see who could shout the other down.

I had taken just about all I could stand of their bloodlust. My days at Hurricane were over, especially after hearing Spats calling for my death, something I still couldn't understand. My winning would have freed the tribe from punishment over the failed attack on Avalanche. Could he have worked out another deal of some kind? Was he the third chief who had agreed to a trial by death, and not Red?

I drove the thoughts from my head. *Focus, Ayrion, focus!*

Flesh Eater finally got tired of circling and rushed me. I dodged and blocked, landing a hard blow to his knee. He punched again, and I ducked, striking a blow to his ribs. He blocked my second swing with his arm, the leather straps acting as makeshift armor.

We continued to dance. The more Flesh Eater tried and failed to hit me, the more enraged he became. Swing after swing, I continued to throw him back, parry and strike, parry and strike. He soon lost all patience and barreled through my next barrage of hits, grabbing my arm in the process and lifting me over his head. I struck him in the face with my stick. His nose snapped, and he screamed, throwing me into the wall.

I braced for the impact, losing both sticks as I slammed into the wood. Pain shot through my left side. Had I broken my arm? I tried moving it and found I could. Barely making it back to my feet, I ducked under Flesh Eater's next swing, and he smashed the plank where my head had been. He recovered quickly and grabbed me by the neck, lifting me into the air.

He was just too strong, and my body was too broken to move like it should. I heard Reevie and Sapphire shouting from the door, yelling at me to do something, to fight, screaming for Flesh Eater to stop.

The masked boy's grip blocked my airway. I couldn't breathe. His fingers pinched my neck, slowly shutting off my blood flow. I only had a few seconds before I would be unconscious, and if that happened, I was done for.

My training kicked in and I grabbed the smallest finger of both his hands and snapped them backward. They came free with a pop. He screamed and released my neck.

The crowd went wild as I stumbled back, gasping for air. More shouts of "Death's Shadow! Death's Shadow!" filled the Pit.

The masked creature dropped to his knees, trying to fix his awkwardly bent fingers. He didn't seem all that worried about me. One of the broken halves of the pole was sticking out of the sand on my right. The split end had a sharp enough point to pierce the boy's neck. I eased my way over and picked it up.

Flesh Eater either didn't see me coming or didn't care, but I managed to make it within a step or two without attack. Loud chants of "KILL HIM! KILL HIM!" filled half the room. The other half were screaming their disappointment and demanding that Flesh Eater get up and finish the job, Spats above the rest.

Flesh Eater's neck was open for the kill. The large vein pumping on the side was waiting to be severed. I drew back my weapon.

Above the din of angry shouts and desperate pleas, I heard a voice. It was muffled, but it was definitely coming from behind the thick mask over Flesh Eater's face. Between the sobs as he tried to put his two small fingers back, I heard him speak for the first time.

"Why hurt Tubby? Why hurt Tubby? Why hurt Tubby?"

I lowered my spear. The crowds cried out all the louder, demanding a bloody end. I could hear Reevie and Sapphire screaming at me through the door to "Kill the monster. Kill Flesh Eater and get out of there!"

I stared down at the helpless creature in front of me and found I couldn't do it. Had all my training been for nothing?

Above me, the tribes were about to come undone. One spark would ignite a fire that would probably burn the entire place to the ground.

And I knew just the spark.

CHAPTER 33

"**O**PEN THE DOOR!" I yelled, leaving Flesh Eater where he was and running for the exit. By the time I got there, Reevie and Sapphire had unlocked the gate and were working to get it open. The boy with the bite in his leg didn't wait that long. He knocked Reevie over as he fought to squeeze through. Sapphire punched the boy in the face, then grabbed his arm and twisted it behind him to keep him from moving.

"Let him go," I said when I reached them. "Things are about to get bad."

"Get in here so I can shut the door," Reevie demanded, grabbing at my arm.

"No. Leave it open."

"What? Are you crazy?" Sapphire pointed at Flesh Eater. "What if he gets loose?"

"That's what I'm hoping for." I yanked Reevie out the door and into the Pit.

"Have you lost your mind?" he shrieked, trying to kick me in the shin.

"Get out here, both of you, and stay behind me."

The tribes were out of their seats with a raging chant of "KILL HIM! KILL HIM! KILL HIM!" I had no idea which *him* they were referring to. At this point, probably both of us. Sapphire cautiously stepped into the arena and scooted back against the wall behind me. "What are we doing, Ayrion?"

"Someone suggested that I should leave the tribes. Do you still think so?" They both nodded, so I continued. "Good, 'cause after tonight, I'm not going to be welcome anywhere."

"Why?" Reevie asked, keeping a close eye on Flesh Eater. "What are you planning to do?"

I looked at Reevie and smiled, then turned to the giant boy still sitting in the sand where I'd left him. "Flesh Eater!" He didn't look up. "FLESH EATER!" Still, he didn't budge. I raised my hands to the sides of my mouth and shouted once more.

"Tubby!"

The boy's head shot up, and he looked straight at me. I pointed at the open door and the awaiting corridor, yelling just one word.

"Run!"

Tubby stood and looked at the door, then at me, then back at the door. Without any further prodding, he ran for his freedom.

Reevie yelped and pressed against my back as the giant boy flew past.

The crowds had stopped chanting. The room was silent. Clearly, it hadn't dawned on them yet what I had just done. That was when the first of the screaming could be heard, as Flesh Eater had no doubt exited the tunnel directly above us, right in back of the Hurricane risers.

I left Reevie and Sapphire cowering by the door and ran across the arena to collect the other half of the pole hook, which I had dropped during my last encounter with the wall. I needed both for what was coming.

By the time I made it back to the door, Reevie was holding some of the gauze from his bag. He quickly wrapped my chest to support what I was sure were broken ribs, then helped me with the rest of my clothing.

We headed back through the corridor leading up behind Hurricane's risers. I poked my head out of the opening to see what was happening, and to make sure I wasn't about to run back into my giant opponent.

It didn't take long to spot him. He was working his way through the back of Hurricane's seating. One look at the giant and they exploded into a crazed panic. Kids running everywhere. In their rush to escape, they threw themselves into the other tribes' sections.

From there, an all-out battle ensued.

Kids were punching and kicking, head-butting and biting. Some were pulling hair, others gouging eyes. It was a weaponless war. Some of the kids were leaping from the stands down into the Pit, trying to get away from the giant monster. Others were thrown in as a result of the fighting. The noise was deafening as the screams and hollers echoed off the stone walls. I could barely hear myself think.

Through the chaos ahead, I caught a glimpse of Red fighting to keep her tribe together as they pushed for the left exit.

This was my chance. "Get the armbands!"

"Which ones?" Reevie asked, opening the flap of his carry bag. "Armbands? What armbands?"

"The red ones," I said, ignoring Sapphire. Reevie dug through his satchel and came out with three strips of red material.

After our recent battle with Avalanche, I'd made sure Reevie kept a full selection of armbands with us at all times. I never knew when they might come in handy.

"Perfect," I said. "Now put those on and stash the blue ones."

Sapphire looked confused. "If we get caught impersonating another tribe, it could mean the end of us."

"It's going to be the end of us if we don't get out of this warehouse. We need to—" I was interrupted by shouts from the other side of the corridor. Two boys exiting the arena made a rush for us, fists up.

Before I could get around Reevie, Sapphire had kicked the first in the chest, doubling him over, and smashed her elbow into the second's face. The impact threw him against the wall, where he bounced off and fell to the ground limp. Before the first boy could catch his breath, she landed a solid blow to his face, and he dropped on top of the other one. Neither moved.

I smiled. "Impressive. And you didn't even have to use your daggers."

She waved airily. "Please. I could have taken those two with both my hands tied behind my back."

"You should ditch that vest."

"Right." Sapphire put her black Guard vest inside Reevie's satchel with mine and tied on the red armband. Within moments, we went from being members of Hurricane to members of Wild-fire. "I can't believe we're about to do this."

"I think it's time we go," Reevie said, peeking out from the end of the corridor. "There's a break near the left wall."

"Do you think you can manage on your own?" I asked.

Reevie nodded.

"Good. Then stay between us, but don't stand too close." I raised my sticks, about to leave, when an unexpected sensation washed over me, like waking from a half-drowsed sleep. I could feel it, the warmth of my magic flooding in, focusing my thoughts. I took a deep breath and let it fill me. I'd forgotten how good it felt.

"Get ready," I said, then tightened my grip and came out swinging.

I ducked to the side as someone's fist flew by my head. Blocking the boy's next swing, I kicked him in the leg. He barely had time to hit the ground before I had clubbed him in the back of the head.

Pushing Reevie out of the way, I stopped the next girl with a slap to the side of her arm, just enough to take it off course, followed with a swift strike to the face. She had a stunned look on her face when she went down.

Behind Reevie, Sapphire was fighting two of Rockslide's Guard, each carrying a shortsword. She was quite proficient with her two daggers as she managed to keep them at bay. I jerked Reevie to the right just as a large boy dove past, expecting to tackle an easy target. The boy landed in the dirt, and I kicked him hard enough to keep him there.

"Behind you!" I didn't need Reevie to tell me. I waited for the two Avalanche beaters to get closer, letting them believe they had caught me off guard.

Three . . . Two . . . One. I leaped to my left, taking Reevie with me. He yelped as the two boys swung their odd-shaped pieces of wood, hitting nothing but air.

I blocked their next two swings and then ducked under a third, jabbing the sharp end of my stick into the first boy's stomach. It wasn't deep enough to do serious damage but was enough to break the skin and make him think I had. He took a couple more wild swings before noticing the blood soaking through his shirt. He dropped his club and ran. The second got a good look at my eyes and decided to follow his friend's example and retreat.

Reevie grabbed my shoulder. "Help her!"

I spun in time to see Sapphire take a kick to the hip and go down. I threw one of my clubs, and it smashed the first guard in the face. Blood poured from his nose, which was now bent awkwardly to the side. I threw myself at the second guard, forcing his attention away from Sapphire. He was at least two or three heads taller than I was. The guard smiled, obviously thinking he had landed easy prey. Apparently, not everyone recognized me by my eyes. All he saw was the red armband.

"After I'm through with you," the guard said, "I'm going to club the cripple and teach your girl what it means to really scream. I hear Wildfire girls have a lot of spirit."

"I'll show you spirit!" Sapphire said, throwing herself at the guard. She attacked him with the ferocity of a panther. He barely had time to get his sword up before she struck left, then countered and struck right, ducking and spinning as she danced around her opponent. His arms were flailing, struggling to hold her at bay. By the time he had realized he was outmatched, she had stabbed him three times. He didn't get back up.

"Come on," I said, pulling her off the fallen kid. "We need to get out of here." I grabbed the guard's sword and left one of my sticks in return.

We continued to fight our way toward the left entrance, me in front and Sapphire bringing up the rear. Several times, we were forced to stop and defend our position. Some ran in fear, others limped, but most went down and didn't get back up.

The room was in complete anarchy. Kids fighting without even looking to see who they were fighting, just so long as the person in front of them was wearing a different-colored armband; and in some cases, even that didn't stop them.

So far, I had managed to keep from killing anyone. I was saving that special treat for Red, or possibly Spats, if I ever saw him. Knowing Spats, he'd probably managed to weasel his way into another retreat, leaving his tribe to fend for themselves. I wondered how much longer it would take before the tribe tossed him over the wall as a reject.

My magic started to wane, which meant we were getting closer to Red. Through the battle ahead, I caught a brief glimpse of the Wildfire chief fighting her way into the corridor that led out of the arena. She was quite deadly with her daggers. Her moves were graceful but direct. She didn't waste energy with flashy, elongated strikes, just enough to get the job done.

It didn't take the three of us long to reach the wall. Getting from there to the passage outside took considerably longer. When we got there, the Wildfire Guard was holding the entrance to give their tribe time to get through.

We kept our heads down and blended in with the rest of the escaping kids with red armbands. In all the chaos, I could have been standing next to Red and she wouldn't have noticed.

I kept a tight grip on Reevie's hand as we pushed our way through the torch-lit corridor. My ribs were poked and prodded to the point of nausea as the throng of scared kids fought to reach the other side. The only thing keeping me upright was the tight dressing Reevie had applied under my shirt and my own determination that Red wasn't going to step foot outside these grounds with my father's ring still in her possession.

I could see the open foyer just ahead over the river of bodies.

We burst through the narrow passageway like water spilling from a dam and followed the tide straight for the doors.

CHAPTER 34

COOKING PITS DOTTED the open grounds like large fire-flies, lending their light to the erupting bedlam inside the stone walls of the old depository. What had been a deadly brawl inside the Pit had turned into a full-scale battle outside; each of those campfires held the weapons that the tribes hadn't been allowed to carry inside.

"Dysentery!" Reevie shouted over the clash of steel and wood and the cries of the wounded and dying.

"Stay close!" I yelled. Reevie pressed against my back as we moved with Wildfire down the steps and around to the left side of the grounds, following the stone wall toward the entrance at the other end.

It was one thing to have survived a battle between two tribes, but to step into an all-out war between all five was sheer insanity. Most of the tribes were struggling to reach the front gate, having no desire to be caught in the middle. There were some, however, who found a certain pleasure in locking blades with their rivals. Those kids mostly wore either white or green armbands.

I tried to keep us near the center of Wildfire as we pushed our way ahead. Red was clearly trying to skirt the main battle and make a run for the gate. I had to give her credit for staying with her tribe and not playing the coward like another chief I knew.

The stone archway leading out of the depository was clogged with fighting, kids with armbands of all colors. Most were in packs, but they were small and scattered all over the place.

I shivered, realizing I had lost my magic once again.

"On me!" Red shouted as a large group of Avalanche beaters attacked from the right while we attempted to get by. I could see Cutter's wide-brimmed hat floating through the crowd, attempted to cut her and her Guard off from the rest of Wildfire.

It wasn't that I cared one whit about Red, but the thought of that smug two-faced mongrel sticking her in the back, and smiling as he did it, didn't sit right with me. It was Cutter who had started this whole mess in the first place when he'd raided Hurricane's warehouse and set Spats up to be killed in an ambush. I'd have rather jumped off Howling Gorge than let him get away with that.

As we neared the outer wall, I guided Reevie and Sapphire away from the others and hid them behind a couple of unused haulers. "Stay here until I get back."

"Where do you think you're going?" Sapphire demanded, taking a step toward me.

"To stop Cutter."

She raised her sword. "Good. I'm coming."

"You need to stay here and protect Reevie. I can't stop Cutter if I'm constantly looking over my shoulder to make sure the two of you are safe."

"I don't need someone looking out for me," she huffed.

"Reevie needs you more than I do. Keep him safe."

Reevie pulled a dark bottle out of his bag, along with a couple of long strips of cloth. "Don't you worry about us," he said as he tied one of the strips around his face and one around Sapphire's. He held his breath and started dousing the rest of the cloth with the liquid from the bottle. "We'll be fine. Do what you need to. We'll be here when you get back." The smell from the bottle burned my nose and left me feeling lightheaded. "Ether," he said, holding up the soaked material. "Anyone who gets close enough will wish they hadn't."

I smiled, remembering being hit by one of his bottles during our last confrontation with Avalanche. Leaving the two of them there, I ran toward the fighting.

My magic was completely gone as I pushed through the Wildfire beaters to reach the front, sword in one hand and stick in the other. There were a few green armbands scattered across the wall of white in front of us. At this point, whichever side of the line you found yourself on was the side you were fighting with.

I blocked with my stick and cut with my blade. The sword was small but light, easily maneuverable in tight spaces. A strike to the wrist knocked a dagger from one kid's hand. The boy next to him went down with a swift kick to the knee. They were dropping as fast as I could make them. But for every white or green armband that went down, three more were there to take their place.

I spun to my right, dodging a quick thrust to my gut. I was about to club the girl in the head when one of my fellow reds decided to beat me to it. But instead of bashing my opponent, he swung wide. I didn't even have time to duck. White dots clouded my vision and everything went black. By the time I realized I was on the ground, the back of my head throbbed.

While fighting to keep from getting trampled, I realized from this perspective that most of the Avalanche beaters were barefoot. From the waist down, everyone looked the same. Nothing identified friend from foe except the direction of the toes. I decided toes that had chosen to point in my direction were fair game. With a smile, I raised the butt end of my stick and bashed the closest set. The owner yelled, hopping up and down. Suddenly, he dropped to the ground in front of me, bleeding. Someone up there had clearly taken advantage of my work.

I moved to the next pair.

All around me, I bashed bare feet. Those unlucky enough to be wearing shoes, I stabbed with the tip of my blade. Kids were going down left and right. I couldn't help but wonder how proud Spats would have been, seeing me *cut their feet*. I cleared a large-enough area around me to not have to worry about getting bludgeoned by my own people when I got back up. Of course, they weren't really my people, so I didn't feel the least bit guilty when I stabbed the red beater responsible for clubbing me in the first place. As soon as he started hopping, I jumped up and whopped him on the head.

The boy didn't have time to hit the ground before I was being forced to block another beater. I rammed my stick into the hefty girl's unprotected midsection and then kicked her into the white-banded wall of fighters behind her, knocking several more down in the process.

Using the momentary break, I turned to see if I could spot where I had left Reevie and Sapphire, but I wasn't tall enough to see anything beyond the second row of beaters. I could see the outer wall, which gave me some indication that I wasn't too far away. To my left, Red and some of her guards were struggling to hold back a growing cluster of Avalanche beaters.

None of her tribe had noticed her predicament, seeing only the white armbands in front of them, so I broke off my fighting at the front and pushed my way through the left ranks. The closer I got, the more I questioned why I was risking my life for hers. As much as I didn't want to admit it, the answer was staring me in the face.

I wasn't going to leave Aramoor.

If it had just been me and Reevie and Sapphire, I wouldn't have questioned it. But we had Bull and the other rejects living at the granary to consider. They were our responsibility in a way. Besides, I didn't think I could stomach the thought of turning tail and running. I was an Upakan warrior. That name meant something. And if we did intend to stay, I wasn't about to let Cutter get away with this.

Breaking free from the last of the Wildfire beaters, I was able to get a better view of the battle. We were about halfway between the Pit and the entrance. I spotted kids wearing the purple armbands of Sandstorm flooding the stone archway leading out of the depository. Noph was pulling his tribe out as fast as he could to avoid getting ambushed by either Cutter or Kore. Intermingled with the purple were the blue bands of Hurricane. Spats had no doubt left them to their own fates and was probably back at the Temple by now, ordering a warm dinner and a hot bath.

Up ahead, I caught my first full glimpse of Red. She was now down to a couple of guards and the little black-haired boy she had taken with her to the Guild meeting. He was carrying a sword but didn't look like he knew what to do with it. If he was supposed to be her guard, he was the worst I'd ever seen.

He never even saw me coming.

"Mind if I borrow that?" I said as I grabbed the sword out of his hand and punched him in the side of the face. His eyes rolled back, and he dropped into the dirt at my feet. As soon as he hit the ground, my magic exploded through my body like a caged animal being set free. I looked at the little kid. Now I knew why Red kept him around. *He* was the one suppressing my gifts. I didn't have time to wonder how he was doing it. Red was now down to a single guard—Toothless.

I lifted the two swords. They felt right, like natural extensions of my body. With my magic coursing through me, I was finally whole again.

Cutter pushed his way through his beaters to get to Red. They had her surrounded. She crouched, two daggers held out in front of her, daring someone to make a move. Blood stained both arms.

"You won't get away with this, Cutter!" she hissed, glancing at the white armbands around her. "The Guild will hear about this!"

Cutter laughed. "If you can't hold on to what's yours, then you don't deserve to have it." He raised his arm. "Kill her . . . slowly."

CHAPTER 35

I HIT CUTTER'S front line before they took their first steps. My magic woke something primal inside me, something I hadn't felt since my trip to Norshag with my father. I gave in to it, letting it fill me. My arms flew with deadly accuracy, swords cutting down those who dared stand in my way.

Cutter's beaters fell in such great numbers that the kids standing in the second and third rows had to be pushed forward just to face me. It wasn't until Cutter drew his own blade and started threatening the lot of them that they began to press.

By this time, I was running on pure adrenaline and magic, my body nearing exhaustion. My injuries from the Pit threatened to overwhelm my other senses. Every breath was excruciating. Red, along with Toothless, fought beside me with everything she had just to keep up.

I danced among the beaters—spinning, dodging, sweeping from one to the next. I glided in and around every blow they sought to land, each beater getting only a single swing before my swords found their flesh. Their frustration at not reaching me only fueled their anger.

"Kill him, you fools!" Cutter screamed.

I weaved between fighters, never staying in one place long enough to be taken. Cutter called for more reinforcements, forcing me to give ground. I couldn't keep this up. Magic or not, my strength was wearing out.

Red never said a word. It might have been that all her attention was on the beaters and their attempts to cut her down, or it could have been she didn't like the idea of owing her life to someone she had just sent to the Pit. Either way, she continued to fight with a fierceness that earned my respect. Unlike me, she had no qualms about killing any kid stupid enough to come within reach of her daggers.

Toothless hollered as one of the Avalanche beaters stuck him in the side with a pick. Another fighter clubbed him over the head and sent him bleeding to the ground.

There was nothing I could do for him but keep fighting. Red was right beside me, her face half-covered in blood. No matter how skilled I was, no matter how much magic I used, in the end, the numbers won out.

Red cried out. I turned as one of the Avalanche beaters pulled his blade from her shoulder. She stabbed him in the gut for his trouble, and he went down cursing. She was off balance, down to a single arm. She could either block or strike but not both.

I yanked her out of the way of a bludgeon she hadn't spotted but lost my footing in the process. The Avalanche fighters rushed forward, sensing the end. I fought harder than I'd ever fought before.

Red and I stood back to back. I took a club to my right side, trying to fend off three at once. The shock of the blow momentarily paralyzed my arm, and I dropped my sword. We were completely surrounded. Red's shoulder was pressed against mine as she fought with her one good arm.

I parried another strike, redirecting the kid's blade away from my head while in the same motion driving the tip of mine down through his thigh. The boy screamed, grabbed his leg, and fell.

"Hold your breath!" someone shouted behind us.

I recognized the voice and elbowed Red. "Hold your breath."

I twisted my head around as a wide splash of liquid struck the kids behind us. The entire line of Avalanche beaters dropped where they were, opening up enough room for me to pull Red back. The stench of the ether was strong enough to cause my knees to wobble.

Sapphire was suddenly there beside us, cutting down anyone who came close enough to be a threat. I pulled Red back as Reevie used whatever ether he had left on the closest beaters.

Cutter had managed to wall us off from the rest of Red's fighters. Even with the small reprieve, there was no way we were going to survive this.

"I told you to stay with Reevie!"

"Since when have I ever listened to you?" Sapphire said, keeping her blade swinging.

I smiled.

"Attack! Attack! Attack!" Cutter was so enraged, I thought he was going to start cutting his own kids down.

I glanced over my shoulder at Sapphire. "I'm glad you didn't listen."

She smiled, then stabbed the next beater in the chest.

Along with Red, we were standing back to back. I cut and stabbed at anything I saw. My mind was clouding and my breath was coming in deep, raspy gasps. I heard a hard crack on my right followed by a soft groan, and felt, more than saw, Sapphire go down beside me. Out of the corner of my eye, I could see Reevie kneeling over her.

The four of us were completely surrounded, not including the unconscious black-haired guard I had knocked out earlier. Red was trying to drag his body closer to her. The little kid clearly meant something. Red's legs were shaking; a moment later, she went down, the loss of blood finally catching up.

I was the last one still standing. I stabbed two more beaters and nearly decapitated a third before they had managed to knock my sword from my hands and overpower me.

"Wait! Don't kill him yet," Cutter shouted.

The beaters stopped but kept their weapons pointed at me, ready to finish the job.

Fatigue washed over me all at once. I could barely lift my arms. The right one ached from the blow it had taken earlier. Sweat dripped from my face as I stood there gasping for air, watching the wide-brimmed hat move through the crowd toward us.

The ranks parted, and Cutter stepped out, making sure to stay just out of reach. "So, you're the one I have to thank for all of this, huh?" he asked, gesturing to the battlefield with his sword. The two tribes were still going at it on our right, those that were still left within the depository's walls. Bodies were strewn everywhere.

"I could use a fighter like you on my guard," Cutter said. "You're wasting your talents in Hurricane, you know." He pointed at Red. "That black-headed twit can't appreciate what you have to offer like I can. Avalanche is the true power behind the Guild—"

"The true ailment, you mean!" Red said in her usual diplomatic way. "You're a disease, Cutter. Anal leakage from a faerie's backside!"

Cutter nodded to one of his beaters, and the boy kicked her in the face.

Red responded by spitting her blood back at him.

"That's more like it," he said with a smirk. "When a man speaks, a girl should hold her tongue."

"When you see one, be sure to let me know," she said. I had to admit, Red's temper might have gotten in the way of her common sense, but she certainly had guts.

Cutter sneered. "I'm going to save you for last. In fact, I think

I'll save you for my boys. They deserve a reward for all the hard work they've put into capturing you."

The battle around us continued to rage. There was no telling which of the tribes were still fighting and how many had made it out.

All I'd wanted was for me, Reevie, and Sapphire to have escaped all this nonsense unscathed, leaving it as far behind us as we could. But, yet again, another one of my plans had gone horribly wrong.

"So, what will it be?" Cutter asked, pointing the tip of his blade in my face. "Come be my new champion, or suffer the fate of your friends? Actually, I'll do you one better. You come join me and I'll even consider letting them live."

I slowly turned to look at the others. Reevie was bent over Sapphire, applying a bloody rag to her forehead, and Red was trying her best to remain upright, blood running down the side of her face.

What choice did I have? I turned to give Cutter my answer when something caught my attention. Something I hadn't expected. "As tempting as your offer is, I don't believe I could ever take the place of your current champion."

"And why is that?"

"Because," I said, turning to point at something behind them, "I think *he* might have something to say about it."

I had barely gotten the words out when cries of fear erupted at the back of Cutter's ranks, and beaters on both sides scattered in all directions. They trampled each other to get out of the way of the rampaging masked giant with dried blood crusted to his mouth.

Cutter raised his sword. "Stop! I said stop!"

Tubby wasn't listening. He roared as he came thundering through the fighters, sending the rest of the Avalanche forces scurrying for the exit. Cutter, seeing his champion was no longer listening to him, didn't waste any time catching up. His hat flew off his head as he knocked kids out of his way.

Flesh Eater stopped and stared at the five of us. If he attacked, there was nothing I would be able to do to stop him. We were completely helpless. I slowly reached for my sword, and Flesh Eater barked another animalistic roar. I froze. But instead of attacking, he turned and chased after Cutter and the fleeing Avalanche forces. I could have sworn that for a brief instant, I had seen him smile.

CHAPTER 36

MY LEGS GAVE OUT and I dropped beside Red. The depository was surprisingly quiet, if you ignored the chorus of moaning from the injured kids scattered across the grounds.

Flesh Eater's sudden arrival had completely thwarted the entire battle. In the time it took Reevie to wrap Sapphire's head and take a look at Red's shoulder, every tribe but Wildfire had exited the premises.

"That thing sure knows how to break up a good fight," Red said with a painful grunt as she struggled to her feet, her legs as unsteady as mine.

"Will you hold still? Colic!" Reevie exclaimed. "You're the worst patient I've ever treated." He shot a glare at me. "Except maybe for him."

The rest of Red's tribe had slowly gathered around. One of the older beaters picked up the small, unconscious boy Red had been cradling. Even Toothless had somehow managed to survive. He was lying on the ground, holding the wound in his side while spewing complaints and curses with every breath.

Reevie finished tying off Red's bandage. "There, that should hold until you decide to attack some other helpless kid walking down the street."

I sighed and gave Reevie a harsh look. The last thing we needed was to anger Red with what remained of her tribe standing behind her.

"I could have you killed for impersonating another tribe, you know," Red said as she inspected Reevie's work. Blood was already seeping through the bandage.

Reevie crossed his arms. "You could, if you want to die an excruciating death."

I gaped. Was he trying to get us all killed?

Red halted her inspection. "Why would you say something like that? Are you going to pull a blade from your underpants and challenge me to a duel?"

"I won't need to."

This time, it was Red who didn't say anything, but her eyes looked troubled.

Reevie snorted. "In case it's escaped your notice, the kids from

Avalanche aren't exactly the most well kempt, and their weapons look even worse. So, whatever they stabbed you with was probably covered in rust and who knows what else. I give you a week before that wound starts to blacken. Once that happens, there's not much you can do but die."

Reevie smiled. "However, if you were to see to it that we left here in one piece, then I might be persuaded to stop by and treat that wound with a mixture of herbs I have at my disposal."

Red looked at me, then at Sapphire, then back at Reevie, and laughed. "I like you, little one," she said. "You got grit. But how do I know you won't just poison me yourself?"

He gave her a stern look. "If I wanted you dead, we wouldn't be talking right now."

She stared at him a moment, then nodded. "You've got yourself a—"

"Actually," I said, interrupting before she could finish, "I want to add something to that."

Red's eyes narrowed, but she let me speak.

"I want my ring."

Her face darkened.

I held my breath. *Had I crossed the line?* At that point, I really didn't care. I wasn't leaving without that ring.

Red took a deep breath, her hand rising slowly to her neck. To my astonishment, she slipped the necklace off.

I waited, my eyes glued to the piece of jewelry hanging from the end.

She eyed the ring for a while before finally stretching out her arm. "I guess you've earned it," she said, almost reluctantly.

I snatched the ring before she could change her mind, spinning it around in my fingers, tracing the white symbol at the front.

Without saying anything more to us, Red turned and gestured toward the entrance. "Let's go!"

On her orders, Wildfire gathered their wounded and headed for the front gate.

The three of us stood there in silence as we watched the last of them disappear into the night.

"Let's go home," I finally said, hanging my father's ring around my neck and sliding my newly acquired swords through my belt. The thought of my bed was the only thing keeping me moving at that point. I put my arm around Reevie, and we helped each other toward the gates.

"What about all of them?" Sapphire asked, looking out across the open yard, bodies covering a good portion of the ground around the small cooking fires. Many were still moving.

"Leave them to their tribes," Reevie said. He spared a quick glance at the wounded before turning and continuing for the exit. "Their people will come for them eventually."

The torches lining the front of the depository disappeared as we headed west on Mora. The stars were still out and bright, but I didn't think they would be for much longer. Dawn couldn't be that far off.

We half-walked, half-limped down the long, empty stretch of road, my thoughts flooded by the horrific events of the night. When I had released Flesh Eater, I hadn't expected it to turn into an all-out war. I'd simply wanted to cause enough ruckus to get us out of there without being seen. I hadn't expected Cutter to use it as a means of executing Red and taking over her tribe. Although I guess I shouldn't have been too surprised. I had just figured that with all the other tribes present, he wouldn't have tried something so brash.

"I definitely didn't wake up this morning thinking this would happen," Reevie said, as if hearing my thoughts and wanting to chime in. "Quite the turn of events with Red. Having her as an ally might prove valuable."

"I doubt I'd go so far as to call her an ally," I said.

"At least we know it wasn't Red who threw you to the wolves—"

I glowered. "No, it wasn't."

"I still can't believe Spats did that," Sapphire said. "I know he's always only cared for himself, but even this is hard to believe. We needed you to win to keep from owing Avalanche all that gold. Now what are we going to do?"

"Who cares?" Reevie said with an unusual lack of sympathy. "I thought we were getting out of this city."

No one said anything. As diverting as it might have been to talk about leaving, I didn't believe any of us actually thought we would do it.

"What about Bull and Mouse and Petal?" I asked. "What about the rest of the rejects?"

"They can come with us."

I looked at Reevie and he smirked. "Fine, so maybe we didn't think this through as much as we should have, but we can't just sit here. The Guild is going to want blood after what happened tonight. And who better to demand it from than us?"

"It's not our fault we're in this mess," I said.

"We're the ones who let Flesh Eater loose," Reevie argued, glancing around nervously at the darkened streets. He looked as though he half-expected the giant boy to come rushing out of one and eat him just for saying his name.

"This is Cutter's fault," Sapphire said. "He's the one who started this whole thing by invading Hurricane to draw Spats out."

Just the mention of Spats's name made my blood boil.

"You know you're going to have to deal with him, don't you?" she asked, more of a statement than a question.

"Who? Cutter?"

"No. Spats. He can't be allowed to get away with what he's done. And not just to you."

"Why hasn't someone done something about him sooner?"

She thought about it a moment. "The Guild. They wouldn't allow it."

"I don't know," Reevie chimed in. "With the mood they're in, they probably wouldn't say anything if Spats woke up with a knife in his gut." He smiled, an unusual expression for him when talking of killing.

"Besides," Sapphire said, "it wouldn't do much good to have tribal chiefs assassinated every time another member wanted their position. We'd have anarchy." She shook her head. "No, we need to find a way to deal with him that won't fall back on us."

"I might have an idea about that," I said. "But not for tonight. Tonight, my ribs are telling me that I need to crawl in bed and get some sleep."

"I couldn't agree more," Reevie said with a yawn.

We had made it as far as Pilneth when a familiar growl echoed off in the distance, stopping us in our tracks. The sound was quickly followed by a couple of high-pitched screams.

"What was that?" Sapphire asked, looking north into Cheapside.

I released Reevie, who had been leaning on me for support, and took a couple of steps toward the far side of the street. "Sounds like some of the locals just had their first run-in with Flesh Eater."

"Well, let's not be next," Reevie said, tugging on my arm.

I didn't budge. Instead, I turned to Sapphire. "Here, take Reevie. You two head back to the granary, and I'll see what I can do about Flesh Eater."

"What's the granary?"

I'd forgotten Sapphire had never been there before. As Spats's head guard, she was rarely afforded the opportunity to leave the Temple, except when escorting Spats around the city.

"Reevie will show you."

"What are you going to do?" Reevie asked, a look of suspicion creeping across his face. "Not something stupid, I hope."

Sapphire had a knowing look in her eye. "You're going after him, aren't you?"

"Who? Flesh Eater?" Reevie snorted. "Have you lost your mind? Did Cutter's boys beat out what little sense you have left?

You can barely stand. Let the patrollers deal with him."

"He's my responsibility."

"And how, for the love of Aldor, do you figure that?"

"I'm the one who turned him loose," I said.

Reevie and Sapphire exchanged a quick glance.

"He has a point," Sapphire said. "We're the ones who opened the door. How do you think you'll feel if a couple of innocent children are eaten tonight because we decided it wasn't our responsibility?"

I could see Reevie's conscience battling his survival instincts. "I'd feel glad it wasn't me." I knew him well enough to know that wasn't true.

Reevie handed me his travel bag, which still held a decent number of supplies. "Make sure he's good and dead this time. We can't have a monster like that roaming the streets of Aramoor, eating people. I have a little more of my ether left if you want to use it." Reevie didn't say anything else, but I could tell from the tension in his shoulders, he didn't like the idea.

"Take Reevie and go. I'll be fine."

"Just be careful," she said.

Reevie threw his arm over Sapphire's shoulders. "Let's go." He didn't even spare a glance in my direction as he limped off, dragging Sapphire with him. Whenever Reevie got this upset, it was because he feared for my safety.

Needless to say, Reevie was upset a lot.

Sapphire offered a sympathetic smile over her shoulder as Reevie dragged her down the street.

My hands rested on my swords as I watched them shrink into the distance. Once out of view, I swung Reevie's bag over my shoulder and headed in the direction of the screams.

I didn't have to go far.

Most of the shouting was coming from the second- and third-floor windows as residents were woken out of their sleep by a giant masked creature roaming the streets. So far, I hadn't found a trail of bodies, so maybe he had already gotten enough to eat during the battle. I shivered at the thought.

I ducked between two buildings, angry voices getting louder the closer I got to the other side. He had to be just ahead. I came to the end of the narrow alleyway and slowly stuck my head out.

No one was there. With my head cocked to the side, I listened for any hint as to which direction he had taken.

The wait wasn't long.

Metal clanged loudly from an alleyway across the road, so I dashed across the street, keeping a wary eye for loose cobbles. When I reached the corner, I stopped and listened. I could hear what sounded like crates being crunched underfoot and another barking growl.

I peeked around the corner, just enough to get a quick look without being noticed. A streetlamp on the other side of the road lit the narrow corridor. In the shadows, I could just make out the large boy digging around in a pile of garbage, something hanging from his mouth. I was afraid to find out what it was.

Flesh Eater took a couple of steps forward, and the streetlamp lit his face enough for me to finally see what he was chewing. I braced myself for the sight of someone's hand or foot, but it was nothing more than an old melon rind.

"What's going on out here?" a man called out behind me, causing me to jump. His hair was a mess, and his shirt was open at the front. He'd clearly just gotten out of bed to see what was going on, most likely ordered to by a frightened wife.

"Shhh," I whispered, raising my finger to my lips. "Don't startle him."

The man cast about. "Startle who, lad? There's no one here."

I pointed back over my shoulder toward the alleyway. "Go back inside. I'll deal with him."

"Deal with who?" he asked, raising his cudgel. He pushed me aside to see for himself.

With a sharp gasp, he turned and ran back up the street. "Good luck to ya, lad," he hissed as he charged up the steps and through the door, slamming it shut behind him.

The alley was quiet, leaving me to wonder what the large pit fighter was up to. I took a deep breath to steady my nerves and scooted back toward the corner of the building. The wood was rough against my cheek as I cautiously slid my head out to look around the corner.

I nearly swallowed my tongue when I realized I was staring directly into Flesh Eater's eyes. Our noses were practically touching.

I screamed, and Flesh Eater screamed. He scampered back into the alley. Realizing he was just as frightened as I was gave me the courage to step out from my hiding place and into the narrow, garbage-packed corridor.

I could hear sniffling behind a stack of crates on the left.

"Flesh Ea . . . uh, I mean, Tubby?"

A crate toppled off the stack, exposing his giant head.

"I'm not going to hurt you, Tubby. It's me, Ayrion. Do you remember me? I'm the one who let you go." I hoped he remembered.

"Arr—un."

"Yes," I said with a smile as I pointed to my chest. "My name is Ayr–ee–un. And you are Tubby."

"Tubby," he repeated, stepping out from behind the crates and into the faint light. He took another couple of steps forward and then stopped.

He was clearly having trouble trusting me. It wasn't like I could blame him. I was the one who had just snapped his fingers. Besides, who knew how long he'd spent caged away like an animal in Cutter's compound? I couldn't imagine what that must have been like.

I reached into Reevie's bag and pulled out an apple, holding it out for him to see. "Here. Would you like this? Are you hungry?" I tried to keep my words gentle.

Tubby took another step.

"It's all right. I'm not going to hurt you." I made a point of sitting down cross-legged while waiting for him to do the same. He eventually plopped himself down a few feet from where I was sitting. I rolled the apple to him, and he picked it up and sniffed it.

"Go ahead. It's good."

Tubby spit the leftover melon shell out and stuffed half the apple into his mouth, biting down. I couldn't really tell because of the mask, but it looked like there might have been a smile. He released a soft moan as the juices dripped down his chin.

I wondered what it was like, being forced to wear that hideous mask. Was it worn just during fights, or was it something he was forced to keep on? Knowing Cutter, it was probably permanent, used as a way to scare his tribe into obedience.

"Will you let me take that thing off your head?" I asked, pointing at his covered face.

Tubby didn't say anything, but he grew very still.

I wasn't sure if his silence was a yes or a no, but I took the risk and calmly stood up, making sure to keep my movements slow and smooth. I proceeded to move around behind him to take a look at the leather casing. So far, so good. There was a sudden pop and crunch as Tubby sank his teeth into the piece of fruit. I breathed a quick sigh of relief and my shoulders relaxed.

He seemed more interested in the apple than me.

The covering was held on by a simple buckle. I carefully reached out to undo it. "Now, I'm going to loosen your mask, Tubby. Is that okay?" I waited for him to nod, but once again, there was no movement, so I took a deep breath and reached for the buckle. I slowly pulled back on the strap and unhooked it from the latch. "I've almost got it. Just . . . a . . . little . . . farther." I carefully lifted the covering from his head. It was heavier than I had expected.

The enormous boy didn't move. I carried the head piece around to the front to get a better look at what I was dealing with.

I still couldn't see his face. His brown hair had grown in thick clumps around his head like creepers up the side of a knotty pine. He looked scarier with the mask off.

Tubby lifted his hands and ran them across his face. He pinched his nose and then played with his ears. A wide grin spread across his face, almost bringing tears to my eyes. "Come on," I said. I walked to the edge of the alley and motioned for him to follow. "We need to go before the patrollers get here. Look." I pulled the last apple from Reevie's stash and held it up for Tubby to see. "I have food. You don't need to eat garbage. You can come home with me." I almost laughed at the thought.

Tubby stood and snatched the apple from my hand. "Home?"

"Yes, you can come home with me. No one's going to hurt you, I promise. And you don't have to wear this thing anymore." I tried stuffing the headdress inside Reevie's satchel, but it was too big and hung halfway out. "Once we get home, we need to look at those fingers of yours."

Tubby raised his hands and looked at his disfigured fingers from where I had popped them out of joint. I wondered how he was coping with the pain. I didn't regret breaking them, but now that I was starting to understand the simple way Tubby's mind worked, I wished it hadn't come to that. I hoped Reevie would be able to set them without any permanent damage.

With his apple hanging from his mouth, Tubby followed me to the head of the alley. I scanned both sides of the street to make sure the way was clear before hurrying us out and down to the next street over. The giant of a boy stayed close, taking short steps to match my stride. He made sure to keep a few steps behind me, like a pet following its master.

We were nearly to the granary when the absurdity of what I was doing caught up with me, and I started to laugh.

My sudden outburst took Tubby by surprise, and he jumped into a defensive stance—hands out in front, head up and sniffing the air as he twisted around looking for danger.

I took a quick step back and reached for my sword. Tubby might have been simple in the head, but it didn't mean the boy wasn't dangerous.

It took a while for Tubby to recognize that the expression on my face wasn't one of anger or fear, but rather amusement.

Tubby mimicked my expression by spreading his bloody jaws and croaking out a garbled laugh of his own. It was the most disturbing sound I'd ever heard, which, of course, had me laughing even harder, which in turn brought an even greater response from Tubby.

I laughed so hard, I was afraid I'd need fresh trousers when we got back—not that I had any. I laughed at myself, at the circumstances that had brought me to this point. I laughed at Tubby, with his hair growing around his head and dried blood crusted to the front of his face. I laughed at my miserable luck and my perverse ability to somehow make it through every time. But, most importantly, I laughed at what I knew was coming.

"Reevie's going to kill me."

CHAPTER

37

AS PREDICTED, Reevie nearly gave birth when I walked into the granary with Tubby in tow. Bull, along with any of the other rejects who still happened to be up, ran screaming at the first sight of the bloody giant. It took quite a while to coax Tubby inside, and even longer to coax everyone else out so I could introduce them to their new roommate.

"Everyone, this is Tubby," I said to those brave enough to do more than peek out from behind some of the old machinery and crates. "Tubby, this is everyone."

Tubby growled, which didn't help the situation. In fact, half the kids took off running for their rooms.

"We need to give him a bath," I said, still frustrated by everyone's reaction to the enormous boy.

"We need to give *you* a bath," Sapphire admonished, making a point of sniffing in my direction.

Mouse, one of our smallest rejects, was the first to greet Tubby. He stepped forward and looked up at the giant kid towering over him. "You gonna eat us?"

Tubby shook his head.

"Good. Then I guess you can stay."

And with that, the others came out to welcome the new reject.

After a very long, very hot bath of my own, I joined Reevie, Bull, and Sapphire, and we began our work on Tubby. We had to clip pins to our noses to bear the smell. It took quite a while to get him into the extra-large basin of soapy water. He seemed frightened of everything. We cut his crusted mop of hair, scrubbed his skin with stiff brushes, and burned his filthy clothing. We went through three tubs of water just to get him halfway presentable.

Reevie treated the damaged skin below Tubby's waist where he had never been properly cleaned. Needless to say, it rounded out one of the longest, roughest nights I'd spent in Aramoor.

By the time we were through, Tubby looked like a new person.

"He's not too hard on the eyes," Sapphire said, standing back to admire our work. Her statement brought a beam to Tubby's now-washed face. She had an admirer.

Over the next couple of days, we focused on helping the wounded recover. Reevie was able to get Tubby's fingers back into place, using the last of the ether. He splinted each one with a metal rod just to keep the big kid from re-dislocating them while they healed. Tubby did everything he could to please us. I think he was afraid that if he didn't make us happy, he would be sent back to Cutter.

I spent most of my time working on the immediate dilemma of how we were going to survive, given our meager provisions. We were going to need food and medicine, and at the moment, we didn't have a way to acquire either. To top it off, the wager Reevie and I had placed on me to win wasn't being honored, because both parties were still standing at the end.

I was sitting in my favorite spot on the granary's roof, gazing out at the white spires and domes rising from the central part of the city, when a voice startled me from my brooding.

"I thought I'd find you up here."

I turned to see Sapphire peeking out of the hatch leading down to the warehouse. She climbed out, taking a moment to coo at Reevie's pigeon cage before sitting on the empty seat beside mine.

"What did you find out? Were you able to find any pickers willing to talk?"

"I did," she said ominously.

"And?"

"And it's bad. Between the ambush with Avalanche and our battle at the Pit, Hurricane has lost over half its original number."

I could feel my heart sink. "That many?" I shook my head.

"Any word as to why Spats tried to have me killed?"

"No." She turned and looked at me. "That's something you can find out for yourself when you deal with him."

I nodded. What Spats had done required justice. I just wanted to make sure I had thought everything through before dishing it out.

"At least the Guild hasn't retaliated for the Pit," she said.

"That's what has me worried. Why haven't they?"

"My guess is because there's more than one person to blame—"

"Yeah, but I was the one who set Flesh Eater loose—"

"Sure, but you weren't the one who openly attacked another tribe and attempted to assassinate their chief." Sapphire leaned back in her chair. "No, I'd say the Guild has enough on their plate just trying to decide how to keep this from turning into an all-out declaration of war. Last time that happened, I heard the Lancers were turned loose and a quarter of the street rats were rounded up and shipped off to the salt mines. No one wants that."

"A more pressing issue is that we don't have enough food, and Reevie says we'll be out of medicine by the end of the week. There's not enough pickers out there to get the job done."

"I agree; we need more workers."

I sighed and leaned back in my chair as well, too many uncertainties overwhelming me at once. I took a deep breath and slowly released it as I gazed at the heart of Aramoor, the sun dipping toward the peaks of the Sandrethin Mountains in the distance. "I say we don't worry about it, at least not now. I just want to sit here and enjoy the view."

"Couldn't agree more," she said, sinking farther into her own chair.

"Protector! Are you up there?"

I groaned. "Well, that didn't last long." I got up to see what they needed.

Sapphire smiled, then followed me to the open hatchway.

"What is it?" I asked, barely making it to the opening before Rat's head popped out.

Petal and Squeaks were waiting anxiously at the bottom of the stairs.

"You're needed outside immediately, sir. There's, uh, there's . . . Well, you'll just have to come and see for yourself."

"Come on," Petal and Squeaks chimed in as they headed back down the next set of steps leading to the main floor. "You need to see this."

Sapphire giggled.

"Don't encourage them," I grumbled.

She shrugged.

On the main floor, we met Reevie as he made his way up from our underground chambers. "What's all the commotion?" he asked, not looking to be in the best of moods. He'd probably been interrupted in the middle of reading another one of his recently purchased—well, *purchased* might not have been the correct word—volumes on the latest medical practices.

"Don't know." I shrugged. "They just said we were needed out front." My hand slid to my waist on instinct, and my fingers skimmed the leather grip of my sword.

By the time we had made it across the warehouse, Bull had slid open the main door far enough for us to get through. The sun was low on the horizon and blinding, the perfect level to hit us in the face. Even squinting, I needed to place my hand over my eyes just to see. I could have used one of father's shaders.

Petal and Squeaks tugged on my sleeves and pointed toward the road.

"What do we do about them?"

Mouse bared his teeth. "Are we under attack?"

The loading yard in front of the granary was filled with kids.

Tubby rushed out the door and took a spot on my left. He lifted his enormous bludgeon and growled out the front hole of his leather mask. He had taken to wearing it whenever he felt the need for intimidation.

The group of kids backed up at the sight of him. A few took off running down the street.

Reevie scooted a little closer, his book gripped firmly to his chest. "What do you think they want?"

From the looks of them, I didn't believe they were there to do battle. There wasn't a single weapon in the lot. Unless you counted sticks for crutches and poles for toting what little belongings they had.

I could tell Tubby was upset by the way he continued shifting his feet. I placed my hand on his arm, which was about as high as my forehead. "Don't worry, Tubby. I don't think they mean us any harm." With that, he lowered his club and let it hang by his leg.

Across the way, a tall, lanky girl in front took a few steps forward. She had straight auburn hair that hung below her waist, and her outfit looked to be nothing more than random pieces of dresses all stitched together for the sake of simple decency. Her hands were trembling, but she kept her back straight.

"What's your business here?" Reevie asked.

"We've come seeking the Protector."

How did that name get out of the granary? Many of the outcasts were now calling me Protector. I had tried more than once to have them find something a little more creative, like *Ayrion*, but the label somehow seemed to stick, especially considering that every time someone new showed up and mentioned my eyes, Reevie would impart his now well-rehearsed explanation as to my heritage and the *correct* definition of the word *Upaka*. It was his way of reassuring our guests that the champion of the Pit wasn't going to kill them in their sleep and feed them to Tubby.

"And . . . what do you want with him?" Reevie asked nervously, passing a quick glance in my direction.

"We . . ." She looked over her shoulder at the group behind her. Those in the front urged her on. "We heard there was a place where no matter who you are, you can still belong."

That was something I had said to Bull. I glanced at him on my right, and he slunk back with a mischievous grin.

The girl continued. "If that's so, and this is that place . . ." She turned to look at those behind her again, and they nodded once more. "Then we've come to join."

Shouts of agreement rose from those in the yard.

"Well, you were looking for more workers," Sapphire said, staring out at the horde of kids in front of us. "Looks like you just got them."

I gawked at the throng of new faces staring back at me and wondered how we were ever going to manage. I came to one simple conclusion. We'd manage the same way we always had. One day at a time.

Dear Reader,

I HOPE YOU enjoyed this second book in the Street Rats of Aramoor series. If you found the story entertaining and would like to see more, then please consider helping me reach that goal by leaving a quick review on Amazon.

Reviews are very important. They help encourage other readers to try the book while at the same time showing Amazon that the book is worth promoting.

Thank you in advance!

Love fantasy merchandise? Stop by the **Aramoor Market** and take a look at the new Aldoran store. New arrivals every month.

<<www.store.michaelwisehart.com>>

Author Note

YOU CAN LEARN more about the World of Aldor on my website. Don't forget to read the *History of Aldor* while you're there. It will give you a better understanding behind the internal struggles and conflicts taking place between those with magic and those without.

My website: www.michaelwisehart.com

For the Latest News
« facebook.com/MichaelWisehart.author »

Acknowledgements

I THANK GOD for the doors and windows He's allowed to open in order for me to reach this point.

I want to thank my Author Team, whose endless talent, time, and dedication have made this project possible:

AUTHOR TEAM

To my illustrator and sister, whose creativity and talent continues to impress—*Janelle Wisehart*

To my content editor, who has spent countless hours advising me on the proper structure of my thoughts—*Nathan Hall*

To my line editor, who managed to take a floundering script and turn it into something readable—*Danae Smith*

To my copy editors, whose patience has managed to surpass my continual lack of commas—*Tammy Salyer, Mia Darien of LKJ Bookmakers, Richard Shealy*

To my cover artists, who have taken a concept in the back of my mind and turned it into a breathtaking reality—*Whendell Souza, Rodrigo Ramos*

To my numerous Beta Readers, whose faithfulness to the story has helped me keep the pages flowing.

About the Author

MICHAEL WISEHART graduated with a bachelor's degree in business before going back to school for film and starting his own production company. As much as he enjoyed film work, the call of writing a novel got the better of him, and on April 14, 2014, he started typing the first words of what would be two new epic fantasy series: The Aldoran Chronicles and Street Rats of Aramoor.

He currently lives and writes in South Georgia.

Visit « michaelwisehart.com »

Character Glossary

Ackelman, Lord [*ack-el-men*] Aramoor lord who had Reevie's dad turned over to the White Tower because his daughter died.

Ayrion [*air-ee-un*] Thirteen-year-old Upakan street rat. Born with two magical gifts. Banished from his home for accidentally killing another Upakan.

Bull [*bull*] Former Avalanche beater who fought Ayrion during a tribal battle. Becomes one of Ayrion's bodyguards.

Cutter [*cut-er*] Chief of Avalanche. Vindictive and cruel.

Dorin [*dor-in*] One of Ayrion's instructors, who favored his whip as a method of teaching.

Egla [*eg-la*] Faerie goddess of the Temple. Her worshippers turned on her. Her creatures ate her.

Enon [*eh-non*] Farmer's son who rode with Ayrion in the back of a wagon on their way into Aramoor.

Fentin [*fen-tin*] Husband of Orilla. Elderly bookstore owner who keeps a place for Reevie to hide when needed.

Finley [*fin-lee*] Cheese merchant on Borell Street.

Flesh Eater / Tubby [*tub-ee*] The Pit champion. Enormous kid known for biting. He fights Ayrion in the Pit.

Flon [*flon*] Upakan boy Ayrion killed.

Forehead [*for-head*] One of the Hurricane Guard. Best known for his ferocious head-butting technique. Large growth on front of head because of head-butting.

Gerrick, Lord [*gare-ick*] Overweight Aramoor lord whose carriage almost ran Ayrion over.

Kira (a.k.a. Red) [*kee-ruh / red*] Chief of Wildfire. Took Ayrion's father's ring.

Kore [*kor*] Chief of Rockslide. Physically imposing.

Neelan [*nee-lun*] Farmer who offered Ayrion a ride into Aramoor.

Noph [*noff*] Chief of Sandstorm. Great tactician.

Orilla [*or-ill-uh*] Wife of Fentin. Makes a fantastic mystery-meat sandwich.

Petal [*peddle*] Small reject girl from Avalanche. Her hair is as golden as a flower petal. Friends with Mouse and Squeaks.

Po [*poe*] One of Kira's head bodyguards. Short and pudgy with black hair.

Mouse [*mow-ss*] Small reject boy from Rockslide. Small enough to squeeze in and out of tiny places for burgling. Friends with Squeaks and Petal.

Reevie [*ree-vee*] Street rat who saved Ayrion and took him in. Healer in training.

Rossen [*rose-en*] Owner of quilt stand on South Avis.

Sapphire [*Saf-fire*] One of Spats's bodyguards who befriends Ayrion. Good with the sword.

Skull Crusher [*skull-crush-er*] The Pit champion before they banned fights to the death.

Spats [*spats*] Chief of Hurricane.

Squeaks [*squeeks*] Small reject from Avalanche. Friends with Mouse and Petal.

Toothless [*tooth-less*] Head guard of Wildfire.

Toots [*toots*] Head watcher at the Temple.

Stop by and visit:
www.michaelwisehart.com

Printed in Great Britain
by Amazon

11250288R00174